Mountain
Windsong

Mountain Windsong

A Novel of the Trail of Tears

ROBERT·J·CONLEY

University of Oklahoma Press
NORMAN

For Evelyn (Guwist),
my wife and my Oconeechee

Also by Robert J. Conley from the University of Oklahoma Press

The Witch of Goingsnake and Other Stories (Norman, 1988)
The Cherokee Medicine Man (Norman, 2005)
Cherokee Thoughts: Honest and Uncensored (Norman, 2008)

The Real People

The Way of the Priests (New York, 1992; reprint, Norman, 2000)
The Dark Way (New York, 1993; reprint, Norman, 2000)
The White Path (New York, 1995; reprint, Norman, 2000)
The Way South (New York, 1993; reprint, Norman, 2000)
The Long Way Home (New York, 1994; reprint, Norman, 2000)
The Dark Island (New York, 1995; reprint, Norman, 2000)
The War Trail North (New York, 1995; reprint, Norman, 2000)
War Woman (New York, 1998)
The Peace Chief (New York, 1998)
Cherokee Dragon (New York, 2000)

Library of Congress Cataloging-in-Publication Data

Conley, Robert J.
    Mountain windsong : a novel of the Trail of Tears /
    Robert J. Conley. — 1st ed.
        p.   cm.
        1. Cherokee Indians — Removal — Fiction.   I. Title.
    PS3553.0494M68   1992
    813'.54 — dc20   92–54150
    ISBN 978-0-8061-2746-0 (paper)   CIP

The paper in this book meets the guidelines for permanence and durability of the Committee on Production Guidelines for Book Longevity of the Council on Library Resources, Inc. ∞

9   10   11   12

Acknowledgments

The idea for *Mountain Windsong* came to me after listening to a recording of Don Grooms, Cherokee, singing his song, "Whippoorwill," the lyrics of which appear, with his permission, in the text of this book.

The lines from Louis Oliver's poem, "Middle Tone," are reprinted from his book, *Caught in a Willow Net,* 1983, with permission of the publisher, The Greenfield Review Press, Greenfield Center, New York.

The excerpts from Mooney are taken from James Mooney, *Historical Sketch of the Cherokee,* 19th Annual Report, the Bureau of American Ethnology, 1900, and those from Royce from Charles C. Royce, *The Cherokee Nation of Indians,* Fifth Annual Report, The Bureau of American Ethnology, 1887. Ralph Waldo Emerson's letter to President Van Buren (1836) is from Ralph Waldo Emerson, *Complete Works,* Centenary Edition, Houghton Mifflin Company, Boston, 1903. The text of the Treaty of New Echota has been reprinted many places, notably in *Treaties and Agreements of the Five Civilized Tribes,* Institute for the Development of Indian Law, Washington, D.C.

Special thanks to Ken Graham and to Adalene Proctor Smith.

ROBERT J. CONLEY

Tahlequah, Oklahoma

Mountain
Windsong

but the Indian can hear the middle note
and the wind! Oh the winds,
the frigid ones that howl
and whistle around the eaves—
the calm soughing ones
that soothe the ear
with the Key sound of the Universe.

Louis Oliver (Littlecoon)

1

I remember the first time ever I heard the windsong in those misty hills above Big Cove. The dogwood was in bloom. My belly was full of hickory-nut soup and chestnut bread that elisi, my grandmother, had made. After we had eaten our fill, Grandpa had led me up the footpath behind the house that took us onto the top of the hill. There was no reason—no practical reason, I mean. We weren't gathering grapes or berries or wild onions. We weren't going hunting. We just climbed the path to the top of the hill and sat down in the sweetgrass among the passion flowers and thistles beneath the dogwood and sourwood trees. Grandpa took his corncob pipe and tobacco pouch out of a pocket of his baggy khaki trousers. He slowly filled the pipe bowl, folded up the pouch and stuffed it back into his pocket, and poked the pipestem in between his tight old-man lips. He reached into the breast pocket of his khaki shirt for a wooden kitchen match which he struck on the sole of his shoe. He held the flaming match cupped in his hands against the gentle breeze which was stirring the air around us. Then he puffed at his pipe, sucking the flame from the match down into the bowl until he had the tobacco lit. He broke the matchstick and shoved the pieces down into the earth, then he leaned back against the trunk of a big white oak and

*puffed contentedly, sending clouds of white, lovely looking smoke
spiraling their way up into the heavens.*

I stretched out on my back in the weeds and folded my hands
behind my head. I was looking straight up into the sky, and I tried
to imagine what it was like on the other side. Grandpa had told me
that it was a gigantic vault over the earth—kind of like a cereal
bowl turned upside-down over a saucer—and we were walking
around on the saucer under the bowl. I couldn't see Grandpa, looking almost straight up the way I was, but his smoke kept drifting
across my field of vision.

The smell of Grandpa's burning tobacco mingled with the fresh
smells of the hills: the dogwood blossoms, the sweetgrass, the mul-
titude of other aromas of the North Carolina Smoky Mountains,
and I loved it. It was just about perfect—being up there on the hill,
my favorite spot, with Grandpa, my favorite person in the whole
world. So I was just laying there like that and enjoying the company
of Grandpa and the smells and the sights and the sounds of the birds
and the chattering squirrels, and it was just then that I heard the
windsong. And it really was a song—or it was just like a song. I
pushed myself up on my elbows and looked around. I guess I almost
expected to see someone—whoever it was making the music, I guess.
And then I looked at Grandpa, but he was just sitting there quietly
smoking his pipe.

"Grandpa," I said.

He just kept puffing.

"What was that?"

"What, chooj?" he said.

He often called me boy like that rather than call me by my right
name, which is LeRoy, and sometimes he called me Sonny. Sonny
is what Daddy usually called me, and Mom called me either Sonny
or LeRoy, but most of the time Grandpa called me chooj, boy.

"That sound, Grandpa," I said. "It sounds like—like a song."

"Oh," he said, and a smile formed on his wrinkled old brown
face, "it is a song. It's a love song."

"A love song?" I said.

"It's the love song of Oconeechee and Whippoorwill."

I don't think I said anything then, but I sat right up and stared at
him. He had that smile on his face and the twinkle in his eyes that
I knew so well, and I could see that he had a story to tell me. He
always looked like that when he had a story to tell. He puffed his
pipe, and the smoke rose up high before it dissipated and vanished
on its way up to God's house on the other side of the Sky Vault.

"Have you heard about that story?" he said.

"No."

*"Well, it was a long time ago," he said. "Back then the Chero-
kees had all this land. Not just our little reservation here that we
have now. We had lots of land—in North Carolina, in Georgia, in
Alabama, in Tennessee. The Cherokee Nation was real big back in
those days."*

*He paused to puff on his pipe, and he pointed off to the north
where the mountains got higher.*

*"There was a town off over there called Soco Gap," he said,
"and there was a man who lived there. He was a chief. His name
was Tsunu lahun ski. White men can't say that. They called him
Junaluska. That wasn't his original name. He changed it to that,
and I'll tell you why he changed it. His original name was Gul kala
ski. That means something that's leaning over and it keeps falling.
That was his first name. But here's why he changed it.*

*"When the United States Army went to war against the Creek
Indians away back in eighteen-hundred-and-thirteen, and Andrew
Jackson was the general, some of the Cherokees joined the U.S.
Army. Sam Houston, he'd been living with a Cherokee family, and
he joined up. So did this man I'm telling you about—this Gul kala
ski. He joined the army. Well, there was a big fight at a place called
Horseshoe Bend, down in the Creek country, down in Alabama."*

*Grandpa pointed south when he said that. Whenever he was tell-
ing a story, he always pointed off in the direction of any place he
mentioned, like it was just down the road there and you could get up
and go over and look at it if you took a mind to. He paused to take
a few deep sucks on his pipe.*

*"There at Horseshoe Bend," he said finally, "this Cherokee
man, He Keeps Falling Over, stepped in between General Jackson
and a Creek who was just about to kill the general, and Falling
Over All the Time saved Jackson's life. He killed that other Indian.*

*"Then the Creeks were hunkered down real good behind a strong
wall of logs across the river from where Jackson's men were at, and
Jackson couldn't get at them. This Cherokee man I'm talking about,
he led some other Cherokees down into the river, and they swam
across and sneaked up behind the Creeks and surprised them. Then
Sam Houston was able to lead an attack from the front, from across
the river, and they whipped the Creeks. So this Cherokee man, he
not only saved the general's life that day, he also pretty much won
the fight for him.*

"'Course Old Hickory, that's what they called Jackson, he got

all the credit. Probably that's what got him elected president later on. And he knew who did it for him. He knew what happened out there. After the fight was over, he went to this man, this Falling Over man, and he said, 'As long as the sun shines and the grass grows,' he said, 'you and me are going to be friends, and the feet of the Cherokees will be pointed East.' That's what he said.

"Well, later on, when Jackson was president, that's when they were trying to make all the Cherokees get out of here, move out west so the white people could have all our land, this man said he would go talk to Jackson. He said that Jackson was his friend and would help. He remembered what Jackson had said to him after the big fight at Horseshoe Bend, and he figured that the president would remember the man who had saved his life and helped to make him a big hero by winning the fight that day. He said the president would remember his promise and would help the Cherokees out. But Jackson wouldn't even let him come in. So that man told his friends, 'detsinu lahungu, I tried and I failed.' And that was how he got his new name, Tsunu lahun ski, He Tried but Failed. Junaluska."

The sound of the windsong grew louder just then, and it was beautiful, but it was also just a little bit eerie, and it made me shiver. Grandpa puffed at his pipe, but it had gone out. He took it out of his mouth and tapped it against his shoe.

"But this story's not about him—not about Junaluska," he said. "It's about that love song in the wind. It's about Junaluska's daughter. Her name was Oconeechee."

Grandpa stopped and took the time to refill his pipe and light it again, and I was so anxious to hear the story that I thought it was taking him an extra long time to attend to that ritual. I even suspected that he was purposefully dragging it out just to make me wait, to build up suspense, I guess, or to test my patience. Off in the distance the rapid pounding of a woodpecker suddenly disturbed the silence, and an urge to get up and search for it intruded into my anxiety over the unfinished tale. My indecision was resolved for me, however, when Grandpa resumed his story.

"Well," he said, "like I told you, that Junaluska, he lived over there at Soco Gap. He was a chief—a town chief—a town war chief. You see, back in those days, we didn't have one big chief like now. Each town had its own government, and they had two chiefs— a war chief and a peace chief. The peace chief, he was the guy in charge of things at home when there wasn't any fighting going on. The war chief's job was to deal with outsiders and to take over any *time there was a war. It was the white man that caused us to get one big chief over all the Cherokees, and because each town already had two chiefs, when we did get that big chief, we called him the principal chief, you know, like the main chief over all the other chiefs.*

"Even with the white man pushing for it, it took a long time for the Cherokees to agree to have one big chief and one government for all the Cherokees. The reason for that is that a long time ago we had that. Or something like that. We had priests who had all the power. They made the people build mounds and temples, and they got carried around wherever they went. They could do just about anything to anybody. Then one time a man had been out hunting, and when he came home, he couldn't find his wife. He went around to his neighbors, and for awhile nobody would tell him anything. Finally one of his neighbors said that while he was gone, the priests came and took his wife away. So the man got some of his friends and neighbors together, and he said to them, 'We've taken just about enough from these priests,' and they all agreed with him. So they killed all the priests. They had themselves a revolution right then. That all probably happened not too long before the first English colony was set up in these parts. Anyhow, the Cherokees wouldn't allow a strong, central government to develop after that. They let each town have its own government with two chiefs and a council and advisors. They had democracy. And that's the kind of town government that this guy Junaluska was a war chief in."

Just about there, Grandpa took a breather to puff on his pipe and to watch the smoke rise, and the way he was watching it, he made it look so interesting that I just sat back and watched it too. Then pretty soon he started talking again.

"This Junaluska had a wife. Her name was Qualla, same as the name they call our reservation here sometimes. And they were very much in love with each other, Junaluska and Qualla. They were happy there in Soco Gap. They were real happy together. You know, chooj, sometimes it seems like a man and a woman are just meant for each other. They belong together. It's like God made them for each other, and He kind of pushed them together. I don't know if it's like that for everyone. If it is, then I guess some folks never find out who it is they're supposed to be with. Maybe that's why the world is so crazy these days. Maybe most people are just running around crazy looking for the one they belong with, and they don't even know they're looking or what it is that's wrong with them. The ones who do find each other, they're the lucky ones. They're

*the ones who know what life's all about. I feel that way about me
and your grandma. And that's how it was with Junaluska and
Qualla. They were just the right people for each other.*

*"Well, they had a little baby, a girl, and her name was Oconee-
chee. I don't know what that word means, because it's not a Cherokee word, but there used to be a small Indian tribe in these parts
with a name that sounded like that same word. I think maybe
Qualla came from that tribe, and so when they had their* usdi, *their
little one, they gave her that name—the name of her momma's
people. But that's just my guess. Anyhow, she was a pretty little
baby, and Junaluska and Qualla were just about as happy as they
could be. But it didn't last long. Qualla took sick, and she died while
Oconeechee was still just a baby. Junaluska, he was so lost and
lonely without his Qualla that he wanted to die and go with her.
He wanted to find her there on the other side of the big Sky Vault.
He knew that she was up there somewhere just waiting for him to
come along. He cried and he called out toward the Sky Vault that
he wanted to go. He didn't want to stay on this world any longer—
not alone, not without Qualla. But one night when he was sleeping,
he had a dream. Or maybe it wasn't a dream. Maybe it was real.
Qualla came down and talked to him. 'You can't come with me,'
she said. 'Not yet. Our baby has lost her mother. You have to stay
for her sake. When she's grown and has found her own man to look
after her, then you can come to me. I'll be waiting for you.'*

*"So Junaluska stayed on this world to raise his little girl, and
even though he missed Qualla so bad that it hurt him, and he never
stopped thinking about her, not for a minute, he loved little Oconeechee very much. And she was a lot like her mother. She was the
only thing old Junaluska was living for. And it was hard times when
he had to raise this little girl. The state governments all around us
and the U.S. government were all ganged up on the Cherokees and
the other Indians. They wanted all Indians to get out west—to
move west of the big river—the Mississippi River."*

"Why did they want that, Grandpa?" I said.

*"Well, it's kind of hard to say. They thought that a white man
was better than an Indian. They thought we were savages. I'm not
too sure what that word means, that* savage, *but I guess it just
means that we didn't live the same way they did. They said savages
steal and kill people. But they stole from us and they killed our
people. So I don't really know what they meant by that. But they
said that Indians were savage, and they didn't want savage neigh-*

bors. But mostly, I think, they just wanted all our land. I think that's why they wanted to kick us out.

"But that's what was going on. Junaluska knew that it was hard times, and he knew that his little girl would need him, so he stayed here. And now that's the place where the story really starts—the story about the windsong."

2

Chief Junaluska's daughter
Beautiful Oconeechee
Was bathing in a mountain stream
Where a warrior chanced to be.
She stepped out of the water,
And it made his heart stand still.
There had never been such beauty
In the life of Whippoorwill.

Oconeechee wore a cotton skirt and blouse her father had purchased for her at Wil Usdi's store. It was lighter weight and not as hot and uncomfortable in the sultry summer as her buckskins were, but even so the cotton material was sticking to her back and legs. Her long black hair clung to the sweat on her neck. Gnats were particularly bothersome. She had finished her noon meal of corn soup and venison and bean bread, all washed down with good, strong coffee, and she was bored. At sixteen, she was full of energy and youthful exuberance, but the chores of the house not only failed to interest her, they couldn't keep her occupied. She finished the tasks assigned her as the woman of the house, and still had hours in her day to fill with some kind of activity. She spent much of that leisure time alone in the woods which surrounded Soco Gap. One reason she kept to herself was that the single young men of Soco Gap were constantly pursuing her, and there was not one among them who could excite her interest.

So the heat of the day and the annoying attacks of the gnats really served as an excuse for her to follow her natural inclination to avoid unwanted company and seek the solace and cool comfort of the nearby mountain stream. She knew a spot seldom frequented by other citizens of Soco Gap, one she regarded almost as her own private sanctuary. It was just below a falls where the mountain waters, icy even in the hot summer months, cascaded down into a wide pool which appeared to stand remarkably calm even though at its side opposite the falls a narrow stream raced on down the mountain. Oconeechee could feel a significant drop in temperature as she made her way down the hillside to stand beside the calm, cool deep blue and inviting pool. She drew in a full breath and surveyed the scene. Then she pulled her blouse off over her head and dropped it on the rocks beside her. She pushed her cotton skirt down around her ankles, stepped out of it, and waded naked into the soothing waters.

Waguli was looking for Soco Gap. The officials in his own town had sent him on a mission. They knew that Lumpkin, the governor of Georgia, and Andrew Jackson, the president of the United States, were threatening to take their land and move them all to someplace far out in the West, toward the Darkening Land. They had heard the story of Junaluska's attempt to visit the president, and they knew of his resulting new name. They had also heard about the treaty that Ridge and Boudinot and others had signed at New Echota, and they knew that big troubles were ahead for all of them. But it had been some time since they had heard any news, and Waguli had been selected to visit the great man at Soco Gap and ask him what he knew.

Waguli had been selected because he was a young man, strong and healthy, and because he had no wife and children to leave behind. He had also been chosen because he was a skilled speaker and a reliable, level-headed young man. And he had never been to Soco Gap. The old men thought it was time he found his way into that part of the country. Waguli traveled alone, and he traveled light. He wore buckskin leggings with a breechclout and moccasins and nothing else but a single eagle feather tied in his scalp lock. He carried his weapons, and he had a blanket roll tied across his back.

Waguli thought he should be near his destination, but the country around was all unfamiliar to him, so he couldn't be sure. He could hear coming from somewhere up ahead the soothing, cool sounds of a rushing mountain stream. Between him and the stream was a high rocky ridge. Soco Gap, he figured, was built someplace along that stream—or at least, somewhere very near it. He headed up the ridge. It was a steep climb on a hot day towards the end of a long journey, yet he moved quickly and surely up the mountainside toward the ridge.

Waguli was not neglecting his duty for his own comfort. He would freshen up in the mountain waters in order to be able to present himself in a dignified fashion to the people of Soco Gap. The stream was narrow and shallow where Waguli first approached it, so he followed it up the mountain until he came to a spot more suitable for bathing. He had been told that Soco Gap was high in the mountains, and so he thought that he was moving in the right direction anyway. Where he finally stopped the ground leveled off a little. The stream was slightly wider and ran a bit more slowly. It even appeared to Waguli that at this point he could wade into water that would at least reach his waist. He looked around himself for a long moment, then leaned his bow, quiver of arrows, and long blowgun across the trunk of a fallen tree nearby. He untied the eagle feather from his hair and tied it to one end of his bow to keep it off the ground. He removed the blanket roll from his back, untied it, and spread it out on the ground, revealing fresh clothing, more formal than that which he wore for traveling. Then he quickly stripped out of his breech-clout, leggings, and moccasins and waded into the stream. The cold water caused him to gasp involuntarily, but the gasp was followed by a long and satisfied sigh of relief from the heat. Finding the deepest spot in the middle of the stream, Waguli bent his knees and allowed himself to sink completely under. He rubbed himself vigorously to remove sweat and salt and trail dirt.

But this was not a pleasure stop. Waguli was on serious business for the people of his town, and he was soon back out of the water. He picked up a comb from his blanket and ran it through the lock of hair which grew from the crown of his otherwise shaven head. Then he knelt to straighten out the fresh leggings, breechclout, and jacket that had been rolled up in the blanket. Waguli felt a hunger pang gnaw at him, but he ignored it. He was completely out of the *gahawisti* that his mother's sister had prepared for him from dried corn for his journey, but he knew that he would be fed generously at Soco Gap. The heat of the day dried him soon, and he pulled on the clean leggings and moccasins and fastened the breechclout in place. All were elaborately decorated with dyed porcupine quills and colored glass trade beads, as was the leather hunting jacket which he chose to carry until he actually had Soco Gap in sight. He tied the eagle feather back in place, rolled his soiled trail clothes up in the blanket, gathered his weapons, and resumed his march upstream.

Oconeechee swam on her back luxuriating in the cool water and delighting in her own nakedness. She knew that at sixteen she already had a body which drove the men of Soco Gap wild with desire, and, of course, she took some secret pride in that fact. For her part, however, she had not felt that kind of urge. She enjoyed her own nakedness alone there in the clear water of her almost secret place listening to the sounds of the woods: the chattering of *saloli,* the squirrel, the rapid hard-driving of *dalala* the woodpecker, the caustic clamour of *dlayhga,* the bluejay, the harsh *ga ga* of *koga,* the crow, even the busy, systematic buzzing of *wadulisi,* the bee. The thought of a man, any man, intruding on her isolation with the other creatures of the woods disgusted her. She knew also that she was becoming an object of scorn in her village. Cherokees felt that something was wrong with a woman who remained a virgin too long after her body had matured. The white missionaries had been working hard to change that attitude, but the people in Soco Gap remained stubborn about some things. Eventually, she knew, if she persisted in her obstinacy, someone would try to force her.

"*Da ji i si,*" she said out loud. "I will kill him."

Up above her on the high ridge there was a sudden flurry. Birds flew toward the treetops, and a squirrel scolded. She stroked the water gently, just enough to hold her up, and let her body sink below the surface as she looked for the cause of the disturbance. She heard it before she could see it. It was the sound of a human being walking. *Asgaya.* A man. She felt a momentary sense of panic lest someone discover her in her favorite haunt. Then she saw him. It was a man all right, a young man. She could tell by his stride. But such a young man. She could see the shine of his shaved head. She had seen old men like that, a few, but never a young man. The young men had all stopped the old practice of shaving their heads. They wore their hair like white men, cut just below the ears or at the shoulders. A few wore it longer. But only some few stubborn old men still shaved their heads except for the *gidhla,* the scalp lock.

She tried to keep still. She didn't want the strange young man to spy her there below him in her pool. He moved on. His pace was quick and deliberate, and he seemed to be making his way toward Soco Gap. Who could he be, she wondered, a Cherokee from some remote and backward village? Or a Shawnee, or a Delaware? He vanished from her sight, and she hurried out of the water and back into her clothes. Maybe she could reach town before him. She would try. She ran as fast as she could, cutting through the woods on mountain trails that a stranger wouldn't know. Her bare feet pounded the hardened dirt street that led her gasping for breath to her father's small log house in the Gap. Junaluska was sitting on a three-legged stool in front of the house smoking a short clay pipe. He stood up when he saw his daughter approaching in such a rush, and laid aside the pipe. As she came up to him, he grabbed her by the shoulders to help her stop.

"What is it?" he said. "What's all the hurry?"

She tried to answer, but couldn't. She took several deep breaths.

"*Edoda,*" she said at last, "Father, has he come yet?"

"*Gago?* Who?"

"The stranger."

"No one has come," said Junaluska. "Catch your breath, and tell me what it is you're talking about."

Oconeechee dropped to her haunches, then sat heavily on the ground and leaned back against the house. Her father picked up his pipe and sat back down on the stool.

"Well?" he said.

"I was bathing, and I saw him walking along the ridge. He was coming this way. I've never seen him before. I've never seen anyone like him."

"What was he like," said Junaluska, "this strange man? Did he have two heads?"

"One," said his daughter. "Shaved."

"Oh, an old-timer."

"No, Father, a young man, but he was like the old-timers. Like what they must have been when they were young. His clothes were different too. All skins. He had no cloth on him."

Junaluska puffed at his pipe, trying to get it going again.

"A young, old-fashioned stranger coming here," he said. "He must be an emissary from one of our distant towns. Let's get ready to greet him. Bring my good coat and my turban. Change your clothes, and prepare some food for our visitor. I'll go tell Elaqui and Gog'ski."

Waguli saw the town just ahead. He dropped his blanket roll to the ground, set aside his weapons, and pulled on the leather hunting jacket. Then he picked up his things and started toward the town walking with a slow and stately gait. Soon he could see the people of Soco Gap gathering to await his arrival.

"So they know I'm coming," he said to himself.

He was anxious, but forced himself to maintain his steady and dignified pace. He could see three men out in front of the rest of the crowd. They wore colorful cloth hunting jackets and turbans on their heads. He had seen those before. A few of the men in his town were beginning to dress that way and to let their hair grow all over their heads like white men. Those three ahead must be the town chiefs and the priest, Waguli guessed. When he reached them, Junaluska was the first to speak.

"*Siyo,*" he said. "*Ayuh* Tsunalahuhski. I am Junaluska, war chief of Soco Gap. This is our peace chief, Gog'ski, Smoker, and this is Elaqui, Snail, our priest. You are welcome here."

"*Wado,*" said Waguli. "Thank you. I am Whippoorwill of the Wolf People from Old Town far in the mountains. I've been sent to ask you the news."

"Good," said Junaluska. "We'll talk, but first, you must be hungry from your journey. Let's eat."

Times were hard in Soco Gap, as they were throughout Cherokee country, yet a feast was spread for Waguli, the Whippoorwill of Old Town, for as soon as the word had spread concerning his approach, every household of the Gap had

pitched in. The food was served at the council house, an old
fashioned, seven-sided structure of logs. Everyone attended,
and everyone ate. There was corn soup and kanuche. There
was cornbread and beanbread. There were grape dumplings.
There was squirrel and rabbit and venison and even some
beef and pork. There were wild onions and there was poke.
There were crawdads. One old woman had even prepared
some wasp soup. And there were several pots of steaming
coffee. Waguli seldom drank coffee for it was not often to be
had at Old Town, but he liked it, and at this feast he drank
more than his fill. Throughout the meal, he was carefully
watched by Oconeechee. No one would notice, she thought,
because everyone was curious about this young, old-fashioned
stranger. Waguli. Whippoorwill.

Since Waguli was an official visitor from another town and
his business had to do with what was happening in the strug-
gle between the Cherokee Nation and the United States, Junaluska was the man in charge. As war chief he was given
charge of any of the external affairs of government. The meal
finished, Junaluska, with Gog'ski, Elaqui, and Oconeechee,
led Waguli to his house. They sat outside on benches and
stools. Oconeechee hovered in the background, not officially
involved in the discussion but allowed to eavesdrop openly.

"We'll tell you all we know," said Junaluska. "It may not
be the latest news, and it may be that some of it you will
already know, but we'll tell you all we know."

"*Wado,*" said Whippoorwill. "Thank you."

"As I'm sure you know already, the *yonegs* want our country. They've offered us some land out west in exchange for
this our homeland. Speaking for all of us, our chief John Ross
has refused the offer."

"We know Cooweescoowee," said Whippoorwill, using
the mixed-blood chief's Cherokee name. "In Old Town we
know him."

"We went to court," Junaluska continued. "We went two
times to the highest United States court. Both times we won.
But Jackson commands the army, and they say that he'll ignore the court."

"The great chief of the white men ignores his own law?"
said Whippoorwill.

"Yes. Are you surprised? Do you know the story of my
name?"

Whippoorwill looked at the ground between himself and Junaluska—Tsunu lahun ski—He Tried but He Failed.

"Yes," he said. "I've heard that story."

"Nothing is sacred to Jackson," said Elaqui, "to this *tseg'sgin,* this devil—not his own word, not gratitude, not friendship, not his own laws. He would cut the ovaries out of his own dead grandmother and sell this for fish bait."

He turned his head and spat in disgust.

"And he is the great leader of all the whites," said Gog'ski. "What kind of men are these?"

"But there are some whites who live with us," said Waguli. "I saw some here when I came, and we even have some at Old Town. They have Cherokee wives. And here, I think, I even saw a white woman."

"Yes," said Junaluska. "She has a Cherokee husband. The good ones, I guess, have come to live with us."

Waguli stared thoughtfully at the ground between his feet. This was all old news. He needed something more current before he could return to Old Town.

"So what do you think?" he asked Junaluska. "Will we have to move? Will we fight? What will become of us?"

"I don't know," said the old man. "John Ross says we mustn't fight. I don't think that we will. Some of our own people, Major Ridge and his son and Elias Boudinot, some others, are beginning to tell people to sign a new treaty, to accept Jackson's offer and move west."

"I know those men," said Waguli, "that Boudinot and the young Ridge. They came to Old Town once. They were going all over and telling the people to stay here. They said the Americans were wrong and couldn't make us leave our homes."

Junaluska sighed, a heavy, sad sigh with the sound of a last breath departing.

"It seems they have changed their opinions," he said. "They are now saying that times have changed, that it will be easier on us if we go now. They say if we resist longer, the U.S. will move us by force."

"They are cowards," said Gog'ski.

"I don't think so," said Junaluska. "I don't know why they've changed their minds, but I don't believe they are cowards."

"Traitors, then," said Elaqui.

"Every man has a right to express his opinion," said Juna-luska. "If they really believe what they're saying now, they should say it."

Elaqui stood up and walked a few paces away from the group, then turned back to face them, his face wearing a heavy scowl.

"I think they've accepted bribes from the government," he said. "That's why they're saying these things. That's why they've changed their minds."

Waguli looked up and, quite by accident, his eyes caught the eyes of Oconeechee, who was standing behind her father. She had been watching him. He could tell. He looked quickly back down at the ground.

"What can I tell them?" he said. "What can I tell the People back at Old Town?"

 3

We were down at the edge of the creek where the water was cold and clear, and Grandpa was holding a cane fishing pole in his leathery old hands. Dragonflies skimmed along the water and occasionally buzzed past our heads. A cool breeze was blowing and carrying away with it the smoke from Grandpa's pipe. A piece of fresh chicken meat was tied to the end of Grandpa's line, and he had let it down on the flat rocks just a few feet out into the water.

"Now just watch," he had said.

Grandma had killed and plucked the chicken for us, and we had taken it, the fishing pole, a long-handled fishnet, and a big plastic bucket with us down to the creek.

"Look," I said.

A fat, sinister-looking crawdad had crept out from under a flat rock and was making his way toward the meat.

"Jisduh," said Grandpa.

"What?"

"That's his name. Jisduh. Watch. There will be more."

He was right. In just a few minutes the meat was covered with them. They were crawling over each other and falling off. Grandpa smiled, and his old eyes seemed to twinkle.

"They like that fresh chicken," he said. *"We'll wait a minute
and let them get really busy with their meal."*

"What then?" I said.

"Get the net."

*I ran to pick up the net, then went back to stand anxiously by
Grandpa, waiting for his next instructions.*

"Get ready to wade out there," he said.

*I sat down and took off my shoes and socks and rolled my jeans
up over my knees.*

*"Now," he said, "wade out real close, but go easy. You don't
want to scare them away."*

*I crept into the cold water, moving slowly and cautiously, trying
not to even ripple the water, watching the flat, slick rocks with their
sharp edges so I wouldn't slip on them or cut my feet and watching
with fascination the crawdads at work so diligently on the piece of
chicken. Somewhere in my mind with all those other thoughts was
the fear that one or more of the small beasts might decide to attack
my bare feet and legs with those terrible pinchers. There were so
many of them by then that I couldn't even count them. I got as close
as I dared. Then I stopped. The water was cold on my feet and legs,
and it felt good.*

*"Get ahold of the line and lift them up," said Grandpa. "Real
slow and easy. Just enough so you can get the net under there and
grab them."*

*I reached out slowly with my left hand and took the line between
my thumb and forefinger. I had the net in my right, and I lowered
it down close to the water. Then I slowly pulled up on the line until
the crawdad-covered meat was up off the rock. My heart was pounding in my chest. Two of the creatures fell off the bait as I lifted it,
but they scrambled right back into the crowd fighting for their share.
They weren't even suspicious. I shoved the net quickly under them
and jerked it up and out of the water.*

"I got them," I shouted.

"Bring them on out," said Grandpa.

*I carried the net to the bucket, and Grandpa took it and shook all
the crawdads off and into the bucket. Excited, I counted our catch.*

"Twelve," I said. "We got twelve of them."

*Grandpa moved the end of the pole and lowered the meat back
into the water. The same thing happened again—and again and
again. Our bucket was full, and most of the chicken had been used.
On Grandpa's last few casts only a few crawdads had appeared to*

*attach themselves to the bait. It seemed to me as if it had taken only
a short while to fill our bucket, but actually, I guess, it had taken
up most of the late afternoon. The sun was low in the west, just
about to vanish beyond the mountains, and it was making lovely red
and yellow and orange and pink patterns over the dark tree-covered
horizon. I thought that we'd be heading right home, but Grandpa
lit his pipe and leaned back on his elbows.*

"Grandpa," I said, "why did they change their minds?"

*"They didn't change their minds," he said. "We caught most of
them."*

*"I don't mean the crawdads," I said. "I mean those men. Those
Cherokees who said we should all move to Oklahoma."*

"Oh. You're talking about our story."

"Yeah."

*He puffed his pipe, and the smoke ran away in the cool evening
breeze.*

*"There wasn't no such thing then as Oklahoma," he said. "The
land was there, of course, but it wasn't Oklahoma yet.*

*"I don't know why they changed their minds, chooj. I guess if
we had us a room full of Cherokees even today and asked them all
that question, they'd all have different answers. Likely we'd get into
a fight over it. Some think they were good, honest men who really
decided that it would just be better for all the Indians if they went on
ahead out west on their own. Others think they betrayed the Cherokee people for money and for better treatment from the government
for themselves and their families. I don't know. But they sure did
change their song. They surprised everyone when they did that, I
guess.*

*"One thing they were right about. Things did start to get rougher
on the Cherokees. Especially those in Georgia. Georgia passed a
bunch of laws they called the anti-Cherokee laws. They said a white
person couldn't go onto Cherokee land without a permit from the
state government. They said Indians couldn't testify in court. White
men would ride out to Cherokee homes and steal from them, and the
Cherokees couldn't complain because they couldn't testify. Things
got bad."*

*"I thought they said white men couldn't go on Cherokee land,"
I said.*

*"They only passed that law so they could get the white people
who were our friends. Those who were trying to help us. They
arrested some missionaries who were out among the Cherokees and*

threw them in prison. But they didn't care about them others, the ones who just wanted to steal from us."

"What did Whippoorwill do?" I asked.

"Oh, he stayed around Soco Gap for awhile. He talked to everybody he could who might know anything more than what he'd already heard. Sometimes somebody's kinfolks would come in to visit from another town, and he'd ask them what news they had.

"And he commenced to get acquainted with Oconeechee."

> She took him home to her father,
> Said, "My love for him is real."
> Junaluska spread the doeskin
> For his child and Whippoorwill.

Waguli had been busy with his assigned task, but he had looked at the beautiful young daughter of Junaluska, and when he felt he could steal a quiet, leisurely moment, he allowed his mind the luxury of dreaming about her. He knew he didn't have time to indulge his own whims and fancies. He was on business vital to the well-being of his people—the people of Old Town. Yet he had looked at her, and she was very beautiful. And somehow he felt that she had—what? Well, she had looked at him, too. He longed for peaceful times and the leisure they allow. He was sitting idly before the house of Junaluska, and he realized with slight irritation that it was this idleness which allowed such thoughts to race through his head. He should be doing something, he thought, but there was nothing for him to do.

Junaluska had said there was to be a meeting at Red Clay in Georgia, an important meeting. Chief John Ross and other Cherokee politicians would be there, along with some men from the white man's government in Washington. Some people from Soco Gap would attend the meeting, and Junaluska had invited Waguli to travel with them.

"Then you'll take home all the latest information," he had said.

Waguli had considered for a moment, then had decided to accept the invitation. They would be leaving the next morning, so for the time being, Waguli was idle. He had been sitting and smoking with Junaluska following their noon meal, and Junaluska had seen Elaqui, the Snail, passing by. He had gone to speak to Snail, leaving Waguli there alone to muse. Oconeechee stepped out of the house.

"Are you going to Red Clay?" she asked.

The question caught Waguli off guard, and he stammered a bit before he answered her.

"Yes," he said. "I'm planning to go."

"Do all the men in your town look like you?"

"What?"

"Do they?"

Waguli was puzzled.

"No," he said. "Turkey is tall and skinny. Some are old. Some short. Like everywhere else, I guess, we have all kinds."

"Silly," said Oconeechee. "I mean do they dress like you and shave their heads? You knew what I meant, didn't you? You were teasing me."

"No, I wasn't teasing. I didn't think of that. I thought it was a strange question you asked me."

Oconeechee laughed, and Waguli relaxed a little, laughing with her.

"Yes," he said. "Well, most of them. A few men, a little older than I, went away with the *yoneg* soldiers, and when they came back home they were changed. We thought they were—strange."

"How did they look?"

"We thought they were like the *yonegs*."

"Did they look like the men here at Soco Gap?"

Waguli looked at the ground.

"Yes."

"Here at the Gap we've been around the whites a long time. Most of the men here who are old enough fought with Jackson against the Red Stick Creeks. They have changed, I guess, from being around the white men so much. I never thought of it much until I saw you."

"Do you think that I look strange?"

Oconeechee looked Waguli up and down, and she smiled.

"Yes," she said, "but I like the strange way you look."

Waguli's pride and pleasure forced a wide grin across his face.

"You are very beautiful," he said.

"Do you want to swim?"

"What?"

"I have a place to swim," she said. "It's almost a secret. No one goes there but me."

"I saw you there," said Waguli.

"When?"

"When I first came here."

"When you walked along the ridge that first day?"

"Yes."

"I saw you, too, but you were just looking straight ahead. I didn't think you saw me. Do you want to go?"

"That would be nice," said Waguli. "It's a warm day, and I have nothing to do until we go to Red Clay."

"Good. I'll tell my father, and we'll go."

"What's your clan?" Waguli said suddenly.

"I'm a Wolf Person."

Waguli's heart sank. A Wolf. Waguli was a Wolf. To touch this beautiful young woman would be incest. Waguli felt that fate had been unmercifully cynical with him. He had never seen such a beautiful woman, had never felt such desire. And then to find out that she was a relative, a Wolf Person, was too cruel. This is what comes of idleness, he thought. Perhaps it will teach me to keep my mind on business. He glanced up to see Junaluska headed back toward the house, and he turned abruptly away from Oconeechee.

"I have to talk to your father about the trip," he said.

Oconeechee was puzzled by Waguli's quick change of mood and abrupt departure, but she thought that he'd return soon. When he didn't and it became obvious to her that he was avoiding even her glance, she left the town alone and walked through the woods to her favorite place, but she didn't swim. She sat beside the water and stared. What, she wondered, had gone wrong? Things had been going so well. What had she said or done?

As Oconeechee walked into the woods two young men of Soco Gap, Badger and Mouse, watched her go.

"There goes that crazy one," said Badger.

"Crazy, yes," said Mouse, "but she sure looks good."

"She turns away from all of us. I used to think there was something wrong with her. You know, that she didn't like men, but that was before that old-fashioned one from Old Town showed up here."

"She likes him," said Mouse. "You can tell. Maybe if you shave your head she'll like you, too."

Mouse laughed at his own joke, but Badger didn't laugh

with him. Badger looked surly, and he was staring after Oconeechee—where she had gone into the woods.

"Let's go after her," he said.

Mouse's laughter stopped abruptly, and his stare followed Badger's.

"You want to?" he said.

"Of course," said Badger. "She's been daring us to, hasn't she? Let's give her what she wants before that stranger gives it to her. Then he can have her, if he still wants her."

"Maybe she won't want him after she's had us," said Mouse with a leer.

"Yes," said Badger. "*Inena.*"

"Yes," said Mouse, "let's go."

She thought about the Old Town Whippoorwill as she watched the almost still water drift in slow and silent circles, gathering itself to rush headlong down the mountain to wherever it was going. It was always going somewhere, and there was always more coming down the mountain to keep the clear, cold pool full. She slipped her feet into the cool, fresh water, and wondered what had suddenly bothered Waguli—Waguli, the mountain whippoorwill. She inched over the sharp rocks to get closer to the edge of the water in order to let it lap around her brown calves, and she considered her feelings. Never before had she had any interest in a man, but this Waguli fascinated her. He was beautiful as only a man can be beautiful, she thought, and she knew that she wanted him. There could be no other. This was the man she had been waiting for even though she had not known she had been waiting for anyone. Waguli had been sent to her. She loved him.

She stood up in the water. It reached just above her knees and it was cold, but it felt good on a warm day. She slipped the blouse and the skirt off over her head and eased herself into the pool, then drifted out toward the deeper waters. Her sadness had somehow vanished and been replaced by a mysterious calm, a contentment. Waguli had turned away from her, but he would come back. She knew that he would. She loved him, and she was certain that he would love her. She took a deep breath and allowed herself to sink beneath the water, then swam with her eyes open, looking at the wonders of that other world until her lungs could no longer hold out.

Then she surfaced and gulped fresh mountain air. She swam back to the bank and stepped gingerly out onto the rocks where she had dropped her clothes. She leaned over the edge of the pool and twisted water out of her hair, then shook it out again in the breeze.

Suddenly Badger stepped out from somewhere and stood before her. He grinned a sideways grin and looked at her nakedness. His sudden appearance startled her, but she quickly regained control of herself. She looked him straight in the eyes, a threatening act to a Cherokee.

"What are you doing here?" she said.

"I've come for you."

"Get away."

"Hold her, Mouse."

She felt hands grab her arms from behind and pull. She struggled, but Mouse pulled her backwards, down onto the rocks. Badger stood over her. He pulled his store-bought shirt over his head and tossed it aside, stepped out of his moccasins, then dropped his trousers. He loomed there, rigid, obviously ready for what he wanted. She made a sound of disgust and struggled more to free herself from Mouse's grip. Mouse was laughing. Badger stepped forward, losing his balance slightly as a sharp-edged rock bit into the sole of his bare foot, and Oconeechee kicked upward, swinging her right leg with all the strength she could put into it. She hit her mark, causing Badger to scream in pain, reach for his crotch with both hands, and double over in agony. Then she gave a quick and hard wrench with her shoulders to her left, the wet skin of her right arm slipping free from Mouse's hold. Mouse grabbed her hair with his right hand, but she had already picked up a fist-sized rock in her right, and she slammed it into the side of his face.

"Ahh."

He released Oconeechee to grab for the pain on the side of his head. Then he dropped to his knees holding his face in his hands, blood running between his fingers. Badger was still doubled up in his misery, and Oconeechee gave him a shove, toppling him into the pool. She picked up her skirt and blouse and ran.

4

We were sitting behind the house on some old metal lawn chairs. Grandpa sat in the green one, and I was in the red one. The paint was wearing thin on both of them, and they had some rust spots. Grandpa was examining a piece of river cane about four feet long that he held in his leathery hands. He rubbed it from one end to the other, then he checked the ends where he had cut it off smooth just at the joints. He held it up and sighted along its length, then turned it around and did the same thing from its other end.

"Looks pretty straight," he said. "Fetch me that reamer over there, chooj."

I ran over to the shed in the direction he had indicated with his chin and looked around in total confusion at the array of things lying and leaning there.

"What?" I said.

"That long rod there with the sharp point," he said.

I put a hand on a metal rod about a yard long and shot Grandpa a questioning look.

"That's it," he said.

I took him the reamer and stepped back to watch. He began goug-

ing and turning the reamer to cut through the tough membrane at the cane's joints. He finally got through the first one and moved the reamer down a foot or so into the cane pole to start on the next. I started to fidget, and then I dragged a bucket over in front of Grandpa, upended it and sat on it.

"What happened at the meeting?" I asked.

"Oh, not much," he said. "It was just like every other church meeting. Budget report. We didn't have hardly enough money to talk about. Never do. Then Louella Birdsong, she made her usual talk about how we need to get more young people in Sunday School."

"I mean the meeting Whippoorwill went to," I said. "At Red Clay."

"Oh," said Grandpa. "That meeting."

He smiled a devious kind of smile that made me think he knew all along what I was talking about. Then he broke through the second membrane with his reamer. The reamer was too short to go all the way through the cane pole, so he pulled it out and turned the pole around to start on the other end.

"It was just like a lot of other meetings, too," he said. "Any time something big's about to happen to people, they have meetings. All the big shots talk. The politicians, you know. They all make speeches. Some will talk one way and some the other. Some will sound kind of sad about it when they talk, and some will get mad and say the other guy don't care about the people. Got no heart, you know. Then when all the big shots get done, some of the little people will want to talk. People just in the crowd there listening, like you and me. They'll talk and it makes them feel big. Most of the crowd, though, they'll just listen. Keep quiet until it's all over. Then they'll turn to whoever's handy nearby, and they'll tell that person what they think about it all. When it's all done, broke up, and they go back home, then whatever it was they gathered up to talk about comes along and happens to them anyhow.

"That's how it was that time. Old Cooweescoowee, that was Chief Ross, he talked about how the United States government was acting illegal. He told the people there that Andy Jackson didn't have no right to do what he was doing. Said that even the U.S. Supreme Court was on our side and Jackson was breaking his own laws. Then he talked about those Cherokees who had signed that treaty, and he said that they were guilty of treason. He reminded everyone that the Cherokee National Council had passed a law making it illegal for anyone to sell Cherokee land, and anyone

caught doing that could be executed. And besides all that, he told them, those men weren't even elected to do anything by the Cherokee people. They weren't chiefs or council members or even delegates appointed for anything. They didn't have any right to sign anything for Cherokees, and the United States didn't have any right to honor anything they had signed.

"Then he went on for a while about our homeland, how much it means to us. He didn't have any need to tell Cherokees how we feel about home, but I guess everyone liked hearing it anyway. You know, people like to hear someone talk when he's saying what they already believe. Finally, he said, we're not going anywhere. We're going to stay right here, because it's our land and we've got the right, but he said that he didn't want anyone to fight. No fighting, he said."

"Well, some others got up that said the same things that he said. Said they agreed with the chief. And that took about just all day long that first day, I guess."

"What was Whippoorwill doing?" I asked.

"Oh, I imagine he was just there in the crowd, listening to everything and watching everything. I imagine that was probably the farthest away from home Waguli had ever been and probably the biggest crowd of people he'd ever seen. And I bet he'd never seen the likes of old John Ross and them other Cherokee big shots all dressed in fancy suits with lace on their shirts just like rich white men. I imagine he was saying to himself, 'I just thought that Junaluska's bunch was like white men. I hadn't seen nothing 'til I came here.' And there was white men there, too. There must have been more whites than Waguli ever thought he'd see.

"So everything that was said had to be said once over again for everybody to get to understand. See, if a man made a talk in Cherokee, somebody would have to say it over again in English so that them who couldn't understand Cherokee would know what he'd said. Then if somebody said something in English, they'd have to do the same thing but the other way around."

"I bet that's why the meeting lasted all day long," I said.

"Well, yeah. That was sure part of the reason, but the meeting wasn't over that first day. They had to gather up again the next morning."

"What happened then?"

Grandpa poked through another membrane in the cane pole. There was one left to do. Then the pole would be hollow all the way through.

"Next morning," he said, "the other guys got up to talk. There

*was some friends of those treaty guys. They said that it wasn't fair
to call them traitors and to talk about killing them. They said that
the longer the Cherokees held out against the United States, the
worse things would be on them. Those treaty signers, they said,
were just trying to make things a little bit easier for everybody, and
they even risked their own lives to do that. They knew, these
speechmakers said, that some people would call them traitors and
would want them killed. They knew about that law, but they loved
their people so much—this is what their friends were saying that
day—they loved their people so much that they were willing to take
a chance.*

"These guys told all the people gathered there that they'd be better off if they got ready and moved out west on their own, if they
didn't try to hold out any longer, stopped resisting the U.S. government. 'It ain't so bad out there,' they said. 'Some of us done went
and looked. It's about like here.' And I guess that they convinced a
few people that they was right. They claimed that old Ross was
putting everyone else in danger for selfish reasons. Said he knew
that they wouldn't really be able to stay. He was just holding out
for more money.

"Well, you know, Cherokees ain't like white folks when it comes
to politics and speechmaking. No matter how much we don't like
what it is we're listening to, we listen. We give the man who's
talking his chance to have his say. So the people let them talk, but
they could tell, I imagine, that the people was getting mad. Most of
the Cherokees liked old Ross, and they didn't like to hear what these
guys were saying. But they had their say, just like the other side
did, and then the white men talked.

"The white men talked in English, and the translator had to say
it over in Cherokee. They said that the people had ought to listen
to their brothers who had just talked. They said that John Ross was
misguided. They said that the governor of Georgia was fixing to let
loose all the white trash of Georgia onto Cherokee lands and the
United States wasn't going to be able to help us none. That scared
some of the folks. The whites said that the government in Washington was just only interested in our safety, and that's why they
wanted us to get out west where it was safe. 'Course, they didn't
say nothing about the Osages.''

"Osages," I said. "Indians?"

"Sure. The Osage Indians lived out there in the west where the
government wanted to send all the Cherokees. Western Arkansas
and Eastern Oklahoma now. That was their land, their home, just

*like this out here was ours, but the government didn't care about
that, I guess. They said that we could have all that land out there.
Never even mentioned the Osages. But the Cherokees knew all
about them anyhow. Some Cherokees. You know, there was already
Cherokees living out west—mostly in Arkansas. They had got tired
of listening to all the arguments and had just gone on and moved.
And they was fighting a big war with the Osages. Some of them
came back home to visit now and then, and they brought the news
from out west. That's how we knew, even though the government
never told us."*

"I hate the government," I said.

*"No use in that, chooj," said Grandpa. "This all happened a
long time ago. The people who were in the government then are all
long dead. Besides, hate just makes you feel bad. Makes you sick.
It eats you up from inside. I don't hate nothing or nobody. There
are some that I sure can't figure out though, and I ain't got much
use for them."*

*"Well," I said, trying to fathom Grandpa's philosophy, "I guess
I ain't got much use for the government."*

*Grandpa kind of smiled. It showed mostly, though, in the little
wrinkles around his eyes. The reamer broke through the final membrane, and Grandpa ran it back and forth and turned it around and
around from first one end of the cane pole and then the other until
he felt like the inside was smooth enough. Then he set the pole and
the reamer aside and got out his pipe and tobacco. He filled his pipe
and lit it and leaned back in his green chair to enjoy his smoke. I
wanted to hear the rest of the story, and I wanted to know what he
was going to do with the hollow cane pole, but Grandpa looked so
relaxed I hated to bother him. I moved back to my red chair and
turned it a little bit so I could sit straight and watch him.*

Oconeechee handed her father his pipe and tobacco pouch
and waited while he filled the bowl. Then she picked from
the fire a stick with a smoldering end and handed it to him.
He lit the tobacco and handed the stick back to her. She
tossed it back into the fire there just outside the house. Junaluska puffed contentedly. Oconeechee fidgeted. Then she sat
on the hard, packed earth there in front of the old man and
watched him smoke.

"So," he said, "there's something on your mind you want
to talk about."

"How did you know?" she asked.

Junaluska chuckled.

"One can tell," he said. "Is it that old-fashioned Indian that has you so distracted?"

"I might as well tell you everything," said Oconeechee, trying to sound put out with her father. "You read my thoughts."

"You have strong feelings for this Whippoorwill?"

"I love him, Father."

"Ah."

The old man puffed his pipe, sending clouds of smoke towards the heavens. In his mind, his thoughts would go with the smoke and find his Qualla up there on the other side of the Sky Vault. He wanted badly to join her up there.

"It's about time," he said, "that you found yourself a young man to take care of you. I'm getting too old. It's about time for me to leave this world and go on to the next. I want to see your mother again."

A wave of sadness swept over Oconeechee at the thought of losing her father, but she soon dismissed it. He would be around for a long while yet, she told herself. He was just saying that. Besides, her thoughts were too much with Waguli to be long distracted.

"He doesn't like me," she said.

"Why do you think that?"

"We were talking, and I thought he liked me. I asked him if he wanted to go with me to swim, and he said that sounded good. Then he walked away and didn't come back."

"Hmm. Maybe it's too early to tell," said Junaluska. "He'll be back soon. Let's see what happens then."

Just then Badger and Mouse appeared from around the corner. Junaluska saw them and spoke.

"'Siyo,'" he said.

Mouse quickly turned his head, but not before Junaluska got a look at the ugly scab and bruise there. Badger muttered a hurried response to Junaluska's greeting, and the two moved on at a fast pace.

"Now what do you suppose is wrong with those two?" Junaluska said.

Oconeechee looked away. The old man saw something in her face and in the way she attempted to look disinterested.

"What could have given Mouse that terrible knock on the side of his face?"

"I don't know," said Oconeechee, but she had a feeling that her father was reading her mind once again.

Waguli had been surprised to discover that Junaluska would not be traveling to Red Clay for the meeting. It was he who had invited Waguli, but when the time came to leave and Waguli had asked him if he was going, the old man had just shaken his head.

"You know my name," he had said. "I already tried, and I failed. I leave it up to others now. Stop in to see me on your way back, though, after the meeting."

Waguli had looked up to find Oconeechee watching him, and he had quickly looked away. He had then joined Elaqui and Gog'ski and a few others who were going to Red Clay. One had offered him a horse to ride, but Waguli had declined. He had never ridden a horse. In Old Town the horse was still considered to be just what his Cherokee name implied—*soghwili*—he carries it on his back—a beast of burden. But the owner of the horse had insisted. He had even offered to teach Waguli how to ride, so Waguli had relented. At Red Clay his legs were sore. I should have walked, he thought. He had endured two days of oratory and had heard nothing new. The threat of the invasion of Georgia rednecks, however, did sound more immediate.

It seemed to Waguli as if the meeting was about to come to a close, and he hoped that he was right about that. The speeches had all been redundant for some time, and the crowd was becoming restless. It was getting dark, the evening of the second day. The people had all been fed and a fire was still burning. It had been lit for cooking and was being kept alive for light. Up on the speaker's platform a Cherokee called for attention.

"Most of us," he said, "will be going home in the morning. When we stop tonight, the meeting will be over. Is there anyone out there with something to say to all of us who has not had the chance to speak? We want everyone to have the opportunity to speak."

He paused for a moment, and the people looked around at one another.

"This is your last chance at this gathering," said the speaker. "Does anyone else have anything to say?"

"I have some things to say."

All eyes turned toward the voice. It was the voice of an old
man, but it was a strong voice, and it spoke a slightly archaic
Cherokee. The old man was standing just behind the fire,
which threw an eerie illumination over his features. He wore
moccasins decorated with dyed porcupine quills, buckskin
leggings, and a breechclout. Draped across his thin shoulders
was a robe of black wolfskin, hanging open in front to reveal
a shrunken but tattooed torso. Tattoos also adorned his neck
and cheeks. A gorget carved from shell dangled before his
chest from a leathern thong around his neck. Like Waguli's,
his head was shaved, but his *gidhla* grew long and shaggy and
hung in disarray down his back until it reached his waist. It
was decorated, however, with several eagle feathers. A brass
ring adorned his nose, and his ears were slit in order to accommodate large plugs, yet he wore no earplugs, so the loose
skin dangled nearly to his shoulders. Even Waguli thought
that the old man was old-fashioned.

His appearance was startling enough in itself. No one could
recall having seen the old man before. It was as if he had just
materialized there and then. But the most amazing thing was
that the old man was flanked on both sides by two large,
snarling black wolves. They were not tied or restrained in
any visible way, yet they stayed close by the old man's side.
The crowd grew absolutely silent.

"I see Cherokees turning into whites," the old man said,
his face seemingly ablaze. "I see white man's clothes, white
man's weapons, white man's animals. I hear white man's talk.
To maintain our balance, we must remain Cherokee. If you
keep these things you have from white men, the Cherokees
will all be driven to the west, to the edge of the world, to the
Darkening Land. Do you want to stay here where you belong? Then listen to me.

"Throw away your steel knives and iron pots and guns.
Burn the white man's clothes you wear. Throw away the
glass beads you use for decoration and learn again how to
prepare the quills of the porcupine for use as decoration.
Speak your own language, the one God gave the Cherokees.
Kill your cats and pigs and horses. Be Cherokees. That is the
only way to be saved."

 5

UNITED STATES AGREE TO
EXTINGUISH INDIAN TITLE
IN GEORGIA

By an agreement between the United States and the State
of Georgia bearing the date April 24, 1802, Georgia ceded
to the United States all the lands lying south of Tennessee
and west of Chattahoochee River and a line drawn from the
mouth of Uchee Creek direct to Nickohack, on the Tennessee
River. In consideration of this cession the United States agreed
to pay Georgia $1,250,000, and to extinguish the Indian title
whenever the same could be done on peaceable and reasonable
terms; also to assume the burden of what were known as the
Yazoo claims.

Georgia charges the United States with bad faith.—Ever since
the date of this agreement the utmost impatience had been
manifested by the Government and the people of the State of
Georgia at the deliberate and careful course which had characterized the action of the General Government in securing relinquishment of their lands in that State from the Creeks and
Cherokees. Charges of bad faith on the part of the United States,
coupled with threats of taking the matter into their own hands,
had been published in great profusion by the Georgians. These
served only to enhance the difficulties of the situation and to

excite a stubborn resistance in the minds of the Indians against any further cessions of territory.

Cherokees ask protection against Georgia's demands.—Shortly following these attempted negotiations, which had produced in the minds of the Indians a feeling of grave uneasiness and uncertainty, a delegation of Cherokees repaired to Washington for a conference with the President touching the situation. Upon receiving their credentials, the Secretary of War sounded the keynote of the Government's purpose by asking if they had come authorized by their nation to treat for a further relinquishment of territory. To this pointed inquiry the delegation returned a respectful and earnest memorial, urging that their nation labored under a peculiar inconvenience from the repeated appropriations made by Congress for the purpose of holding treaties with them having in view the further purchase of lands. Such action had resulted in much injury to the improvement of the nation in the arts of civilized life by unsettling the minds and prospects of its citizens. Their nation had reached the decisive and unalterable conclusion to cede no more lands, the limits preserved to them by the treaty of 1819 being not more than adequate to their comfort and convenience. It was represented as a gratifying truth that the Cherokees were rapidly increasing in number, rendering it a duty incumbent upon the nation to preserve, unimpaired to posterity, the lands of their ancestors. They therefore implored the interposition of the President with Congress in behalf of their nation, so that provision might be made by law to authorize an adjustment between the United States and the State of Georgia, releasing the former from its compact with the latter so far as it respected the extinguishment of the Cherokee title to land within the chartered limits of that State.

The response of the Secretary of War to this memorial was a reiteration of the terms of the compact with Georgia and of the zealous desire of the President to carry out in full measure the obligations of that compact. The manifest benefits and many happy results that would inure to the Cherokee Nation from an exchange of their country for one beyond the limits of any State and far removed from the annoying encroachments of civilization were pictured in the most attractive colors, but all to no purpose, the Cherokees only maintaining with more marked emphasis their original determination to part with no more land. Seeing the futility of further negotiations, the Secretary of War addressed a communication to the governor of Georgia advising him of the earnest efforts that had been made to secure further concessions from the Cherokees and of the discouraging results, and inviting an expression of opinion from him upon the subject.

Governor Troup's threatening demands.—Governor Troup lost no time in responding to this invitation by submitting a declaration of views on behalf of the government and people of the State of Georgia, the vigorously aggressive tone of which in some measure perhaps compensated for its lack of logical force. After censuring the General Government for the tardiness and weakness that had characterized its action on this subject throughout a series of years and denying that the Indians were anything but mere tenants at will, he laid down the proposition that Georgia was determined at all hazards to become possessed of the Cherokee domain; that if the Indians persisted in their refusal to yield, the consequences would be that the United States must either assist the Georgians in occupying the country which is their own and which is unjustly withheld from them, or, in resisting the occupation, to make war upon and shed the blood of brothers and friends. He further declared that the proposition to permit the Cherokees to reserve a portion of their land within that State for their future home could not be legitimately entertained by the General Government except with the consent of Georgia; that such consent would never be given; and, further that the suggestion of the incorporation of the Indians into the body politic of that State as citizens was neither desirable nor practicable. The conclusion of this remarkable state paper is characterized by a broadly implied threat that Georgia's fealty to the Union would be proportioned to the vigor and alertness with which measures were adopted and carried into effect by the United States for the extinguishment of the Cherokee title.

Response of President Monroe.— . . . The President expressed it as his opinion that the Indian title was not in the slightest degree affected by the compact with Georgia, and that there was no obligation resting on the United States to remove the Indians by force, in the face of the stipulation that it should be done *peaceably* and on *reasonable* conditions. The compact gave a claim to the State which ought to be executed in all its conditions with good faith. In doing this, however, it was the duty of the United States to regard its strict import, and to make no sacrifice of their interest not called for by the compact, nor to commit any breach of right or humanity toward the Indians repugnant to the judgment and revolting to the feelings of the whole American people. The Cherokee agent, Ex-Governor McMinn, was shortly afterward ordered, "without delay and in the most effectual manner, forthwith to expel white intruders from Cherokee lands."

Alarm of the Cherokees and indignation of Georgia.—The views expressed by the governor and legislature of Georgia upon this subject were the cause of much alarm among the Cherokees, who, through their delegation, appealed to the magnanimity of the American Congress for justice and for the protection of the rights, liberties, and lives of the Cherokee people. On the other hand, the doctrines enunciated in President Monroe's special message, quoted above, again aroused the indignation of the governor of Georgia, who, in a communication to the President, commented with much severity upon the bad faith that for twenty years had characterized the conduct of the executive officers of the United States in their treatment of the matter in dispute.

Message of President John Quincy Adams.— . . . the President declared that it ought not to be disguised that the act of the legislature of Georgia, under the construction given to it by the governor of that State, and the surveys made or attempted by his authority beyond the boundary secured by the treaty of 1826 to the Creek Indians, were in direct violation of the supreme law of the land, set forth in a treaty which had received all the sanctions provided by the Constitution; that happily distributed as the sovereign powers of the people of this Union had been between their general and State governments, their history had already too often presented collisions between these divided authorities with regard to the extent of their respective powers. No other case had, however, happened in which the application of military force by the Government of the Union had been suggested for the enforcement of a law the violation of which had within any single State been prescribed by a legislative act of that State. In the present instance it was his duty to say that if the legislative and executive authorities of the State of Georgia should persevere in acts of encroachment upon the territories secured by a solemn treaty to the Indians and the laws of the Union remained unaltered, a superadded obligation, even higher than that of human authority, would compel the Executive of the United States to enforce the laws and fulfill the duties of the nation by all the force committed for that purpose to his charge.

CHEROKEE PROGRESS IN CIVILIZATION

Notwithstanding the many difficulties that had beset their paths and the condition of uncertainty and suspense which had surrounded their affairs for years, the Cherokees seem to have continued steadily in their progress toward civilization.

The Rev. David Brown, who in the fall of 1825 made an extended tour of observation through their nation, submitted, in December of that year, for the information of the War Department, an extended and detailed report of his examination, from which it appeared that numberless herds of cattle grazed upon their extensive plains; horses were numerous; many and extensive flocks of sheep, goats, and swine covered the hills and valleys; the climate was delicious and healthy and the winters were mild; the soil of the valleys and plains was rich, and was utilized in the production of corn, tobacco, cotton, wheat, oats, indigo, and potatoes; considerable trade was carried on with the neighboring States, much cotton being exported in boats of their own to New Orleans; apple and peach orchards were quite common; much attention was paid to the cultivation of gardens; butter and cheese of their own manufacture were seen upon many of their tables; public roads were numerous in the nation and supplied at convenient distances with houses of entertainment kept by the natives; many and flourishing villages dotted the country; cotton and woolen cloths were manufactured by the women and homemade blankets were very common; almost every family grew sufficient cotton for its own consumption; industry and commercial enterprise were extending themselves throughout the nation; nearly all the merchants were native Cherokees; the population was rapidly increasing, a census just taken showing 13,563 native citizens, 147 white men and 73 white women who had intermarried with the Cherokees, and 1,277 slaves; schools were increasing every year, and indolence was strongly discountenanced; the nation had no debt, and the revenue was in a flourishing condition; a printing press was soon to be established, and a national library and museum were in contemplation.

HISTORICAL DATA
ZEALOUS MEASURES FOR REMOVAL
OF EASTERN CHEROKEES

While the events connected with the negotiations and the execution of the treaty of 1828 with the Western Cherokees were occurring those Cherokees who yet remained in their old homes east of the Mississippi River were burdened with a continually increasing catalogue of distressing troubles. So soon as the treaty of 1828 was concluded it was made known to them that inducements were therein held out for a continuance of the emigration to the Arkansas country. Agent Montgomery was instructed to use every means in his power to facilitate this scheme of removal, and especially among those Cherokees who resided within the chartered limits of Georgia.

Secret agents were appointed and $2,000 were authorized by the Secretary of War to be expended in purchasing the influence of the chiefs in favor of the project. A. R. S. Hunter and J. S. Bridges were appointed commissioners to value the improvements of the Cherokees who should elect to remove.

After nearly a year of zealous work in the cause, Agent Montgomery was only able to report the emigration of four hundred and thirty-one Indians and seventy-nine slaves, comparatively few of whom were from Georgia. Nine months later three hundred and forty-six persons had emigrated from within the limits of that State. The hostility manifested by the larger proportion of the Cherokees toward those who gave favorable consideration to the plan of removal was so great as to require the establishment of a garrison of United States troops within the nation for their protection.

President Jackson's advice to the Cherokees.—Early in 1829, a delegation from the nation proceeded to Washington to lay their grievances before President Jackson, but they found the Executive entertaining opinions about their rights very different from those which had been held by his predecessors. They were advised that the answer to their claim of being an independent nation was to be found in the fact that during the Revolutionary war the Cherokees were the allies of Great Britain, a power claiming entire sovereignty of the thirteen colonies, which sovereignty, by virtue of the Declaration of Independence and the subsequent treaty of 1783, became vested respectively in the thirteen original States, including North Carolina and Georgia. If they had since been permitted to abide on their lands, it was by permission, a circumstance giving no right to deny the sovereignty of those States. Under the treaty of 1785 the United States "give peace to all the Cherokees and receive them into favor and protection." Subsequently they had made war on the United States, and peace was not concluded until 1791. No guarantee, however, was given by the United States adverse to the sovereignty of Georgia, and none could be given. Their course in establishing an independent government within the limits of Georgia, adverse to her will, had been the cause of inducing her to depart from the forebearance she had so long practiced, and to provoke the passage of the recent act of her legislature, extending her laws and jurisdiction over their country. The arms of the United States, the President remarked, would never be employed to stay any State of the Union from the exercise of the legitimate powers belonging to her in her sovereign capacity. No remedy for them could be perceived except removal west of the Mississippi River, where alone peace and protection could be afforded them. To continue where they were could promise nothing but interruption and disquietude. Beyond the Mississippi the United States, possessing the sole sovereignty, could say to them that the land should be theirs while trees grow and water runs.

The delegation were much cast down by these expressions of the President, but they abated nothing of their demand for protection in what they considered to be the just rights of their people. They returned to their country more embittered than before against the Georgians, and lost no opportunity, by appeals to the patriotism as well as to the baser passions of their countrymen, to excite them to a determination to protect their country at all hazards against Georgian encroachment and occupation.

The President of the United States about the same time gave directions to suspend the enrollment and removal of Cherokees to the west in small parties, accompanied by the remark that if they (the Cherokees) thought it for their interest to remain, they must take the consequences, but that the Executive of the United States had no power to interfere with the exercise of the sovereignty of any State over and upon all within its limits. The President also directed that the previous practice of paying their annuities to the treasurer of the Cherokee Nation should be discontinued, and that they be thereafter distributed among the individual members of the tribe. Orders were shortly after given to the commandant of troops in the Cherokee country to prevent *all persons,* including members of the tribe, from opening up or working any mineral deposits within their limits. All these additional annoyances and restrictions placed upon the free exercise of their supposed rights, so far from securing compliance with the wishes to the Government, had a tendency to harden the Cherokee heart.

TREATY NEGOTIATIONS RESUMED

Rival delegations headed by Ross and Ridge.— . . . Early in February, 1835, two rival delegations, each claiming to represent the Cherokee Nation, arrived in Washington. One was headed by John Ross, who had long been the principal chief and who was the most intelligent and influential man in the nation. The rival delegation was led by John Ridge, who had been a subchief and a man of some considerable influence among his people. The Ross delegation had been consistently and bitterly opposed to any negotiations having in view the surrender of their territory and a removal west of the Mississippi. Ridge and his delegation, though formerly of the same mind with Ross, had begun to perceive the futility of further opposition to the demands of the State and national authorities. Feeling the certainty that the approaching crisis in Cherokee affairs could have but one result, and perceiving an opportunity to enhance his own importance and to secure the discomfiture of his hitherto more powerful rival, Ridge caused it to be intimated to the United States authorities that he and his delegation were prepared to treat with them upon the basis previously laid down by President Jackson of a cession of their territory and a removal west.

Rev. J. F. Schermerhorn was therefore appointed, and instructions were prepared authorizing him to meet Ridge and his party and to ascertain on what terms an amicable and satisfactory arrangement could be made. . . .

Council at New Echota.—During the session of this council notice was given to the Cherokees to meet the United States commissioners on the third Monday in December following, at New Echota, for the purpose of negotiating and agreeing upon the terms of a treaty. The notice was also printed in Cherokee and circulated throughout the nation, informing the Indians that those who did not attend would be counted as assenting to any treaty that might be made. In the mean time the Ross delegation, authorized by the Red Clay council to conclude a treaty either there or at Washington, finding that Schermerhorn had no authority to treat on any other basis than the one rejected by the nation, proceeded, according to their people's instructions, to Washington. Previous to their departure, John Ross was arrested. This took place immediately upon the breaking up of the council. He was detained some time under the surveillance of a strong guard, without any charge against him, and ultimately released without any apology or explanation. At this arrest all his papers were seized, including as well all his private correspondence and the proceedings of the Cherokee council. In accordance with the call for a council at New Echota the Indians assembled at the appointed time and place, to the number of only three to five hundred, as reported by Mr. Schermerhorn himself, who could hardly be accused of any tendency to underestimate the gathering. That gentleman opened the council December 22, 1835, in the absence of Governor Carroll, whose health was still such as to prevent his attendance. The objects of the council were fully explained, the small attendance being attributed to the influence of John Ross. It was also suggested by those unfriendly to the proposed treaty as a good reason for the absence of so large a proportion of the nation, that the right to convene a national council was vested in the principal chief, and they were unaware that that officer's authority had been delegated to Mr. Schermerhorn.

The articles as agreed upon were reported by the Cherokee committee to their people, and were approved, transcribed, and signed on the 29th.

The council adjourned on the 30th, after designating a committee to proceed to Washington and urge the ratification of the treaty, clothed with power to assent to any alterations made necessary by the action of the President or Senate.

In spite of the opposition of Mr. Ross and his party, the treaty was assented to by the Senate by one more than the necessary two-thirds majority, and was ratified and proclaimed by the President on the 23rd of May, 1836. By its terms two years were allowed within which the nation must remove west of the Mississippi.

The Ross party refuse to acquiesce.—John Ross and his delegation, having returned home, at once proceeded to enter upon a
vigorous campaign of opposition to the execution of the treaty.
He used every means to incite the animosity of his people
against Ridge and his friends, who had been instrumental in
bringing it about and who were favorable to removal. Councils
were held and resolutions were adopted denouncing in the se-
verest terms the motives and action of the United States authorities and declaring the treaty in all its provisions absolutely null
and void. A copy of these resolutions having been transmitted to
the Secretary of War by General Wool, the former was directed
by the President to express his astonishment that an officer of
the Army should have received or transmitted a paper so disre-
spectful to the Executive, to the Senate, and through them to the
people of the United States. To prevent any misapprehension on
the subject of the treaty the Secretary was instructed to repeat
in the most explicit terms the settled determination of the President that it should be executed without modification and with all
the dispatch consistent with propriety and justice. Furthermore,
that after delivering a copy of this letter to Mr. Ross no further
communication should be held with him either orally or in writing
in regard to the treaty.

> From Charles C. Royce,
> *The Cherokee Nation of Indians*, 1887.

 6

TREATY WITH THE CHEROKEE, 1835

Articles of a treaty, concluded at New Echota in the State of Georgia on the 29th day of Decr. 1835 by General William Carroll and John F. Schermerhorn commissioners on the part of the United States and the Chiefs Head Men and People of the Cherokee tribe of Indians.

WHEREAS the Cherokees are anxious to make some arrangements with the Government of the United States whereby the difficulties they have experienced by a residence within the settled parts of the United States under the jurisdiction and laws of the State Governments may be terminated and adjusted; and with a view to reuniting their people in one body and securing a permanent home for themselves and their posterity in the country selected by their forefathers without the territorial limits of the State sovereignties, and where they can establish and enjoy a government of their choice and perpetuate such a state of society as may be most consonant with their views, habits and condition; and as may tend to their individual comfort and their advancement in civilization.

And whereas a delegation of the Cherokee nation composed of Messrs. John Ross Richard Taylor Danl. McCoy Samuel Gunter and William Rogers with full power and authority to conclude a treaty with the United States did on the 28th day of February 1835 stipulate and agree with the Government of the United States to submit to the Senate to fix the amount which should be allowed the Cherokees for their claims and for a cession of their lands east of the Mississippi river, and did agree to abide by the award of the Senate of the United States themselves and to recommend the same to their people for their final determination.

And whereas on such submission the Senate advised "that a sum not exceeding five millions of dollars be paid to the Cherokee Indians for all their lands and possessions east of the Mississippi river."

And whereas this delegation after said award of the Senate had been made, were called upon to submit propositions as to its disposition to be arranged in a treaty which they refused to do, but insisted that the same "should be referred to their nation and there in general council to deliberate and determine on the subject in order to ensure harmony and good feeling among themselves."

And whereas a certain other delegation composed of John Ridge Elias Boudinot Archilla Smith S. W. Bell John West Wm. A. Davis and Ezekial West, who represented that portion of the nation in favor of emigration to the Cherokee country west of the Mississippi entered into propositions for a treaty with John F. Schermerhorn commissioner on the part of the United States which were to be submitted to their nation for their final action and determination:

And whereas the Cherokee people, at their last October council at Red Clay, fully authorized and empowered a delegation or committee of twenty persons of their nation to enter into and conclude a treaty with the United States commissioner then present, *at that place or elsewhere* and as the people had good reason to believe that a treaty would then and there be made or at a subsequent council at New Echota which the commissioners it was well known and understood, were authorized and instructed to convene for said purpose; and since the said delegation have gone on to Washington city, with a view to close negotiations there, as stated by them notwithstanding they were officially informed by the United States commissioner that they would not be received by the President of the United States; and that the Government would transact no business of this nature with them, and that if a treaty was made it must be done here in the nation, where the delegation at Washington last winter *urged that it should be done for the purpose of promoting peace and harmony among the people;* and since these facts have also been corroborated to us by a communication recently received by the commissioner from the Government of the United States and read and explained to the people in open council and therefore believing said delegation can effect nothing and since our difficulties are daily increasing and our situation is rendered more and more precarious uncertain and insecure in consequence of the legislation of the States; and seeing no effectual way of relief, but in accepting the liberal overtures of the United States.

And whereas Genl William Carroll and John F. Schermerhorn were appointed commissioners on the part of the United States, with full power and authority to conclude a treaty with the Cherokees east and were directed by the President to convene the people of the nation in general council at New Echota and to submit said propositions to them with power and authority to vary the same so as to meet the views of the Cherokees in reference to its details.

And whereas the said commissioners did appoint and notify a general council of the nation to convene at New Echota on the 21st day of December 1835; and informed them that the commissioners would be prepared to make a treaty with the Cherokee people who should assemble there and those who did not come they should conclude gave their assent and sanction to whatever should be transacted at this council and the people having met in council according to said notice.

Therefore the following articles of a treaty are agreed upon and concluded between William Carroll and John F. Schermerhorn commissioners on the part of the United States and the chiefs and head men and people of the Cherokee nation in general council assembled this 29th day of Decr 1835.

ARTICLE 1. The Cherokee Nation hereby cede relinquish and convey to the United States all the lands owned claimed or possessed by them east of the Mississippi river, and hereby release all their claims upon the United States for spoliations of every kind for and in consideration of the sum of five millions of dollars to be expended paid and invested in the manner stipulated and agreed upon in the following articles. But as a question has arisen between the commissioners and the Cherokees whether the Senate in their resolution by which they advised "that a sum not exceeding five millions of dollars be paid to the Cherokee Indians for all their lands and possessions east of the Mississippi river" have included and made any allowance or consideration for claims for spoliations it is therefore agreed on the part of the United

States that this question shall be again submitted to the Senate for their consideration and decision and if no allowance was made for spoliations that then an additional sum of three hundred thousand dollars be allowed for the same.

ARTICLE 2. Whereas by the treaty of May 6th 1828 and the supplementary treaty thereto of Feb. 14th 1833 with the Cherokees west of the Mississippi the United States guarantied and secured to be conveyed by patent to the Cherokee nation of Indians the following tract of country "Beginning at a point on the old western territorial line of Arkansas Territory being twenty-five miles north from the point where the territorial line crosses Arkansas river, thence running from said north point south on the said territorial line where the said territorial line crosses the Verdigris river; thence down said Verdigris river to the Arkansas river; thence down said Arkansas to a point where a stone is placed opposite the east or lower bank of Grand river at its junction with the Arkansas; thence running south forty-four degrees west one mile; thence in a straight line to a point four miles northerly, from the mouth of the north fork of the Canadian; thence along the said four mile line to the Canadian; thence down the Canadian to the Arkansas; thence down the Arkansas to that point on the Arkansas where the eastern Choctaw boundary strikes said river and running thence with the western line of Arkansas Territory as now defined, to the southwest corner of Missouri; thence along the western Missouri line to the land assigned the Senecas; thence on the south line of the Senecas to Grand river; thence up said Grand river as far as the south line of the Osage reservation, extended if necessary; thence up and between said south Osage line extended west if necessary, and a line drawn due west from the point of beginning to a certain distance west, at which a line running north and south from said Osage line to said due west line will make seven millions of acres within the whole described boundaries. In addition to the seven millions of acres of land thus provided for and bounded, the United States further guaranty to the Cherokee nation a perpetual outlet west, and a free and unmolested use of all the country west of the western boundary of said seven millions of acres, as far west as the sovereignty of the United States and their right of soil extend:

Provided however That if the saline or salt plain on the western prairie shall fall within said limits prescribed for said outlet, the right is reserved to the United States to permit other tribes of red men to get salt on said plain in common with the Cherokees; And letters patent shall be issued by the United States as soon as practicable for the land hereby guarantied."

And whereas it is apprehended by the Cherokees that in the above cession there is not contained a sufficient quantity of land for the accommodation of the whole nation on their removal west of the Mississippi the United States in consideration of the sum of five hundred thousand dollars therefore hereby covenant and agree to convey to the said Indians, and their descendants by patent, in fee simple the following additional tract of land situated between the west line of the State of Missouri and the Osage reservation beginning at the southeast corner of the same and runs north along the east line of the Osage lands fifty miles to the northeast corner thereof; and thence east to the west line of the State of Missouri; thence with said line south fifty miles; thence west to the place of beginning; estimated to contain eight hundred thousand acres of land; but it is expressly understood that if any of the lands assigned the Quapaws shall fall within the aforesaid bounds the same shall be reserved and excepted out of the lands above granted and a pro rata reduction shall be made in the price to be allowed to the United States for the same by the Cherokees.

ARTICLE 3. The United States also agree that the lands above ceded by the treaty of Feb. 14 1833, including the outlet, and those ceded by this treaty shall all be included in one patent executed to the Cherokee nation of Indians by the President of the United States according to the provisions of the act of May 28 1830. It is, however, agreed that the military reservation at Fort Gibson shall be held by the United States. But should the United States abandon said post and have no further use for the same it shall revert to the Cherokee nation. The United States shall always have the right to make and establish such post and military roads and forts in any part of the Cherokee country, as they may deem proper for the interest and protection of the same and the free use of as much land, timber, fuel and materials of all kinds for the construction and support of the same as may be necessary; provided that if the private rights of individuals are interfered with, a just compensation therefor shall be made.

ARTICLE 4. The United States also stipulate and agree to extinguish for the benefit of the Cherokees the titles to the reservations within their country made in the Osage treaty of 1825 to certain half-breeds and for this purpose they hereby agree to pay the persons to whom the same belong or have been assigned or to their agents or guardians whenever they shall execute after the ratification of this treaty a satisfactory conveyance for the same, to the United States, the sum of fifteen thousand dollars according to a schedule accompanying this treaty of the relative value of the several reservations.

And whereas by the several treaties between the United States and the Osage Indians the Union and Harmony Missionary reservations which were established for their benefit are now situated within the country ceded by them to the United States; the former being situated in the Cherokee country and the latter in the State of Missouri. It is therefore agreed that the United States shall pay the American Board of Commissioners for Foreign Missions for the improvements on the same what they shall be appraised at by Capt. Geo. Vashon Cherokee sub-agent Abraham Redfield and A. P. Chouteau or such persons as the President of the United States shall appoint and the money allowed for the same shall be expended in schools among the Osages and improving their condition. It is understood that the United States are to pay the amount allowed for the reservations in this article and not the Cherokees.

ARTICLE 5. The United States hereby covenant and agree that the lands ceded to the Cherokee nation in the forgoing article shall, in no future time without their consent, be included within the territorial limits or jurisdiction of any State or Territory. But they shall secure to the Cherokee nation the right by their national councils to make and carry into effect all such laws as they may deem necessary for the government and protection of the persons and property within their own country belonging to their people or such persons as have connected themselves with them: provided always that they shall not be inconsistent with the constitution of the United States and such acts of Congress as have been or may be passed regulating trade and intercourse with the Indians; and also, that they shall not be considered as extending to such citizens and army of the United States as may travel or reside in the Indian country by permission according to the laws and regulations established by the Government of the same.

ARTICLE 6. Perpetual peace and friendship shall exist between the citizens of the United States and the Cherokee Indians. The United States agree to protect the Cherokee nation from domestic strife and foreign enemies and against intestine wars between the several tribes. The Cherokees shall endeavor to preserve and maintain the peace of the country and not make war upon their neighbors they shall also be protected against interruption and intrusion from citizens of the United States, who may attempt to settle in the country without their consent; and all such persons shall be removed from the same by order of the President of the United States. But this is not intended to prevent the residence among them of useful farmers mechanics and teachers for the instruction of Indians according to treaty stipulations.

ARTICLE 7. The Cherokee nation having already made great progress in civilization and deeming it important that every proper and laudable inducement should be offered to their people to improve their condition as well as to guard and secure in the most effectual manner the rights guarantied to them in this treaty, and with a view to illustrate the liberal and enlarged policy of the Government of the United States towards the Indians in their removal beyond the territorial limits of the States, it is stipulated that they shall be entitled to a delegate in the House of Representatives of the United States whenever Congress shall make provision for the same.

ARTICLE 8. The United States also agree and stipulate to remove the Cherokees to their new homes and to subsist them one year after their arrival there and that a sufficient number of steamboats and baggage-wagons shall be furnished to remove them comfortably, and so as not to endanger their health, and that a physician well supplied with medicines shall accompany each detachment of emigrants removed by the Government. Such persons and families as in the opinion of the emigrating agent are capable of subsisting and removing themselves shall be permitted to do so; and they shall be allowed in full for all claims for the same twenty dollars for each member of their family; and in lieu of their one year's rations they shall be paid the sum of thirty-three dollars and thirty-three cents if they prefer it.

Such Cherokees also as reside at present out of the nation and shall remove with them in two years west of the Mississippi shall be entitled to allowance for removal and subsistence as above provided.

ARTICLE 9. The United States agree to appoint suitable agents who shall make a just and fair valuation of all such improvements now in the possession of the Cherokees as add any value to the lands; and also of the ferries owned by them, according to their net income; and such improvements and ferries from which they have been dispossessed in a lawless manner or under any existing laws of the State where the same may be situated.

The just debts of the Indians shall be paid out of any monies due them for their improvements and claims; and they shall also be furnished at the discretion of the President of the United States with a sufficient sum to enable them to obtain the necessary means to remove themselves to their new homes, and the balance of their dues shall be paid them at the Cherokee agency west of the Mississippi. The missionary establishments shall also be valued and appraised in a like manner and the amount of them paid over by the United States to the treasurers of the respective missionary societies by whom they have been established and improved in order to enable them to erect such buildings and make such improvements among the Cherokees west of the Mississippi as they may deem necessary for their benefit. Such teachers at present among the Cherokees as this council shall select and designate shall be removed west of the Mississippi with the Cherokee nation and on the same terms allowed to them.

ARTICLE 10. The President of the United States shall invest in some safe and most productive public stocks of the country for the benefit of the whole Cherokee nation who have removed or shall remove to the lands assigned by this treaty to the Cherokee nation west of the Mississippi as a permanent fund for the purposes hereinafter specified and pay over the net income of the same annually to such person or persons as shall be authorized or appointed by the Cherokee nation to receive the same and their receipt shall be a full discharge for the amount paid to them viz: the sum of two hundred thousand dollars in addition to the present annuities of the nation to constitute a general fund the interest of which shall be applied annually by the council of the nation to such purposes as they may deem best for the general interest of their people. The sum of fifty thousand dollars to constitute an orphans' fund the annual income of which shall be expended towards the support and education of such orphan children as are destitute of the means of subsistence. The sum of one hundred and fifty thousand dollars in addition to the present school fund of the nation shall constitute a permanent school fund, the interest of which shall be applied annually by the council of the nation for the support of common schools and such a literary institution of a higher order as may be established in the Indian country. And in order to secure as far as possible the true and beneficial application of the orphans' and school fund the council of the Cherokee nation when required by the President of the United States shall make a report of the application of those funds and he shall at all times have the right if the funds have been misapplied to correct any abuses of them and direct the manner of their application for the purposes for which they were intended. The council of the nation may by giving two years' notice of their intention withdraw their funds by and with the consent of the President and Senate of the United States, and invest them in such manner as they may deem most proper for their interest. The United States also agree and stipulate to pay the just debts and claims against the Cherokee nation held by the citizens of the same and also the just claims of citizens of the United States for services rendered to the nation and the sum of sixty thousand dollars is appropriated for this purpose but no claims against individual persons of the nation shall be allowed and paid by the nation. The sum of three hundred thousand dollars is hereby set apart to pay and liquidate the just claims of the Cherokees upon the United States for spoliations of every kind, that have not been already satisfied under former treaties.

ARTICLE 11. The Cherokee nation of Indians believing it will be for the interest of their people to have all their funds and annuities under their own direction and future disposition hereby agree to commute their permanent annuity of ten thousand dollars for the sum of two hundred and fourteen thousand dollars, the same to be invested by the President of the United States as a part of the general fund of the nation; and their present school fund amounting to about fifty thousand dollars shall constitute a part of the permanent school fund of the nation.

ARTICLE 12. Those individuals and families of the Cherokee nation that are averse to a removal to the Cherokee country west of the Mississippi and are desirous to become citizens of the States where they reside and such as are qualified to take care of themselves and their property shall be entitled to receive their due portions of all the personal benefits accruing under this treaty for their claims, improvements and *per capita;* as soon as an appropriation is made for this treaty.

Such heads of Cherokee families as are desirous to reside within the States of No. Carolina Tennessee and Alabama subject to the laws of the same; and who are qualified or calculated to become useful citizens shall be entitled, on the certificate of the commissioners to a pre-emption right to one hundred and sixty acres of land or one quarter section at the minimum Congress price; so as to include the present buildings or improvements of those who now reside there and such as do not live there at present shall be permitted to locate within two years any lands not already occupied by persons entitled to pre-emption privilege under this treaty and if two or more families live on the same quarter section and they desire to continue their residence in these States and are qualified as above specified they shall, on receiving their pre-emption certificate be entitled to the right of pre-emption to such lands as they may select not already taken by any person entitled to them under this treaty.

It is stipulated and agreed between the United States and the Cherokee people that John Ross James Starr George Hicks John Gunter George Chambers John Ridge Elias Boudinot George Sanders John Martin William Rogers Roman Nose Situwake and John Timpson shall be a committee on the part of the Cherokees to recommend such persons for the privilege of pre-emption rights as may be deemed entitled to the same under the above articles and to select the missionaries who shall be removed with the nation; and that they be hereby fully empowered and authorized to transact all business on the part of the Indians which may arise in carrying into effect the provisions of this treaty and settling the same with the United States. If any of the persons above mentioned should decline acting or be removed by death; the vacancies shall be filled by the committee themselves.

It is also understood and agreed that the sum of one hundred thousand dollars shall be expended by the commissioners in such manner as the committee deem best for the benefit of the poorer class of Cherokees as shall remove west or have removed west and are entitled to the benefits of this treaty. The same to be delivered at the Cherokee agency west as soon after the removal of the nation as possible.

ARTICLE 13. In order to make a final settlement of all the claims of the Cherokees for reservations granted under former treaties to any individuals belonging to the nation by the United States it is therefore hereby stipulated and agreed and expressly understood by the parties to this treaty—that all the Cherokees and their heirs and descendants to whom any reservations have been made under any former treaties with the United States, and who have not sold or conveyed the same by deed or otherwise and who in the opinion of the commissioners have complied with the terms on which the reservations were granted as far as practicable in the several cases; and which reservations have since been sold by the United States shall constitute a just claim against the United States and the original reservee or their heirs or descendants shall be entitled to receive the present value thereof from the United States as unimproved lands. And all such reservations as have not been sold by the United States and where the terms on which the reservations were made in the opinion of the commissioners have been complied with as far as practicable, they or their heirs or descendants shall be entitled to the same. They are hereby granted and confirmed to them—and also all persons who were entitled to reservations under the treaty of 1817 and who as far as practicable in the opinion of the commissioners, have complied with the stipulations of said treaty, although by the treaty of 1819 such reservations were included in the unceded lands belonging to the Cherokee nation are hereby confirmed to them and they shall be entitled to receive a grant for the same. And all such reservees as were obliged by the laws of the States in which their reservations were situated, to abandon the same or purchase them from the States shall be deemed to have a just claim against the United States for the amount by them paid to the States with interest thereon for such reservations and if obliged to abandon the same, to the present value of such reservations as unimproved lands but in all cases where the reservees have sold their reservations or any part thereof and conveyed the same by deed or otherwise and have been paid for the same, they their heirs or descendants or their assigns shall not be considered as having any claims upon the United States under this article of the treaty nor be entitled to receive any compensation for the lands thus disposed of. It is expressly understood by the parties to this treaty that the amount to be allowed for reservations under this article shall not be deducted out of the consideration money allowed to the Cherokees for their claims for spoliations and the cession of their lands; but the same is to be paid for independently by the United States as it is only a just fulfilment of former treaty stipulations.

ARTICLE 14. It is also agreed on the part of the United States that such warriors of the Cherokee nation as were engaged on the side of the United States in the late war with Great Britain and the southern tribes of Indians, and who were wounded in such service shall be entitled to such pensions as shall be allowed them by the Congress of the United States to commence from the period of their disability.

ARTICLE 15. It is expressly understood and agreed between the parties to this treaty that after deducting the amount which shall be actually expended for the payment for improvements, ferries, claims, for spoliations, removal subsistence and debts and claims upon the Cherokee nation and for the additional quantity of lands and goods for the poorer class of Cherokees and the several sums to be invested for the general national funds; provided for in the several articles of this treaty the balance whatever the same may be shall be equally divided between all the people belonging to the Cherokee nation east according to the census just completed; and such Cherokees as have removed west since June 1833 who are entitled by the terms of their enrolment and removal to all the benefits resulting from the final treaty between the United States and the Cherokees east they shall also be paid for their improvements according to their approved value before their removal where fraud has not already been shown in their valuation.

ARTICLE 16. It is hereby stipulated and agreed by the Cherokees that they shall remove to their new homes within two years from the ratification of this treaty and that during such time the United States shall protect and defend them in their possessions and property and free use and occupation of the same and such persons as have been dispossessed of their improvements and houses; and for which no grant has actually issued previously to the enactment of the law of the State of Georgia, of December 1835 to regulate Indian occupancy shall be again put in possession and placed in the same situation and condition, in reference to the laws of the State of Georgia, as the Indians that have not been dispossessed; and if this is not done, and the people are left unprotected, then the United States shall pay the several Cherokees for their losses and damages sustained by them in consequence thereof. And it is also stipulated and agreed that the public buildings and improvements on which they are situated at New Echota for which no grant has been actually made previous to the passage of the above recited act if not occupied by the Cherokee people shall be reserved for the public and free use of the United States and the Cherokee Indians for the purpose of settling and closing all the Indian business arising under this treaty between the commissioners of claims and the Indians.

The United States, and the several States interested in the Cherokee lands, shall immediately proceed to survey the lands ceded by this treaty; but it is expressly agreed and understood between the parties that the agency buildings and that tract of land surveyed and laid off for the use of Colonel R. J. Meigs Indian agent or heretofore enjoyed and occupied by his successors in office shall continue subject to the use and occupancy of the United States, or such agent as may be engaged specially superintending the removal of the tribe.

ARTICLE 17. All the claims arising under or provided for in the several articles of this treaty, shall be examined and adjudicated by such commissioners as shall be appointed by the President of the United States by and with the advice and consent of the Senate of the United States for that purpose and their decision shall be final and on their certificate of the amount due the several claimants they shall be paid by the United States. All stipulations in former treaties which have not been superseded or annulled by this shall continue in full force and virtue.

ARTICLE 18. Whereas in consequence of the unsettled affairs of the Cherokee people and the early frosts, their crops are insufficient to support their families and great distress is likely to ensue and whereas the nation will not, until after their removal be able advantageously to expend the income of the permanent funds of the nation it is therefore agreed that the annuities of the nation which may accrue under this treaty for two years, the time fixed for their removal shall be expended in provision and clothing for the benefit of the poorer class of the nation; and the United States hereby agree to advance the same for that purpose as soon after the ratification of this treaty as an appropriation for the same shall be made. It is however not intended in this article to interfere with that part of the annuities due the Cherokees west by the treaty of 1819.

ARTICLE 19. This treaty after the same shall be ratified by the President and Senate of the United States shall be obligatory on the contracting parties.

ARTICLE 20. [Supplemental article. Stricken out by Senate.]

In testimony whereof, the commissioners and the chiefs, head men, and people whose names are hereunto annexed, being duly authorized by the people in general council assembled, have affixed their hands and seals for themselves, and in behalf of the Cherokee nation.

I have examined the foregoing treaty, and although not present when it was made, I approve its provisions generally, and therefore sign it.

Wm. Carroll,
J. F. Schermerhorn.

Major Ridge, his x mark,
Te-gah-e-ske, his x mark,
James Foster, his x mark,
Robert Rogers,
Tesa-ta-esky, his x mark,
John Gunter,
Charles Moore, his x mark,
John A. Bell,
George Chambers, his x mark,
Charles F. Foreman,
Tah-yeske, his x mark,
William Rogers,
Archilla Smith, his x mark,
George W. Adair,
Andrew Ross,
Elias Boudinot,
William Lassley,
James Starr, his x mark,
Cae-te-hee, his x mark,
Jesse Half-breed, his x mark,

Signed and sealed in presence of—
Western B. Thomas, secretary.
Ben F. Currey, special agent.
M. Wolfe Batman, first lieutenant, sixth U.S. Infantry, disbursing agent.
Jon L. Hooper, lieutenant, fourth infantry.

C. M. Hitchcock, M.D., assistant surgeon, U.S.A.
G. W. Currey,
Wm. H. Underwood,
Cornelius D. Terhune,
John W. H. Underwood.

In compliance with instructions of the council at New Echota, we sign this treaty.

Stand Watie
John Ridge

March 1, 1836
Witnesses:

Elbert Herring,
Wm. Y. Hansell,
Alexander H. Everett,
Samuel J. Potts,
John Robb,
Jno. Litle,
D. Kurtz,
S. Rockwell.

Whereas the western Cherokees have appointed a delegation to visit the eastern Cherokees to assure them of the friendly disposition of their people and their desire that the nation should again be united as one people and to urge upon them the expediency of accepting the overtures of the Government; and that, on their removal they may be assured of a hearty welcome and an equal participation with them in all the benefits and privileges of the Cherokee country west and the undersigned two of said delegation being the only delegates in the eastern nation from the west at the signing and sealing of the treaty lately concluded at New Echota between their eastern brethren and the United States; and having fully understood the provisions of the same they agree to it in behalf of the western Cherokees. But it is expressly understood that nothing in this treaty shall affect any claims of the western Cherokees on the United States.

In testimony whereof, we have, this 31st day of December, 1835, hereunto set our hands and seals.

James Rogers,
John Smith,
Delegates from the western Cherokees

Test:
Ben F. Currey, special agent.
M. W. Batman, first lieutenant, Sixth Infantry.
Jno. L. Hooper, lieutenant, Fourth Infantry.
Elias Boudinot.

Schedule and estimated value of the Osage half-breed reservations within the territory ceded to the Cherokees west of the Mississippi, (referred to in article 5 on the foregoing treaty,) viz:

Augustus Clamont one section			....	$6,000
James	"	"	"	....	1,000
Paul	"	"	"	....	1,300
Henry	"	"	"	....	800
Anthony	"	"	"	....	1,800
Rosalie	"	"	"	....	1,800
Emilia D., of Milhanga			....	1,000
Emilia D., of Shemianga			....	1,300

$15,000

I hereby certify that the above schedule is the estimated value of the Osage reservations; as made out and agreed upon with

Col. A. P. Choteau who represented himself as the agent or guardian of the above reservees.

March 14, 1835   J. F. Schermerhorn

Supplementary articles to a treaty concluded at New Echota, Georgia, December 29, 1835, between the United States and Cherokee people.

Whereas the undersigned were authorized at the general meeting of the Cherokee people held at New Echota as above stated, to make and assent to such alterations in the preceding treaty as might be thought necessary, and whereas the President of the United States has expressed his determination not to allow any pre-emptions or reservations his desire being that the whole Cherokee people should remove together and establish themselves in the country provided for them west of the Mississippi river.

ARTICLE 1. It is therefore agreed that all the pre-emption rights and reservations provided for in articles 12 and 13 shall be and are hereby relinquished and declared void.

ARTICLE 2. Whereas the Cherokee people have supposed that the sum of five millions of dollars fixed by the Senate in their resolution of ———— day of March, 1835, as the value of the Cherokee lands and possessions east of the Mississippi river was not intended to include the amount which may be required to remove them, nor the value of certain claims which many of their people had against citizens of the United States, which suggestion has been confirmed by the opinion expressed to the War Department by some of the Senators who voted upon the question and whereas the President is willing that this subject should be referred to the Senate for their consideration and if it was not intended by the Senate that the above-mentioned sum of five millions of dollars should include the objects herein specified that in that case such further provision should be made therefor as might appear to the Senate to be just.

ARTICLE 3. It is therefore agreed that the sum of six hundred thousand dollars shall be and the same is hereby allowed to the Cherokee people to include the expense of their removal, and all claims of every nature and description against the Government of the United States not herein otherwise expressly provided for, and to be in lieu of the said reservations and pre-emptions and of the sum of three hundred thousand dollars for spoliations described in the 1st article of the above-mentioned treaty. This sum of six hundred thousand dollars shall be applied and distributed agreeably to the provisions of the said treaty, and any surplus which may remain after removal and payment of the claims so ascertained shall be turned over and belong to the education fund.

But it is expressly understood that the subject of this article is merely referred hereby to the consideration of the Senate and if they shall approve the same then this supplement shall remain part of the treaty.

ARTICLE 4. It is also understood that the provisions in article 16, for the agency reservation is not intended to interfere with the occupant right of any Cherokees should their improvement fall within the same.

It is also understood and agreed, that the one hundred thousand dollars appropriated in article 12 for the poorer class of Cherokees and intended as a set-off to the pre-emption rights shall now be transferred from the funds of the nation and added to the general national fund of four hundred thousand dollars so as to make said fund equal to five hundred thousand dollars.

ARTICLE 5. The necessary expenses attending the negotiations of the aforesaid treaty and supplement and also of such persons of the delegation as may sign the same shall be defrayed by the United States.

In testimony whereof, John F. Schermerhorn, commissioner on the part of the United States, and the undersigned delegation have hereto set their hands and seals, this first day of March, in the year one thousand eight hundred and thirty six.

J. F. Schermerhorn.

Major Ridge, his x mark,	John A. Bell,
James Foster, his x mark,	Jos. A. Foreman,
Tah-ye-ske, his x mark,	Robert Sanders,
Long Shell Turtle, his x mark,	Elias Boudinot,
John Fields, his x mark,	Johnson Rogers,
James Fields, his x mark,	James Starr, his x mark,
George Welch, his x mark,	Stand Watie,
Andrew Ross,	John Ridge,
William Rogers,	James Rogers,
John Gunter,	John Smith, his x mark.

Witnesses:

Elbert Herring,	John Robb,
Thos. Glascock,	Wm. Y. Hansell,
Alexander H. Everett,	Saml. J. Potts,
Jno. Garland, Major, U.S. Army,	Jno. Litle,
C. A. Harris,	S. Rockwell.

7

Back at Soco Gap Waguli again did his best to avoid Oconeechee. It was not easy for him to do. She was still the
most beautiful woman he had ever seen, and she seemed
to be everywhere he turned. But his horror at the thought of
incest was great.

Waguli spent some time, along with Elaqui and Gog'ski,
telling Junaluska what had happened at Red Clay. Mostly
Junaluska sat and listened and nodded his head as if to say
that everything he was hearing was simply a confirmation of
what he had known all along.

"It's what I expected," he said. "That's one reason I didn't
go. It will make no difference one way or the other. I guess
the important thing is—did you learn something there to tell
them back at Old Town?"

Waguli shrugged.

"No," he said. "Not really. Unless that things are even
worse than what I heard here. The bad things, it seems, are
coming even faster than we thought."

"John Ross still counsels us to resist?"

"Yes. Though there are some who say he is only trying to
get more money."

"Of course."

Elaqui and Gog'ski excused themselves, leaving Junaluska
and Waguli alone. The two men stared at the ground between
them. It seemed there was nothing more to be said on the
subject of the meeting at Red Clay. Casually, even carelessly,
the two men began walking toward the edge of the village
and beyond.

"You know my daughter," said Junaluska, when he was
sure that they were beyond the hearing of anyone else.

Waguli was startled by the question. He looked up at Junaluska. Then he looked away again.

"Yes," he said.

"Oconeechee."

"Yes."

"Do you find her attractive?"

Waguli did not immediately answer the painful question.
He walked on a few steps, still staring at the ground.

"What man would not?" he said. "She is very beautiful."

The old man smiled.

"She thinks you don't like her."

"Why would she think that?" said Waguli. "I like her—
too much."

Junaluska stopped walking and turned to face Waguli. He
looked the younger man in the eyes. Waguli fidgeted under
the gaze.

"Why too much?" asked Junaluska. "Do you have too
many wives already?"

"I have no wives," said Waguli, "but we are both Wolf
People, Oconeechee and I."

Junaluska threw back his head and began to laugh, and Waguli wondered if the old man had suddenly lost his wits. It
happens to old ones sometimes, he thought. There was nothing funny here. The contemplation of incest was not a laughing matter.

"I don't understand," he said. "What's funny?"

Junaluska allowed his laughter to subside. He took a couple
of deep breaths and wiped at his eyes.

"Is that what bothered you?" he asked.

"Of course."

"My friend," said Junaluska, "my daughter is a Wolf Person. That much is true. But she's not of the same Wolf People

as you are. Her mother was not a Cherokee. Oconeechee belongs to the Wolf People of her mother's tribe. She lives here among us without a clan. She's alone—except for her old father."

Waguli stared at Junaluska for a long moment in a confused mixture of astonishment, shock, and anticipation. So the beautiful Oconeechee was not his relative after all! His heart beat faster in his chest. He turned and paced away from Junaluska, then turned abruptly and walked back to him again. He held back the shout of joy that wanted to burst forth from deep inside him.

"Not a Cherokee?" he said, and he started to laugh.

"So you don't think your strange man likes you?" said Junaluska to his daughter. His face wore a sly half smile, and his old eyes twinkled. Oconeechee's back stiffened, and she stretched herself as tall as she could.

"He will," she said.

"He wants to marry you."

"What?"

"I think you heard," said the old man.

"Did he say so?"

"Yes. He did."

"But he left."

Junaluska sat down heavily with a loud groan on the stool outside his house.

"He had to get back to Old Town with the news, but he's coming back. It's all arranged. You have a husband, my daughter. Now bring me my pipe and tobacco. I want to smoke."

Oconeechee fought off an urge to talk back to her father. She went inside the house and returned shortly with the pipe and tobacco pouch. It seemed to her that Junaluska took an insufferable amount of time filling the pipe bowl. She fetched him a small live coal balanced in the crotch of a stick, and he used it to light the pipe. She watched impatiently as he puffed to get the pipe going and the great clouds of smoke rose above his head. Finally she could stay quiet no longer.

"Am I to be married?" she said.

"Yes. I just told you."

"But why did he ignore me? Why did he stop being friendly?"

"You told him that you are a Wolf Person," said Junaluska.

"I am."

"So is he."

Oconeechee opened her lips as if to speak, but no sound came out of her mouth. She thought. Then she began to laugh.

"Of course," she said. "He couldn't have known that my mother was not a Cherokee, so he thought we were relatives."

"Yes," said Junaluska, and he was laughing too. Soon the laughing stopped, and Oconeechee knelt before her father and put her hands on his knees.

"I am very happy," she said.

"Waguli is a good man," said Junaluska. "He'll take good care of you. I know."

The Sun finished her long day's crawl along the underside of the Sky Vault, and at its far western edge, the Sky Vault raised itself up enough to allow her to go out onto the other side. It was dark. Junaluska still sat and smoked. Oconeechee looked out from the house.

"Are you coming to bed, Father?" she asked.

"Soon," said the old man. "You go ahead."

He smoked until the tobacco in his pipe was all used up, then he stood up, laid the pipe down on the stool, and started to walk. He walked slowly but deliberately toward the edge of town, and while he walked, he stared at a lone, bright star just to the right of and below the moon. And suddenly there appeared before him a beautiful young face. It was a face much like his daughter's face, but it was not his daughter. It was a face from long ago.

"I'm coming now," he said. "I'm coming to you."

He was just outside the town, and he kept walking into the woods. He was guided only by the beautiful face, yet his step was as sure as if he were walking down the street of Soco Gap at noon. He kept walking, yet he came no nearer to the beautiful face than when he had first seen it. But the features were clear to him. He could see the clear brown skin, the bright, moist, nearly black eyes.

"I'm coming," he said again. "She's taken care of now. She has a husband—a good man. She'll be all right now."

Then the beautiful face opened its lips, and a voice sweet and clear and strong came forth into the night.

"Come," it said.

Grandpa had some black walnut root and some bark, and he had put them in an old white enamel pot with a little bit of water in the bottom. He had built a small fire back behind the house, and the little chipped pot was sitting on the fire to boil. The piece of cane pole was all reamed out, nice and smooth, and he had set it aside. I still didn't know what he was up to, and I didn't want to ask him, because it seemed somehow more fun if I just watched and listened and did what he told me to do, and then somewhere along the line I would maybe figure it out, or it would just sort of become obvious, or if none of that happened, he would finish it eventually, and then if I didn't know what it was by looking, he would either tell me what it was, or, what was more likely, he would use it so that I could see what it was. Anyhow, that was why I didn't ask him about the cane pole. It seemed more fun to me the other way.

So the cane pole was leaning against the back wall of the house, and Grandpa was boiling that walnut root and bark. We took up our usual seats there behind the house, and Grandpa filled up his pipe and lit it, and there we sat just watching that stuff boil and smelling it. Every now and then Grandpa would tell me to put some more wood on the fire, and every now and then he would get up and look in the pot to make sure there was enough water in there or something. I didn't know. But as usual, I was just happy to be there with him, watching him do the things that he did, watching his smoke rise up and disappear and learning things. I didn't ask Grandpa about what he was doing, but I did ask about some things that were on my mind, and I had a question that had been bothering me for some time, so when I saw that he was settled down for awhile with his pipe, I asked.

"Grandpa," I said, "did Waguli come back?"

"What?"

"Waguli was supposed to marry Oconeechee," I said, "but he had to go back to Old Town first, and then her daddy died. Did Waguli come back?"

"Oh," said Grandpa, like he'd just figured out what I was asking. I knew, though, that he'd understood me the first time. He was just teasing me by making me ask again. "Oh," he said, "Waguli. Well, not right away. He didn't get back as soon as he meant to. First off, it was a long ways on over to Old Town, and he had to

walk. That took awhile. Then he had to tell everyone in town what he had learned on his trip, and that took awhile. Everyone had questions, and they had to talk about the problems. Everyone had an opinion and had to give it to everyone else. I bet they talked about it for four days at least. Then, especially because they were what we call real conservative there at Old Town, I imagine that they all went to the water."

"Went to the water?" I said.

"Don't you know about that? About going to the water?"

"No," I said. "What is it?"

"I thought you knew about that," he said, and his eyes had that twinkle in them that made the skin around them wrinkle up even more than usual. He took a couple of puffs on his pipe.

"No," I said again.

"Well, I guess I'll have to tell you about that."

My legs were beginning to feel too short for comfort in the red lawn chair, and besides, I wanted to get closer to Grandpa to hear about going to the water, so I got my bucket again and set it down in front of his chair. I sat on the bucket facing him, and I put my elbows on my knees and my chin in my hands and waited to hear more.

"Put another stick on that fire, chooj," he said.

I jumped up and ran to the woodpile and picked up a small split log.

"That one's too big," he said.

I dropped it and found one smaller, an unsplit one that my fingers would almost reach around, and I held it up for him to see.

"That'll do," he said.

I put it on the fire and went back to my bucket seat and reassumed the same posture I had just abandoned.

"They used to go to the water when things were really bad," said Grandpa. "When it seemed like there was nothing else to do. It was kind of like a last resort, and it was a very powerful, very special ceremony. They didn't do it for just any reason either. It was only for all the people. Maybe all the people in just one town, or maybe all the Cherokee people. They call it, Elohi Gaghusduhdi. That means kind of like, it's propping up the world, you know?"

"Yeah," I said, but I really wasn't sure. I guessed it was really important, though. "What did they do?"

Grandpa got up from his chair with a kind of a groan. He walked over to the fire, and then he knelt down beside it. He picked up a small stick and gouged around in the water with the roots and bark in it.

"Ahh," he said, "that'll be ready pretty soon now." He straightened himself up with another groan and went back to his chair and sat down again. "What did they do? Well, they picked one man from each clan. Waguli might have been the man from the Wolf Clan. He could have been. If it was him, he had to get some tobacco. Not just any old tobacco. Tsola gayuhnli. They call that old tobacco or sometimes ancient tobacco, but what it really means is sacred tobacco. He had to get some of that. So did the other six guys."

"Grandpa," I said, "are you smoking sacred tobacco?"

"Well, chooj,*" he said, exhaling a beautiful puff of smoke that looked bluish to me as it hovered around his head for an instant before rising to dissipate, "I guess maybe I am. I grow it right here. It's that old kind. Anyhow, those seven guys, they had a place to go to. It was down by a stream. They knew where it was, and they all had to go there at midnight, and then they put all their tobacco in a pile on the west bank. Then Waguli, if he was the one, because he was from the Wolf Clan, and it always went first, he got up and stood by that pile of tobacco, and he faced the east. Then he said some words. He had to know those words. It couldn't be just any words. They had to be said just right. And it was a long thing that he had to say. Then he said the same thing over again until he had said it four times. Then he stepped out of the way, and the next guy came up and did the same thing. Said the same words. Said them four times. Just like Waguli done it. Finally all seven men, one from each clan, had said those same words over four times. All just alike."*

"What did they say, Grandpa?" I asked.

"Oh, it was a long thing. I can't tell you all the words. You ain't supposed to say them unless you're going to the water. It's kind of like spending money. If you waste it just because you have it, then some time will come when you need it, and you won't have any. Wasting them sacred words is kind of like that. But what they did was they called on Thunder. You know, Thunder is our special friend. He's a friend to the Cherokees. So they called on Thunder to use his powers to help them out of their trouble, but they had to do it in a special way.

"Well, when they were all done saying it four times, Waguli went back to the tobacco pile there, and he filled his pipe and lit it. Then he blew smoke to the east. Then he walked around that pile of tobacco to the north, and he blew smoke to the north. Then he

*walked around to the west and blew smoke, and then to the south.
He made a circle around that tobacco. Then he moved away, and
the next guy did the same thing. All of them did that."*

*Grandpa's pipe had burned out, and he got up and moved to the
fire again. He tapped the burnt tobacco out of his pipe bowl into the
flames, tucked the pipe into his shirt pocket, and studied the stuff in
his pot again.*

"I think it's ready," he said. "Fetch me that cane pole."

*I ran to get the pole, and I was kind of excited. I figured that I
was about to find out just what it was for. I got back to Grandpa's
green chair before he did, because he had gotten up and walked over
to the house to get a small paintbrush off a window ledge there. He
brought the brush back and sat down, and I handed him the pole.*

*"Now get that rag over there," he said, "so you won't burn your-
self, and bring me that pot."*

*Well, I got the rag and I got the pot. I took the pot over to
Grandpa, and he motioned me to set it down on the ground there
between his feet. He was holding that cane pole and looking it up
and down, and he turned it around and around in his dark, wrinkled
hands. I couldn't figure what he was studying so hard. It looked just
the same to me all up and down. But pretty soon he was satisfied
that he'd seen it good enough, I guess, because he stopped studying
so hard. He held it in his left hand, and with his right hand he
dipped the brush into the pot.*

"You made paint," I said.

*"Well, it's a kind of dye, chooj," he said, and he painted a dark
brown ring around the pole real close to one end. Then he held the
pole away from himself a little and studied that brown ring, kind of
nodding his head a little like he was pleased with what he had done.
The dye was a nice, rich brown, and it did look good against the
yellow of that cane. Then he painted another ring real close to that
one, so close that they made a kind of stripe. Then he skipped down
a couple of inches, I guess, and he did the same thing again, and
then in the space between the two stripes, he drew in some little
crosses or what looked like plus signs to me. He made four of them
inside the band between the stripes going around the pole. He moved
a little ways down the pole and started again.*

"Grandpa?" I said.

"Ummm?"

"What did Waguli and the other guys do next?"

*"Well, they waited a little while, and then they did the whole
thing all over again."*

"The whole thing? All the long words and the smoking and the circles and everything?"

"That's right. The whole thing. Then they waited some more and did it again. They did that all night long until they had done it seven times, and when they did it that seventh time, it was dawn. Anyhow, I imagine that they did that. It makes sense. It's what Cherokees do in real bad times like that. That's probably what they did there at Old Town."

He had finished painting on the cane pole, and he held it out to look at his work. He was apparently satisfied, and he held it out toward me.

"Here," he said. "Put it back where you got it awhile ago and let it dry."

I took it, careful not to get my hand near any of the places Grandpa had drawn designs with the black walnut dye. I held it for a moment and studied what Grandpa had done.

"Grandpa," I said, "there's seven of them. Those bands that you made. There's seven."

"Oh, yeah?" he said, like he was surprised, but I thought he probably had made seven of them on purpose, and he knew it all the time. He wasn't really surprised when I told him that.

"Yeah," I said. "Seven. And in each band there's four crosses."

"Well," he said, "I wonder what that means."

 8

LETTER TO MARTIN VAN BUREN,
PRESIDENT OF THE UNITED STATES
1836

Sir:

The seat you fill places you in a relation of credit and near-
ness to every citizen. By right and natural position, every
citizen is your friend. Before any acts contrary to his own
judgment or interest have repelled the affections of any man,
each may look with trust and living anticipation to your government. Each has the highest right to call your attention to such
subjects as are of a public nature, and properly belong to the
chief magistrate; and the good magistrate will feel a joy in meeting such confidence. In this belief and at the instance of a few
of my friends and neighbors, I crave of your patience a short hearing for their sentiments and my own: and the circumstances
that my name will be utterly unknown to you will only give
the fairer chance to your equitable construction of what I have
to say.

Sir, my communication respects the sinister rumors that fill
this part of the country concerning the Cherokee people. The
interest always felt in the aboriginal population—an interest

naturally growing as that decays—has been heightened in regard to this tribe. Even in our distant State some good rumor of their worth and civility has arrived. We have learned with joy their improvement in the social arts. We have read their newspapers. We have seen some of them in our schools and colleges. In common with the great body of the American people, we have witnessed with sympathy the painful labors of these red men to redeem their own race from the doom of eternal inferiority, and to borrow and domesticate in the tribe the arts and customs of the Caucasian race. And notwithstanding the unaccountable apathy with which of late years the Indians have been sometimes abandoned to their enemies, it is not to be doubted that it is the good pleasure and the understanding of all humane persons in the Republic, of the men and the matrons sitting in the thriving independent families all over the land, that they shall be duly cared for; that they shall taste justice and love from all to whom we have delegated the office of dealing with them.

The newspapers now inform us that, in December, 1835, a treaty contracting for the exchange of all the Cherokee territory was pretended to be made by an agent on the part of the United States with some persons appearing on the part of the Cherokees; that the fact afterwards transpired that these deputies did by no means represent the will of the nation; and that, out of eighteen thousand souls composing the nation, fifteen thousand six hundred and sixty-eight have protested against the so-called treaty. It now appears that the government of the United States choose to hold the Cherokees to this sham treaty, and are proceeding to execute the same. Almost the entire Cherokee Nation stand up and say, "This is not our act. Behold us. Here are we. Do not mistake that handful of deserters for us"; and the American President and the Cabinet, the Senate and the House of Representatives, neither hear these men nor see them, and are contracting to put this active nation into carts and boats, and to drag them over mountains and rivers to a wilderness at a vast distance beyond the Mississippi. A paper purporting to be an army order fixes a month from this day as the hour for this doleful removal.

In the name of God, sir, we ask you if this be so. Do the newspapers rightly inform us? Men and women with pale and perplexed faces meet one another in the streets and churches here, and ask if this be so. We have inquired if this be a gross misrepresentation from the party opposed to the government and anxious to blacken it with the people. We have looked at the newspapers of different parties and find a horrid confirmation of the tale. We are slow to believe it. We hoped the Indians were misinformed, and that their remonstrance was premature, and will turn out to be a needless act of terror.

The piety, the principle that is left in the United States, if only in its coarsest form, a regard to the speech of men, forbid us to entertain it as a fact. Such a dereliction of all faith and virtue, such a denial of justice, and such deafness to screams for mercy were never heard of in times of peace and in the dealing of a nation with its own allies and wards, since the earth was made. Sir, does this government think that the people of the United States are become savage and mad? From their mind are the sentiments of love and a good nature wiped clean out? The soul of man, the justice, the mercy that is the heart's heart in all men, from Maine to Georgia, does abhor this business.

In speaking thus the sentiments of my neighbors and my own, perhaps I overstep the bounds of decorum. But would it not be a higher indecorum coldly to argue a matter like this? We only state the fact that a crime is projected that confounds our understandings by its magnitude, a crime that really deprives us as well as the Cherokees of a country for how could we call the conspiracy that should crush these poor Indians our government, or the land that was cursed by their parting and dying imprecations our country, any more? You, sir, will bring down that renowned chair in which you sit into infamy if your seal is set to this instrument of perfidy; and the name of this nation, hitherto the sweet omen of religion and liberty, will stink to the world.

You will not do us the injustice of connecting this remonstrance with any sectional and party feeling. It is in our hearts the simplest commandment of brotherly love. We will not have this great and solemn claim upon national and human justice huddled aside under the flimsy plea of its being a party act. Sir, to us the questions upon which the government and the people have been agitated during the past year, touching the prostration of the currency and of trade, seem but motes in comparison. These hard times, it is true, have brought the discussion home to every farmhouse and poor man's house in this town; but it is the chirping of grasshoppers beside the immortal question whether justice shall be done by the race of civilized to the race of savage man, whether all the attributes of reason, of civility, of justice, and even of mercy, shall be put off by the American people, and so vast an outrage upon the Cherokee Nation and upon human nature shall be consummated.

One circumstance lessens the reluctance with which I intrude at this time on your attention my conviction that the government ought to be admonished of a new historical fact, which the discussion of this question has disclosed, namely, that there exists in a great part of the Northern people a gloomy diffidence in the *moral* character of the government.

On the broaching of this question, a general expression of despondency, of disbelief that any good will accrue from a remonstrance on an act of fraud and robbery, appeared in those men to whom we naturally turn for aid and counsel. Will the American government steal? Will it lie? Will it kill?—We ask triumphantly. Our counsellors and old statesmen here say that ten years ago they would have staked their lives on the affirmation that the proposed Indian measures could not be executed; that the unanimous country would put them down. And now the steps of this crime follow each other so fast, at such fatally quick time, that the millions of virtuous citizens, whose agents the government are, have no place to interpose, and must shut their eyes until the last howl and wailing of these tormented villages and tribes shall afflict the ear of the world.

I will not hide from you, as an indication of the alarming distrust, that a letter addressed as mine is, and suggesting to the mind of the Executive the plain obligations of man, has a burlesque character in the apprehensions of some of my friends. I, sir, will not beforehand treat you with the contumely of this distrust. I will at least state to you this fact, and show you how plain and humane people, whose love would be honor, regard the policy of the government, and what injurious inferences they draw as to the minds of the governors. A man with your experience in affairs must have seen cause to appreciate the futility of opposition to the moral sentiment. However feeble the sufferer and however great the oppressor, it is in the nature of things that the blow should recoil upon the aggressor. For God is in the sentiment, and it cannot be withstood. The potentate and the people perish before it; but with it, and its executor, they are omnipotent.

I write thus, sir, to inform you of the state of mind these Indian tidings have awakened here, and to pray with one voice more that you, whose hands are strong with the delegated power of fifteen millions of men, will avert with that might the terrific injury which threatens the Cherokee tribe.

With great respect, sir, I am your fellow citizen,

Ralph Waldo Emerson

9

Oconeechee watched her father
Join her mother in the sky,
Then she went to find her lover,
Say I'm yours until I die.
She went up the Oconoluftee,
Down the Little Tennessee,
Up the Nantahala,
Down the Hiwassee.

The body of Tsunalahuhski, known to the world as Junaluska, was laid out on the cot that he had slept on in his own house. While his clan sisters bathed the corpse and anointed it with bear's oil, Oconeechee went to the woods alone. The funeral was not her business, for she was of another clan. She took with her the sharp scissors her mother had gotten in earlier years from the English trader and went to her favorite spot by the water. There she wailed and cropped her long, beautiful hair up close to her ears. The old clan sisters dressed the newly washed body in Junaluska's best clothes, and the body was placed in a wooden coffin. Holes were drilled in the box to allow the soul to escape, and the remains of the old man who had tried but failed were placed in the ground. His pipe and tobacco pouch were put in there with him, and he was buried. Oconeechee came back from the woods and stood beside the grave while they sang and prayed, and, like all the others, she tossed a handful of dirt into the grave, but when the others were gone, she stayed alone and she wept.

Back at the house, a clan brother of Junaluska's was going through the house with burning twigs of cedar. The sisters who had handled the corpse had gone away. They would not be seen again for four days. Oconeechee stood outside the house. The clan brother came out, his task accomplished, and saw her.

"It's all right now," he said. "You can go in."

She stood staring at the house as the clan brother walked away. She knew what he meant, that the house had been purified by the incense of the cedar following the death. But she did not want to go inside. The house would not be the same without her father in there. She had not known her mother, but she had not known life without her father. She suddenly felt very much alone. She had not led a normal life among the Cherokees. A child ordinarily lived among the relatives of its mother, and Oconeechee's mother had not been a Cherokee. Her clan was the Wolf Clan of her mother's people, but she did not know her mother's people. She did not speak their language. She was alone.

The flames of the cooking fire before the house had burned themselves down but not completely out, and on an impulse, Oconeechee bent to pick up a faggot with a red-hot end. She blew on it, and it almost flamed out. She went inside the house and placed the faggot on a cot, then knelt beside it and blew again. Soon the cot was burning. She stood and watched it for a moment, then, sure the flames would grow, went back outside. Elaqui was standing in the street watching. He nodded his approval. She walked over to the old man.

"Can you tell me," she said, "how to find Old Town?"

It was May of 1838 when seven-thousand United States soldiers under the command of General Winfield Scott arrived in the Cherokee Nation with orders to remove the Cherokees by force.

Under Scott's orders the troops were disposed at various points throughout the Cherokee country, where stockade forts were erected for gathering in and holding the Indians preparatory to removal. From these, squads of troops were sent to search out with rifle and bayonet every small cabin hidden away in the coves or by the sides of mountain streams, to seize and bring in as prisoners all the occupants, however or wherever they might be found. Families at dinner were startled by the sudden gleam of bayonets in the doorway and rose up to be driven with blows and oaths along the weary miles of trail that led to the stockade. Men were seized in their fields or going along the road, women were taken from their wheels and children from their play. In many cases, on turning for one last look as they crossed the ridge, they saw their homes in flames, fired by the lawless rabble that followed on the heels of the soldiers to loot and pillage. So keen were these outlaws that in some instances they were driving off the cattle and other stock of the Indians almost before the soldiers had fairly started their owners in the other direction. Systematic hunts were made by the same men for Indian graves, to rob them of their silver pendants and other valuables deposited with the dead. A Georgia volunteer, afterward a Colonel in the Confederate service, said: "I fought through the civil war and have seen men shot to pieces and slaughtered by thousands, but the Cherokee removal was the cruelest work I ever knew."

To prevent escape the soldiers had been ordered to approach and surround each house, so far as possible, so as to come upon the occupants without warning. One old patriarch, when thus surprised, calmly called his children and grandchildren around him, and, kneeling down, bid them pray with him in their own language, while the astonished soldiers looked on in silence. Then rising he led the way into exile. A woman, on finding the house surrounded, went to the door and called up the chickens to be fed for the last time, after which, taking her infant on her back and her two other children by the hand, she followed her husband with the soldiers.

From James Mooney,
Historical Sketch of the Cherokee, 1900.

Old Town was set along the side of a creek in the mountains. The soldiers came in the early morning before the dawn and Waguli was awakened by the noise. When he came out of the house there were soldiers at either end of town, mounted on their horses, rifles in hand. They called out and others came out of their homes. Some ran toward the mountains, but there they found soldiers behind trees and rocks, rifles trained on them, bayonets fixed. They ran back again to the creek in front of their town, and there across the creek were foot soldiers holding their rifles with fixed bayonets at the ready. Little children began to cry and run for their mothers. Some began to wail. They had lived long enough with rumors and fear. They knew what this was. One soldier on a horse began shouting something, but his language was strange to most of the people of Old Town, for they knew only the Cherokee tongue. The soldiers began moving slowly, closing in on the people. The wailing and crying grew in volume.

Waguli stood in the middle of the crowd, and he shared in the general panic. Cooweescoowee had said that they should not fight, and surely the people in Old Town were not equipped to take on all these soldiers, some of them mounted, all armed with guns and bayonets. Many of the people in Old Town were women and children. Many more were old people. And Cooweescoowee had said that they should not fight. But Cooweescoowee had not said what they should do if the soldiers showed up with their rifles and long knives and began to drive the people from their homes. They had no right to do this. Waguli's panic slowly gave over to a sense of outrage. His home was invaded. His people were threatened. His honor and dignity were insulted. The circle of soldiers grew tighter, and the people crowded closer and closer together in fear.

Waguli suddenly reached forth and grabbed the barrel of a rifle, shoving it upward with his right hand. With the heel of his left, he bashed the chin of the soldier behind the gun. The assaulted trooper staggered backward under the impact of the sudden blow. Stunned, he almost fell to his knees as his legs grew rubbery beneath him. Another soldier, reacting quickly, grabbed Waguli from the left side, and Waguli spun on him, grabbing him by the jacket front and flinging him aside, knocking two more off their feet. He turned to his right in time to raise a knee into the stomach of the soldier running at him from that direction, then he ran for the water. Several rifles were raised and aimed at Waguli's back as he fled, but before they were fired, one of the soldiers on horseback shouted, and the rifles were lowered. Then two mounted soldiers turned their horses and raced after Waguli. He was halfway across the creek when the first rider reached his side. The soldier raised his rifle and swung it through the air, smashing the butt against the back of Waguli's head. Waguli took two

more labored strides through the water and pitched forward
on his face.

When Waguli regained his senses, his hands were tied behind his back and a soldier was pulling him to his feet. He
staggered, but he did not fall. Another rope was looped around
his shoulders and arms and pulled tight, burning his skin.
The soldier holding the other end of the rope climbed onto
the back of a horse. Waguli's head began to clear, and he
could see that the people were all lined up, men, women, and
children. He was in the line, too, behind a soldier's horse.
Up ahead one of the soldiers shouted out something Waguli
could not understand, and the line began to move. When the
Indians did not begin immediately to walk, soldiers pushed
them and nudged them with bayonets. Waguli was pulled by
the soldier on the horse holding the rope. They were headed
down the mountain. The long walk had begun.

> But Whippoorwill went out a hunting,
> And the soldiers captured him.
> They say he fought with honor,
> And he never did give in.
> Whippoorwill would not surrender,
> So they took away his pride,
> Marched him clear to Oklahoma
> With his hands behind him tied.

Oconeechee was tired. Her muscles ached and her feet were
swollen and cut from her long walk through the unfamiliar
mountains. She was hungry, too, but she knew from the directions she had been given that she was almost at the end of
her journey. At Old Town she would find Waguli. Then she
would eat and rest, and everything would be all right. She
would be married to Waguli, and in his arms, once again
she would find happiness. Waguli would drive away the lone-
liness that had oppressed her spirit ever since her father had
gone to join her mother in the land above the Sky Vault.
Oconeechee stopped to catch her breath and rest her limbs,
and she heard from somewhere up in the roof of the forest
the mocking voice of a bluejay trying hard to imitate the cry
of the red-tailed hawk.

"You don't fool me," she said. "I know who you are."

The jay cried out again, and Oconeechee moved on. A green lizard scurried up the side of a red oak tree. Each step was painful, but the fire in her heart sustained her. "Everything begins with fire," she had often heard her father say, "and everything ends with fire." This fire in her breast was a beginning. She knew that. She walked on. A mockingbird settled on a low branch ahead, almost in her path. As she approached his perch, he fluttered off again. Then she heard the rippling sound of running water, and she knew she was almost there. She quickened her pace, ignoring the pains that shot through her limbs with each step she took. Old Town was just ahead, and Waguli.

The water was cold and soothing to her hot and battered feet as she waded into the stream to cross over to the other side. A mountain trout slithered past her legs, and crawdads scurried under rocks. Her body begged her to stay and bathe it in the cool waters, but the flame in her heart and the gnawing in her stomach said no. She emerged on the opposite bank and turned to head upstream. Again she quickened her pace. It would be just there, just around the bend. She had never been to Old Town, but Elaqui's directions were astonishingly accurate. All along the trip she had seen things just as he had described them. So she knew. It was just there. She walked on, breathing faster, ignoring the pain. Her heart was racing, too. Was it because of the physical strain or the anticipation? She couldn't tell.

She rounded the bend and saw the town. She had been right. The old man, Elaqui, had been right. It was just there. But something was wrong. She hurried on, but getting closer, she could tell what it was that had troubled her sight. No one was moving about. She saw no life. She stopped and stared in disbelief, then she started walking slowly toward the deserted town. From somewhere a dog barked, a lonely, mournful sound. At last she was standing in the middle of the town. She looked around in desperation, but there was no one to turn to.

"Waguli," she said. "Waguli?"

The only answer was the mournful bark of the hidden dog. Then slowly the terrible truth came to her mind, the unthinkable became lucid thought, and she gave it trembling voice.

"The soldiers came," she said.

10

We had just finished lunch. We had fried squirrel, and mashed potatoes and gravy, and corn and brown beans, and it was all real good. Grandma never fixed anything that wasn't real good. And we had pan-fried corn bread to go with it all, and afterwards some big cinnamon rolls that Grandma was just famous for all over the reservation. I was so full, I wanted to go lay down somewhere and sleep it off like an old dog would do, but Grandpa got up from the table and went over to his bureau and picked up his pipe and his tobacco pouch, and he stuck them in his pocket.

"Come on, chooj," he said. "Let's go for a walk."

You couldn't go anywhere from Grandpa's house without going either uphill or downhill. There just isn't any such thing around those parts as flat. This time we went downhill, and pretty soon we went into the woods. Grandpa was just strolling along like he wasn't going anyplace in particular and wasn't in any hurry to get there. And that was okay with me, because I was so full I sure didn't want to be in any hurry. One time Grandpa stopped and stood real still. I walked up beside him, and he put a hand on my shoulder, and with his other hand he pointed up ahead to a slender birch tree.

I remember that it was a birch, because that was one of the few trees that I knew when I saw one. And he said, "galegi." There was the biggest blacksnake that ever I saw, and it was just kind of inching its way up that tree. I'd never seen a snake climb a tree before, and it made me feel nervous. I was sort of used to watching for snakes on the ground where I stepped, but I never thought about having them up over my head. I guess Grandpa could see that I felt like that, because he just smiled a little bit and patted me on the back.

"He's not interested in us," he said. "We're a little bit too big for him to swallow. Come on."

We walked on a little farther, a little deeper into the woods, and then Grandpa stopped again. He looked around on the ground until he found a suitable spot, then he sat down, kind of between the big exposed roots of an old tree, and he leaned back on the tree. He took out his pipe and tobacco and fired it up. Off in the distance I could hear the hammering of a woodpecker, and all around me were the songs of a dozen different birds and the scolding chatter of squirrels. It seemed to me like a good time for Grandpa to continue the story he'd been telling me about Whippoorwill and Oconeechee, so I got all ready to hear more, but Grandpa, he was just leaning back against that tree and puffing on his pipe. Pretty soon I had used up all my patience. I just couldn't take it any longer.

"Grandpa," I said, "did they get all the Cherokees?"

"Who?"

"Those soldiers," I said, and I think that there was at least a little tone of exasperation in my voice, because I knew that he knew what I was talking about. He just always did that to me when I asked him a question like that. "The soldiers who got Whippoorwill. Did they get all the Cherokees?"

"No," he said. "No, they didn't get them all. If they had, we wouldn't be sitting here today. Not here in this spot. We might be around, I guess. Maybe. But we'd be out in Oklahoma, probably, or maybe out in California where some of them have got to, but we wouldn't be here."

He straightened out his right leg and reached deep into his big pocket to pull out his pocket knife, and then he pulled open its biggest blade. He held the knife out toward me.

"Here," he said. "You see that honey locust over there?"

I took the knife and I looked across where I thought he was looking, but I didn't know a honey locust tree. I couldn't tell which tree he meant.

"No," I said, but I walked on over to one of the trees. "This one?"

"No, chooj, the next one over. There with the pods on it that look like beans."

I moved over and put my hand on the honey locust.

"Yep. Now cut me that lowest branch."

I reached up and put my hand around a low branch and looked back at Grandpa.

"Yeah," he said. "Cut it clean, and cut it up close to the trunk. That's good. Right there."

I gripped the branch as hard as I could, and then I sank the knife blade into its wood.

"The soldiers came on a whole family. All of them together having a meal. The old man was named Tsali. Tsali and his wife had two grown sons and one young one. Tsali's brother and his wife and kids were there with them, and Tsali's two grown boys, they had families, too. They were all of them visiting and having a meal together, and the soldiers came. Well, Tsali and his family, none of them could talk any English or even understand any of it, but they sure enough could tell what those soldiers wanted. They knew, so Tsali just told them to get up and do what they was told. He didn't want anyone in his family to get hurt. So the soldiers lined them all up out on the road headed down the mountain."

"Just like they did with Whippoorwill," I said.

"Just like. They had to leave their food on the table, and all their extra clothes and blankets. They had to leave all their belongings behind. The soldiers wouldn't let them take anything. And they started to march them down the mountain.

"Well, Tsali's grown boys were getting pretty hot, I guess, and they wanted to fight those soldiers, but their daddy kept telling them to do what the soldiers wanted and not to fight. He didn't want anyone to get hurt. He had also heard that Chief John Ross had said he didn't want any Cherokees fighting the soldiers, and he wanted to do what the chief had said.

"Tsali was getting old by this time. Oh, he probably wasn't as old as me, but he was getting old and so was his wife, and his wife, she didn't move quite as fast as the soldiers wanted them to move along. So finally one of those soldiers kind of prodded the old woman in the backside with his bayonet. He probably thought that was kind of funny. But Tsali didn't think it was funny at all. Not a bit. Just like I wouldn't think it was funny if anyone did anything like that *to your grandma. No sir. I'd probably do just what old Tsali did."*

Grandpa had been talking so much that he had let his pipe go out, so he stopped talking and found a match in his pocket. By then I had managed to get the branch he wanted cut off the locust tree, and I had gone back over to sit by him to listen to the story. He got his pipe relit and puffed on it a few times.

"What was that, Grandpa?" I said.

"What? What was what?"

Grandpa was looking around like he was trying to find something I had seen somewhere, but he knew what I meant. He knew I hadn't seen anything.

"What did he do?" I said. "Tsali."

"Oh. Well, he hollered out in Cherokee, 'Get them now,' and he jumped on that soldier that had jabbed his wife. And his brother and each of his boys, they each jumped on a soldier. They grabbed the guns away from them and knocked them down, and the soldiers all jumped up and commenced to running headlong down the hill like scared jackrabbits."

I laughed out loud at the image of the soldiers running downhill away from Tsali and his family, and Grandpa paused for awhile to let me have my laugh.

"But one of them never got up," he said, and I stopped laughing. "One soldier was dead."

"Who killed him?" I said.

"Oh, I don't know. Maybe it was Tsali. Maybe he killed that soldier that had poked his wife. I kind of like to think that was it, but I don't really know. Nobody does, I guess. Maybe it was one of the others, his brother or one of his sons. Anyhow, one of them had killed a soldier, and the other soldiers had all run off scared, so Tsali and his family turned around and went back up the mountain, but they didn't go back home. Maybe they went by the house to pick up some things, but they didn't stay there. They went way up in the mountains, way up where they didn't think the soldiers would ever find them, and they found some of their friends along the way, and they took them along with them. Pretty soon there was a pretty good bunch of them up there. Not nearly as many as were caught, but a pretty good bunch."

"And the soldiers couldn't find them?" I said.

"Well, no, they couldn't. But they wanted Tsali and his bunch real bad. So when they had just about everybody all rounded up and put in their stockades, they found Wil Usdi, the little white man

*that had growed up with the Cherokees and could talk Cherokee,
and they told him to go find Tsali. They told him to say that if
Tsali and his brother and his sons would surrender, they would stop
hunting Cherokees. Those few who were hid out up there in the
hills could stay there, at least for awhile, until the government figured out something to do with them. The big general figured they
was so few that it really wouldn't matter much. So Colonel Thomas—that's what the white men called Wil Usdi—he went and
found Tsali and the others, and he give them that message."*

"What did Tsali do?" I asked.

*Grandpa had picked up the branch of honey locust that I had
fetched him, and he was whittling on it with his pocket knife, cutting
off little pieces about six or seven or eight inches long and laying
them aside.*

*"He talked it over with his family, and they went on in. They
knew that the soldiers would kill them, because they had killed that
soldier."*

"But he asked for it," I said. "He had it coming."

*"Maybe so, chooj, but the soldiers didn't see it that way. They
put four stakes in the ground, and they tied Tsali to one, and the
other three men, his two sons and his brother, they tied each of them
to one. They decided that Tsali's little boy was too young, and they
let him live. Then they got some Cherokees out of the stockade, and
they made them into a firing squad. They made them shoot Tsali
and the others. They did that, I guess, so that the Cherokees would
know that they was absolutely whipped. Couldn't do nothing.
Couldn't say nothing. Just do as they was told—like dogs."*

*I got so mad, I had tears welling up in my eyes, but I didn't say
anything. I was afraid that if I did Grandpa would hear in my voice
that I was crying, and I didn't want him to know that, so I just kept
quiet, and I looked at the ground, and I listened.*

*"They did keep that one promise, though," he said. "They
didn't go after them others. Them few who was hid out in the hills.
And that's where Oconeechee was—with them in the hills."*

Waguli had walked the entire way from Old Town, down the
mountain, through mountain streams, and across the plain to
the stockade. He thought when he first saw it from a distance
that it looked like an army fort. Constructed of logs, it was a
stockade fence built in a square. At one corner stood a guard
tower. A closer view told Waguli that the enclosure was

much too small to be a fort. And when the gate was opened
and he was thrust inside along with the others, he saw that it
was only a fence. There was nothing inside—no buildings,
no huts, no chairs or benches even. There was nothing but
people, Cherokee people, men, women, and children of all
ages. They were crowded into the foul-smelling compound.
Women wailed and children cried and screamed out of fear
and hunger and physical discomfort.

All the long walk, Waguli had nurtured a growing rage
and bitter hatred. Inside the makeshift, temporary prison, he
was overcome with an instant horror at the inhumanity of his
captors, their cold indifference to human suffering, their ca-
sual acceptance of so much misery and terror, and their ready
participation in its creation. The horror led to a nausea, a
great, dull sickness deep in his guts and his heart. If he could
only vomit all this sickness up, he thought—but, of course,
he couldn't. He could retch his very innards up, he knew, and
the scene around him wouldn't change. He looked around
until he found a spot against the wall, and he sat down in the
dirt, knees drawn up, head hanging low on his chest. He
closed his eyes, but he could still smell the filth, still hear the
wailing and the crying and the screaming. Someone untied
his ams, but he sat in a daze as if stunned by a blow, scarcely
acknowledging the act of kindness, not even taking note of
who it was that had done the good deed. He would rather die
than remain in this place, he thought. He resolved that he
would not remain.

He began to dig. The white men had treated him like a
dog, so, he reasoned, he would dig like one. He would scratch
a hole under the fence and crawl out and run. The ground
was hard and rocky, and soon his fingers were torn and bleeding, yet still he scratched. He longed for dog claws on his
hands. Some few watched him at first, then others. They
crowded around him to shield him from the line of sight of
the guard in the tower. By and by one knelt down to help,
and then another. By nightfall they had dug beneath the bot-
toms of the poles, and in the dark, they scratched their way
outside. Waguli lay on his back and dropped, first his arms,
then his head and shoulders, into the hole. He wriggled on
his back, shoving with his heels. The rough butts of the
stockade poles raked his chest and belly flesh as he forced

himself under the fence. His arms were free. No one grabbed them. Then his head was out, but still he couldn't look around. He was expecting a blow, a kick, a shot, but none came. Finally he got all the way through, and came quickly to his feet in a crouch and looked around. There were no soldiers near. No one had seen him. His heart pounded inside his chest. The blood seemed to race through his veins. Off in the distance the soldiers' campfires gleamed in the night. They didn't want to be too near the stink, Waguli thought. Another Indian was emerging from the hole, and Waguli ran.

11

Waguli heard the shots behind him, but he didn't look back. He ran. He was in unfamiliar country, so he didn't know where he was running to, but he ran. He ran to get beyond the campfires of the soldiers, to disappear into the darkness, to vanish from the sight of these cruel white men. He ran. He heard the white soldiers behind him shouting. He couldn't understand the words, but he understood the anger and urgency in their tone. He ran. Then he heard the horses, heard the pounding of their hooves as they came up behind him, heard the panting of the big animals as they closed in.

Then came the powerful impact, the blow that knocked him off his feet, as the big *soghwili* bashed into him, sideswiped him from behind, and sent him sprawling forward on his face in the dark. He didn't see the ground coming at him for the general blackness. He felt it as it abruptly stopped his forward motion. He rolled as he landed, and a second beast ran over him as he rolled, kicking him, barely missing trampling him underfoot with its sharp, ironclad hooves. The horse screamed and reared, apparently as frightened by the near miss as was Waguli. Waguli scrambled desperately to his feet, intending to attack the rider of the frightened animal, to pull him to the ground, but instead he felt the biting lash of a rawhide rope across his back. He whirled to face the wielder of this weapon, but the other soldier, similarly armed, had regained control of his beast, and he lashed Waguli across the shoulders. A third mounted soldier rode up, and then a fourth. Waguli found himself surrounded by stamping, snorting beasts mounted by white devils with whips. His mind told him to clutch one of the biting ropes as it struck him, to yank hard and pull at least one of his tormentors to the ground, but every time he reached for one, another bit into his flesh.

Eventually he staggered and fell to his knees. He huddled there while the blows continued to lacerate his back until a sharp, commanding voice brought a halt to the torture. There was a brief pause, then he felt his arms wrenched behind his back, felt the rough ropes being wrapped around his wrists and pulled tight, felt them again tear into his flesh. Again he was captive. Again he was bound.

Oconeechee stood alone in Old Town. There was not much sign of violence. A pole had been knocked out from under a corner of an arbor in front of one house, causing it to collapse. There was no sign of looting. People's personal belongings were still in their homes. But there were no people. There was no Waguli. The dog continued to bark. Oconeechee sank to her knees and began to wail. Slowly, cautiously, from around the corner of a vacant house to her back, a lone figure emerged. He watched her. He listened. Then, when she paused for a breath, he spoke.

"Are you Cherokee?"

Oconeechee ceased her wailing, and fear made her stiff. Yet the voice spoke Cherokee.

"Yes," she said, but she did not turn.

"Who are you?"

"My name is Oconeechee."

"I have never heard that name," said the voice.

Oconeechee stood slowly and turned to face the stranger who questioned her.

"I am not a real Cherokee," she said. "I belong to the Wolf Clan of another people. My mother's people. My father was Tsunalahuski of Soco Gap."

"Ah," said the man, "I know of him. He is a great man."

"He is no longer with us on this earth," said Oconeechee, "and I am left alone. I don't know my mother's people. I don't speak their language. I was raised a Cherokee, yet I have no Cherokee clan. I am alone. I was going to marry Waguli of this town here, so I came to find him."

"He is gone," said the stranger. "Everyone is gone. The soldiers came and took them. I was away hunting. When I came home, this is what I found. I was hiding when I heard you here. My name is Wildcat. I belong to the Deer People. My wife and my children were here. My parents. All my friends. All my relatives."

"My Waguli was all I had. What will we do?"

"We have to leave here," said Wildcat. "I have heard that after the soldiers leave, the Georgians come in to steal everything. Sometimes they're just behind the soldiers. They haven't come here yet, but they could come any minute."

"We can go hide in the woods," said Oconeechee.

"First you need some new clothes. We can get them for you from my house, and I'll get my things, too. We'll take all we can use. Come with me. Hurry."

Oconeechee followed Wildcat to his house, where he gathered up a change of clothes for himself, his tobacco, pipe, and weapons. He found a dress for Oconeechee. It was made of soft doeskin. Oconeechee thanked Wildcat and ran with the dress to the creek. She bathed quickly, then put on the new dress. Wildcat came out of his house with his goods tied into a bundle.

"Are you ready to go?" he asked.

"Where will we go?"

"I heard that some of our people are hiding high up in the mountains in the old caves where the white men will never find them. I think I can find them, though. Let's go before the Georgians get here."

"I hate to let them steal all the things of your town," said Oconeechee.

"Let's leave them only ashes," said Wildcat.

He struck flame to his own house first, then helped it

spread throughout the town. They watched it burn, and then they left.

Waguli was back inside the stockade, his hands still tied behind his back, the wounds to his flesh festering along with the bitterness in his heart. He was seated as before, leaning against the logs, his knees drawn up, his head hanging. This time, though, the guard in the tower had been instructed to watch Waguli. He had been identified as a troublemaker. No one was to go near him. If anyone approached too near, the guard would shout and aim his rifle. Then they would move away to a safe distance. When mealtime came, a soldier would come inside the compound and give Waguli's nearly raw salt pork to another prisoner to feed to him. Waguli refused to eat the white man's meat, and soon they didn't even bother to try anymore. His insides growled their hunger at him, but the gnawing pain in his stomach was somehow satisfying to Waguli. He decided that he would starve himself to death.

> They broke his noble spirit,
> Filled his heart so full of pain,
> He would not give Oconeechee
> Only half a man.
>> Whippoorwill, Whippoorwill,
>> Don't you know how she's searched all these hills?
>> She's searched every glen and glade
>> Not knowing why you went away.
>> Can't you feel she loves you still, Whippoorwill?

He tried to concentrate on his own pain and hunger. He kept his head down and his eyes closed. He tried to shut out the sights and sounds and smells of the stockade, and the visions in his mind and the ache in his heart that had been left there by the beautiful daughter of old Tsunalahuski, the lovely Oconeechee, the only love of his life. None of it worked. A screaming child would force him to open his eyes, and he would see the human misery all around him. He saw the soldier bring the bottle of whiskey and entice the young Cherokee woman outside the compound. He saw her return later, too long gone to have satisfied just one man, staggering drunk from the white man's crazy water and the white man's lust. He saw the child sick with dysentery screaming in its helpless mother's arms, and he later saw it dead. He saw the young woman who had drunk the whiskey in a pathetic attempt to escape the pain lying passed out in her own vomit. And when he closed his eyes, he still saw them. The images swam in his mind, and they only grew stronger the tighter he squeezed his eyelids shut.

He heard the crying children, and he heard the mothers' wailing because they could do nothing to ease the pain and hunger and fear felt by their little ones. He heard the groans of the old men and old women as they valiantly attempted to suffer with patience. And he heard the laughter and the cursing of the soldiers, and he thought that he would swell and burst with his fermenting rage. But of all the physical horror, the pain of his wounds, the clangor of terror in his ears, the ghastly sights before his eyes, the worst were the smells. Fetid odors of human waste, the stench of sickness, the scent of death, the rank smell of rotten meat, the general rankness of unwashed bodies crowded together in too close proximity, all combined to produce a suffocating, mephitic assault on his nostrils and lungs and a savage and virulent affront to the dignity of humankind.

Yet the deepest pain of all came with thoughts of Oconeechee. Where could she be, he wondered. Was she in a camp like this? Or was she dead? He tried to recall her beauty, and then he tried to drive the image from his mind. If only he knew she was safe somewhere, then perhaps he could endure this white man's hell. Or if he knew that she was dead, he could feed on his hatred, nurture it and let it grow. He longed for the ability to weep—or to vomit. He could do neither. His whole being, physical, mental, spiritual, was one massive, dull ache. Slowly, complete realization of the total significance of all these things came into Waguli's mind, and it was cataclysmic, earth shattering. It was more than the unhappiness of Waguli and Oconeechee, more than the cruel, needless suffering of the wretches around him in the stockade, more than the thefts and the deaths. All of these were bad enough, but it was more than all of them combined. It was like the crack of doom.

They had gone to the water, and they had done everything right. The old men had seen to that. They should have been saved. The ceremony had always worked in the past. The People had always prospered. It had never failed them before. Waguli couldn't understand why it had failed this time. If the going to the water couldn't save them, nothing could. There was no hope. None. Nothing but defeat, disaster, despair, and death.

Then he remembered the old prophet he had heard at Red Clay. He tried to recall the old man's exact words. What had he said? It came to him as if in a vision. He saw the old man materialize as before, saw the two black wolves at his sides, heard him speak the prophetic words of warning, of impending doom.

I see Cherokees turning into whites. I see white man's clothes, white man's weapons. I heard white man's talk. To maintain our balance, we must remain Cherokee. If you keep these things you have from white men, the Cherokees will all be driven to the west, to the edge of the world, to the Darkening Land. Do you want to stay here where you belong? Then listen to me.

Throw away your steel knives and iron pots and guns. Burn the white man's clothes you wear. Throw away the glass beads you use for decoration and learn again how to prepare the quills of the porcupine for use as decoration. Kill your cats and pigs and horses. Be Cherokees. That is the only way to be saved.

That was the answer. If only the people had listened to the old man. He thought about the people in Soco Gap, how they wore their hair, the way they dressed, how he, himself, had thought they looked and acted like whites. He told himself they were to blame. But then he remembered his own steel knife, and he recalled how proud of it he had been when he first acquired it. He considered all the steel pots in Old Town and all the glass beads on even his own clothing. We are all to blame, he told himself. None of us heeded the warning. Now it is too late.

Waguli's rage began to cool. It was displaced by an abject heaviness of heart and mournful regret. Then he saw that a white man was beginning to move among the Cherokees there in the compound. He appeared to be concerned and compassionate. He was not a soldier, but soon soldiers joined him, and they opened the gates and accompanied a small number of women and children to the outside. Waguli wondered where they were being taken. He wondered if others would be taken later. Soon they returned, and others were taken out.

"They are taking them to the river to bathe," he heard someone say in Cherokee. "The preacher is making them do it."

When all the women with children had been allowed to go to the river, the old people were taken out, those who were not too sick to be moved. Finally younger men were allowed to go. The preacher and soldiers came to Waguli, and the preacher said something to the soldiers. The soldiers seemed to protest, but the preacher became more firm. Waguli was pulled to his feet, and his hands were untied.

"Come, my son," said the preacher, and Waguli was surprised to hear Cherokee words spoken by a white man. He allowed himself to be conducted, along with the others, to the river, and he waded into the soothing waters and bathed his wounds. He bathed, but he felt filthy again as soon as he was back inside the stockade, and as soon as he was back inside, the soldiers bound his wrists again. Again the ropes chaffed his still raw and tender flesh. This time, however, the bonds were not pulled so cruelly tight. At the next mealtime, the preacher returned again with the soldiers, and Waguli was again released.

"You must eat," said the preacher, and Waguli, lacking the strength to resist and the will to refuse, accepted the food. He no longer worried about whether or not it was fit to eat. He could not taste. He did not care. He ate.

I didn't want this summer ever to end. I never had wanted summers with Grandpa to end, but this one seemed to me somehow more important than all the others. It was more necessary, it seemed, more immediate, more vital. And so when Mama came to take me to the clinic for the physical exam I had to have for school, it made me sad. It meant the summer was almost over. She took me right back to Grandpa's house after the exam, but just the taking of it reminded me how soon the essential, life-supporting summer would end, and I would be back in the city in school.

When Mama drove up to the house she had barely stopped the car, and I jumped out. I ran inside the house ahead of her. Grandma was there baking bread. She had flour all over her, and she smelled nice.

"Hi, Grandma," I said, and I gave her a quick hug and a kiss. "Where's Grandpa?"

"He's out back," she said with an indulgent smile, and I ran out the back door. I heard Mama through the screen door say, "In one door and out the other," but I didn't pay that any mind. There sat Grandpa in his green chair. He had the pieces of the honey locust he had cut all lined up on the ground beside his chair. They had been sharpened on one end and looked to me like giant toothpicks, except

*that the other end was blunt. Grandpa had one of them in his hands,
and he had some fluffy stuff, too, and some string or thread. He had
some of that fluffy stuff on the blunt end of the stick, and he was
wrapping the thread around real close and tight to hold the fluff on.*

"What's that?" I said.

"'Siyo, chooj," he said.

"Oh. Hi, Grandpa. What's that fluffy stuff?"

"Bull thistle down," he said.

*"Oh, I know what that is. You showed me once. They grow
down beside the road."*

"Yeah. Them's the ones."

*I wanted to ask him next what they were for, why he was tying
them to the sticks like that, but I didn't. Instead I pulled my red
chair around where I could watch him real close. He finished with
the one he had in his hands and reached down for another, and he
took some more of the thistle down and started to work on that one.
I noticed the cane pole leaning over against the house where I had
last seen it, but Grandpa had done some more to it since then. It had
strips of leather tied around it in two different places, and from one
of the leather pieces a pheasant feather dangled. Well, I didn't lose
interest in what Grandpa was doing, but it was taking him so long
to do it, and there were four more sticks on the ground beside his
chair, that I guess I did start to get just a little bored. I was looking
around, and over there by the shed in the midst of all the stuff that
was lying around there, I saw a green lizard crawling on a stick of
firewood. I went after him.*

*"Don't catch him by his tail, chooj," said Grandpa. "If you do,
he'll just break it off."*

*I didn't even know that Grandpa had seen the lizard or knew
what I was doing, but I guess that nothing much ever escaped
Grandpa's attention. He always seemed to know just about everything that was going on around him. Well, I caught the lizard, not
by his tail, and I held him in my hand and felt his little heart beat.
He was a real pretty one. In just a little while I let him go again. I
put him right back on the log, just where I had found him, and he
ran off of it and skittered underneath the edge of the shed.*

*Every now and then I looked back at Grandpa, and he would
still be just tying that fluffy stuff to his sticks. I wandered off a little
ways, and there crawling up the side of a small tree was a praying
mantis. He was big and a real pretty green color. I put my hand up
above him, and he crawled right onto it. Then I lowered my hand*

so I could watch him right in front of my face, and he seemed to be watching me, too. I walked back over to where Grandpa was sitting, real slow, because I didn't want to let him fall off my hand.

"Look, Grandpa," I said.

"Udolanuhsdi," he said.

"Is that his name?"

"That's what we call him in Cherokee," said Grandpa. "Can you say it? Udolanuhsdi."

"Udolanuhsdi," I repeated.

"Good," he said. "Put him over there in the garden when you're done visiting with him. He takes care of gardens."

"How does he do that?" I asked.

"He eats up the bugs that eat the garden plants."

I carried the praying mantis over to the garden and let him crawl off my hand onto the leaf of a tomato plant, and I squatted down there and watched for awhile, but no other bug came along for him to eat. Finally, I went back to Grandpa, and he was just tying up the last stick. I got kind of excited then all over again about what it was he was doing, because I figured that I was just about to find out what it was. He was almost done. He finished it, and he put it down with the others, six of them altogether. Then he gestured toward the shed.

"You see that old cardboard?" he asked me.

I ran to pick up an old pasteboard box that was there in the midst of the other stuff lying around.

"It's got something in it," I said.

"Bring it here. Let me see."

I picked up the box and carried it over to Grandpa where he sat. There was an old electric motor or something in the box. He looked at it.

"Oh," he said, "just dump that out over there."

I ran back to where I had gotten the box and dumped the motor out on the ground. Grandpa pointed off to his left, off to the side of the shed.

"Put it over there," he said. I ran out and put the box down. "A little farther back." I scooted it back some with my foot. "That's good."

As I started back toward Grandpa, he was getting up out of his chair with a good, loud groan, and then he walked over to where the cane pole, all decorated up so nice, was leaning against the house. He picked up the pole and went back to his chair, bent over, and picked up one of the tufted sticks. He poked the stick, sharpened end first, down one end of the pole, then pointed the other end of the pole at the cardboard box. He brought the end of pole he had put the stick in up to his lips, and then there was a loud poof sound and a thud, and only then did I know what he had been making all this time. He had made a blowgun, and he had shot a dart right into the box. I ran to the box and looked at the dart sticking about half its length through the cardboard.

"Wow," I said.

Grandpa had bent over to get another dart.

"Come on, chooj,*" he said. "You try it."*

He poked another dart in and handed me the blowgun. I aimed it and blew, but the dart only went out a few feet and fell to the ground.

"Try again," said Grandpa, poking another dart in. "Take a big breath and then puff it out hard, all at once."

Well, I sucked in all the breath I could and put the gun to my mouth. My cheeks were all pooched out with the wind I had stored up in them, and my belly was poked out, too. Then I blew it all out hard, just like he said, and the dart flew right over the box.

"I missed," I said.

"That's okay. You got the idea now. Here. Take a better aim this time. Just point the pole right at the box, and do it just like you did that last time."

He had loaded the gun again, and again I filled up my lungs and my cheeks and again I blew, and this time there was a thud.

"I hit it."

"Yeah," said Grandpa. "You sure did. Try another one."

I hit the box again. I was thrilled.

"The old-timers used to hunt with these," said Grandpa. "They'd hunt little things with them."

"Did Whippoorwill have one?" I said.

"Oh, yeah. Sure. He'd have one. 'Course he didn't have it once they got him in that prison. He didn't have anything in there. Nobody did. Maybe just a few blankets for a whole lot of people. And it started to get cold while they were living like that. Just waiting. Nothing to do."

"What were they waiting for?"

"First thing, I guess," he said, "they was just waiting to get everybody all rounded up. They had to have some place they could hold the ones they caught 'til they caught them all and would move

*them west. But then they caught all of them they were going to
catch. They knew that those few were still out there, but they had
promised Tsali, you know, before they killed him, that they would
quit, and they did. So they had all the people they wanted, and they
had them in those prisons, and they were ready to move them out,
but Chief John Ross held it all up."*

"Why'd he do that?"

*"Well, I guess the soldiers took some of the people and moved
them out west, and it was real bad. Old Ross, he went to the army
and told them the Cherokees could move themselves, and they had
to argue about it for awhile. Finally, they let him do it. So for all
the rest of the people, it was Cherokees who led them on out there.
It was bad enough that way, but it was a whole lot worse for that
first bunch—the ones the army took."*

"Which ones did Whippoorwill go with?" I asked.

*"He fought them," said Grandpa, "and he tried to escape. I just
imagine that the soldiers took him. I bet they did. The soldiers took
him, I guess."*

He could tell most of what they wanted him to do by their
gestures, but when he couldn't, there were plenty of interpre-
ters around—Cherokees who could speak English, a few
whites who could speak Cherokee. His hands were once
again bound behind his back. No one told him why. He
imagined it was because he had tried to run away from them.
He had been pulled to his feet by soldiers. They had pushed
him into line. They had some wagons and some horses, but
not even enough for the very young and the very old and the
very sick. Many walked. Waguli walked. He walked with his
hands tied behind his back. Soldiers rode along beside them,
mounted on horses, carrying their long rifles with attached
long knives, carrying their long ropes, the kind they had
whipped him with. The wounds on his back and shoulders
were not yet healed. The wound to his heart was beginning
to heal. It was beginning to scab over, and beneath the scab
was a kind of numbness, a callous of sorts, a not caring anymore, a not hoping, a spirit that was dead. It was June, and
it was hot.

Somewhere up ahead a soldier shouted something, and the
column began to move. Waguli walked, his head down. His
feet, his legs, his back and shoulders all ached, but it was a

profoundly dull ache. He didn't think about it. He walked.
The horses and wagons ahead of him stirred up dust as thick
as a cloud, a fog of dust, and he walked through it, he
breathed it, he felt it cake on his skin. From out of the noise of
the wagon wheels, the wagons creaking, the horses' hooves,
the horses' snufflings and blowings, and the blustering banter
of the soldiers, he heard the woeful cry of an infant. He
walked on.

He had ceased wondering about his destination. He had
begun to believe that there was no destination, that the soldiers were just to going to march them around until they
dropped dead, one by one. He had heard that they were being
taken out west, farther west than he had ever imagined, but
they were not moving west. He had enough awareness left
about him to know that. They were moving southeast. It
must be another trick of the soldiers. He walked on. Then
finally he saw where they were going. It was another prison,
like the one he had been kept in, but a little larger. He
thought that he would be put in there, but instead, the soldiers brought more people out of this second stockade and
put them in line. Soon they were moving again. This time
they went south. And they went to yet another camp and
picked up more people. Waguli wondered how many of these
prisons the white men had for Cherokees, how many Cherokees were penned up like animals. They had walked for three
days, and all they had done was add to the length of the file.
They had not emptied any one of the three prisons. Waguli
had decided that he and the others were the captives of a race
of madmen.

On the morning of the fourth day, they began to walk
again. This time they headed west. West: the direction of the
color black, *guhnage,* the direction of despair, the pathway to
the Darkening Land at the edge of the world, the place from
which no human being ever returned. In his torpor he moved
along with his head down, legs moving mechanically, lungs
indifferently sucking in trail dust along with air. Once he
wandered out of the line, and he didn't even know it until a
mounted soldier rode up and rudely pushed him back in place.
Nudged by the trooper's horse, he staggered and nearly fell.
Then he resumed his previous pace. The jar of the big animal
against his body, the faltering of his steps, the loss of balance

came almost as a relief to the monotony of the plodding journey, the journey with no end, the trek to nowhere.

From up ahead in the line, he heard an awful wailing. It was the sound of death. It was a Cherokee female's piercing mourning cry. He trudged on. Soon he saw off to the side of the trail the body of an old man. A woman knelt beside the body. Two young Cherokees stood waiting with shovels, watched by a soldier sitting in his saddle, holding his rifle. The line continued to move. Not even death would slow its progress, Waguli thought. The trip had just begun, and already they were dying. Why not? Already he was dead inside. He wondered why his body kept moving, why his lungs kept drawing in the dusty air. Why? Why? Why?

13

The few who remained free hid in the mountains. They were free, but they were poor and they were hungry. They had abandoned everything they owned when they ran from the soldiers, and when some of them went sneaking back to their homes to see if they could gather any of their belongings, they found their homes looted or burned or both. They gathered what they could from the woods and from the mountain streams, but there was never enough. They were always hungry, but the children did not cry. The children knew they were hiding, and they were afraid that if they cried, the soldiers would hear them and come for them. They hungered in silence.

Oconeechee was there with them, led to them by Wildcat. When there was food she ate a little, but she gave most of her share to the small children with their hungry eyes. She went out into the woods like the others, and searched for food. What she found, she gathered and carried back to the camp to put into the common store. The young men went out hunting. Some had managed to escape with guns, but the only powder they had was what was in the horns they wore slung from their shoulders, and they had but a few lead balls. It didn't matter, though, because they were afraid to use the guns for fear the soldiers would hear the noise and come for them. The men with knives in their belts used the sharp blades to cut branches and make weapons. They made bows and arrows and spears and blowguns, and with these they hunted. Mostly they found squirrels and rabbits.

One day late, Wildcat came home with a deer. There was much rejoicing, but even then there was not enough for everyone. Oconeechee stood back from the crowd. She did not want to call attention to the fact that she was not eating, but Wildcat noticed. He walked over to her side.

"You didn't get your share," he said.

"I'm all right. The little ones need it," said Oconeechee.

"You need it, too," said Wildcat, "to keep up your strength. You have been gathering food. You've been working like all the rest of us."

"*Wado,* Wildcat. Thank you for worrying about me, but I'm all right. Besides," she said, "I'm leaving tomorrow."

Wildcat's face betrayed surprise, almost shock, and a little disappointment.

"Where will you go?" he said. "There are soldiers everywhere out there. It's not safe—especially for a beautiful young woman."

"I have to go find Waguli. If they have him in one of their pens, I'll find a way to get him out."

"You'll just get yourself put in."

"Then I'll be with him."

"Probably you won't even find him. There are many prisons. They have thousands of Cherokees in them. You don't even know where these prisons are. How can you find him? While you're looking for Waguli, the soldiers will find you. Maybe you won't wind up in prison with Waguli. Maybe you'll wind up in some other prison, or maybe the soldiers will just kill you."

"I have to try to find him, Wildcat. I love him. Without him, I have no reasons to live. Do you understand?"

Wildcat put his hands on Oconeechee's shoulders and gave her a gentle squeeze. He took a deep breath and sighed.

"Yes," he said. "I understand your feelings. But we have all lost someone. We can only go on with our lives. Here. Little one, I know Waguli. Don't throw away your own life searching in vain for a man who is probably already dead."

Oconeechee pulled herself away from Wildcat and gave him a hard look.

"What do you mean?" she said. "How can you say that?"

"I know him. Waguli would not let the white soldiers take him. He would fight. If he tried to fight, they killed him. You won't find him, Oconeechee. Stay here with us."

"No," she said. "I'm leaving in the morning."

She turned and walked away from Wildcat, going into the darkness of the woods. She had not thought that Waguli might be dead. She did not want to consider that as a possibility. But she knew that Wildcat was right about one thing. Waguli would fight. He would not easily submit to imprisonment. She walked deeper into the night woods, away from the low sounds of the refugee camp. Tears of anger and frustration blinded her eyes. Low-hanging branches caught at her hair. Finally, she stopped and leaned on the trunk of a tree. Her breath came in quick pants. Then she heard the voice in the night woods, the unmistakable sound of the whippoorwill. She held her breath for silence and waited and listened. It called again, softly, surely, calmly, and the voice was reassuring. Oconeechee's breaths became more regular. She wiped her eyes and searched the darkness. She was suddenly calm and very determined. The whippoorwill spoke again.

"Waguli?" she said.

And the voice, speaking for the fourth time, answered her.

"Yes, Waguli," she said, "I am coming. I'm coming for you. I'll find you."

She slept well that night, and in the morning she was up early and ready to leave, but she found all the people gathered together waiting for her. She stood and looked at them, from one face to another. They were solemn faces. She waited. Finally Wildcat spoke.

"You are leaving us now?" he asked.

"Yes," she said. "I told you."

"I know," said Wildcat. "I won't argue with you anymore,

but there are some things you should know before you leave. We talked about you last night—when you went off into the woods. Everyone here knows what you mean to do, and why you are doing it. This man is Grasshopper. He escaped from the white man's prison. Before you leave, listen to what he has to say."

The man introduced as Grasshopper stepped forward. He looked at the ground, and spoke softly.

"I was in the white man's prison," he said. "It was awful. It was filthy. People were sick, and some were dying in there. I couldn't stand it. I was in the same prison with your Waguli. He had fought with them, so they kept him tied. They had beaten him, too. Inside the prison, I untied his arms. Then he started to dig with his hands like a dog. Some people gathered around him so the soldiers couldn't see what he was doing. Then I helped him dig, and so did another man. We dug under the fence, and then Waguli crawled out. So did I, and so did the other man. Maybe more did. I don't know. The soldiers saw us and shot the other man, but Waguli ran, and I ran. I don't know where he went, but he escaped. I saw him crawl out, and I saw him run."

"Then he's free," said Oconeechee. "He's free, and he's out there somewhere. I must find him."

"There's more," said Wildcat. "Wait."

"There was another man," said Grasshopper. "His name was Tsali. He killed a soldier. He was up here in the mountains somewhere. There are others, you know. We are not the only ones who escaped. This Tsali, he was with the others. Anyway, the soldiers sent Wil Usdi to find him. They said that they would leave the rest of us alone if Tsali would go down to them and let them kill him. He did. I saw them shoot Tsali."

For a moment there was silence. Then Wildcat spoke again.

"You hear, Oconeechee?" he said. "If you stay here, you'll be safe. The soldiers are not going to come after us now."

"Then it is even more safe for me to go look for Waguli," said Oconeechee. "He escaped from the prison, and the soldiers won't come."

"But the Georgians," said Wildcat. "They are not soldiers. We still have to watch out for the Geogians. We're hiding up here in the mountains, and the soldiers have said they won't come looking for us. They didn't say it would be safe for us to come down."

"Do you know, Grasshopper," said Oconeechee, "where the other free Cherokees are hiding?"

"I know."

"Can you tell me how to find them?"

"I will take you to them."

Waguli lost track of the days. One day was like the last. Time had ceased to exist. He no longer lived in the normal world in which he had grown up. He was one of a group of ghosts moving west toward the Darkening Land, and time was standing still. People around him were dying. He had lost count of them, too, the dying ones. He remembered seeing old ones and little ones being buried beside the trail while the rest of the ghosts kept moving. The dying didn't seem to matter. They were all dead already. Some of them, like Waguli, kept moving for some unknown reason, but they were all dead. Some still wailed when one of their number fell over and ceased moving, but Waguli would not wail. He would not weep. He would not mourn for the dropping over of someone who had long been dead, as he was dead. He was a ghost. He wished that his body would go ahead and drop over so it could be covered with the strange earth and his spirit could be freed from its dreary existence. Beside the trail some were digging a shallow grave while a family gathered around and wailed and keened and wept. The body of an infant lay there among them, awaiting the hasty preparation of its final resting place. It would be unmarked. The family would not be back to visit it. Waguli did not look deliberately at this scene. He saw it peripherally as he trudged past. It entered his brain with the other images, the images which had become blurred into one, so many that he had lost count. One more ghost had decided to stop moving. Why would not his ghost make that same decision?

They had walked for two days through the wooded mountain trails, existing on supplies that the refugees had given them from their own meager store. Oconeechee had not wanted to take from them, but they had insisted. They had voted, Wildcat had said, and one could not go against the voice of the people. They had walked for two days when Grasshopper stopped in the trail and held up his hand for silence.

"We are here," he said. "Wait."

Grasshopper walked on ahead to a spot on the trail where he could be seen clearly from the caves up ahead.

"It is I," he called out, "Grasshopper. I have come back, and I've brought a friend."

"Come ahead, Grasshopper," came an answering voice. "Bring your friend."

Grasshopper looked back over his shoulder at Oconeechee waiting there in the trail.

"*Inena,*" he said. "Let's go."

Oconeechee hurried ahead to catch up with Grasshopper. Then the two of them walked together on up the trail. Soon she could see the people gathered at the mouths of the caves, waiting to greet Grasshopper and to meet the stranger he had brought into their midst. The people were curious about Oconeechee, and she was anxious to ask them her questions, but, true to tradition and in spite of the fact that they had little, the people first prepared a meal to share with their guests. It was a meager meal, and all ate sparingly, but all ate. At the back of the crowd Oconeechee saw two familiar faces. Badger and Mouse lurked in the shadows and stared at her with hard faces. The face of Mouse was marked with an ugly scar. So those two escaped somehow, she thought.

Quickly she dismissed them from her mind. They weren't worth consideration. They had tried their luck with her before, and she had taught them a lesson, a hard lesson. Yet, still, Cherokees had long memories. She suppressed a shudder and forced her mind back to present concerns. The meal was ended and it was the time for talk. Wildcat told her tale for her to the people in the cave. He told of her love for Waguli and their plans for marriage. He told of Waguli's capture and escape. He did not tell of Waguli's recapture, as he did not know about that. He told of Oconeechee's search for her missing lover. The people in the cave had heard of Waguli, they had heard of Oconeechee's father, and they were sympathetic. But they couldn't help. They had no new information. None of them had seen Waguli. They gave Oconeechee a place to sleep in the cave and promised her provisions for the trail in the morning. Early the next morning she accepted the provisions, thanked the people, and left the cave. She was alone, and she did not know where she was going. She knew only that she must find Waguli.

> She went up the Oconoluftee,
> Down the Little Tennessee,
> Up the Nantahela,
> Down the Hiwassee.

14

Whippoorwill, Whippoorwill,
Don't you know how she's searched all these hills?
She's searched every glen and glade
Not knowing why you went away.
Can't you feel she loves you still, Whippoorwill?

Finally they stopped. The soldiers gathered the long line of Cherokees together beside a big river, and there they camped. Waguli did not know the river. He did not know where he was. He was west of his home, on the trail west. He knew no more. Fires were built, and the soldiers distributed food: corn, a little bacon, corn meal, and coffee. The Cherokees cooked their own food. Waguli was untied so that he could cook and eat, but he did not cook. Another Cherokee man saw him sitting listlessly and approached him.

"You're not cooking," said the man.

Waguli handed the man his food ration.

"You take it," he said.

He thought that he had given his food away, but a short while later, he was surprised when the man brought it back to him prepared to eat. Waguli stared for a moment, then accepted the food.

"*Wado*," he said.

"My name is Pheasant," said the man. "My wife cooked your food."

"I am Waguli. I am alone."

Waguli thought for a fleeting moment of his lost Oconeechee. He hoped that she was safe somewhere. He was glad
that she had not become his wife. If she had, she would be
here on this trail to the Darkening Land with him, sharing
his misery.

"When they give us food to cook," said Pheasant, "my
wife will cook for you. You can eat with us."

Waguli nodded. He picked up the tin cup Pheasant had
brought him and slurped some of the hot coffee. He had developed a taste for the white man's black drink.

"Waguli," said Pheasant, "they keep you tied. Why?"

"I fought them," Waguli answered, "when they came to
my town, and when they put me in their prison, I tried to
escape."

"Will you try to escape again?"

Waguli thought long and hard. He recalled the beatings he
had received from the white soldiers. He reminded himself
that he had no idea where he was, and he thought that even
if he did manage to escape, he would find himself in strange
country surrounded by white people. He thought of Oconeechee. He did not know where she was or whether she was
safe or even alive. He did not want to share this kind of life
with her. It was not even a kind of life, he thought. It was a
kind of death. He remembered the old Cherokee prophet and
the things he had said, and then he looked at the white man's
tin cup in his hand which contained the white man's *kawhi*.

"No," he said. "It's useless. Already I tried, and I failed."

Waguli nearly chuckled at himself when he realized how
close he had just come to saying the name of the man who
had almost become his father-in-law. He sensed the chuckle,
a kind of wry reaction somewhere inside him, but it did not
surface.

"I'll talk to the soldier chief," said Pheasant. "I'll tell him
that you won't try to escape again. Maybe he won't tie you
up anymore."

"You talk the white man's language?" said Waguli.

"Yes. Enough."

Pheasant did talk to the soldier chief. Waguli saw them
talking together. And the soldiers did not bind Waguli again
that night. He did sense that they continued to watch him
closely. It was more comfortable sleeping without the ropes,

even though he could still hear the children weeping throughout the night.

In the morning there were six big, flat white man's boats in the water. Waguli had seen white men in boats like these on the rivers near his home. They were not like the Cherokee dugout canoes. They were larger, and they were made of planks. Big rectangular things which lay flat on the water, they carried large oars, and the boatmen also used long poles with which to push and guide them down the river. These boats, though, were larger than the ones Waguli had seen before, and he had never seen so many at once. Each boat had its own crew of white boatmen, a rugged-looking bunch. They reminded Waguli of the Georgians he had encountered. They wore no shoes or boots and had their trousers rolled up to just under their knees.

The soldiers began shouting, and the Cherokees were soon herded onto the six rocking platforms. Some of the children began to scream in fear. It was chaotic, but soon the boats were loaded, and they began to float downriver. They floated most of the day, then stopped and unloaded again. Another camp was made. More food was distributed. Again Pheasant's wife prepared Waguli's ration for him, and for the first time in days, he could not say how many days, Waguli looked around himself. He saw Pheasant and his wife and child, and knew he would remember them. As dull as his senses had become, he was not yet insensitive to simple kindness.

Again they slept on the bank of the river. Waguli expected the soldiers to begin yelling early the next morning and to load them once more onto the flat boats. He was surprised. He slept late. When he sat up and looked around, he saw that some were still sleeping. The soldiers stood around casually watching the Cherokees, and some of the people were bathing in the river. Except for the usual distribution of rations, nothing else happened that day.

The next day was almost the same. Waguli did talk a little to Pheasant, and he learned the names of Pheasant's wife— Sally, a white woman's name, and child—Yudi, a small boy. In the afternoon a wagon came. It was loaded with new clothes, white men's clothes. Pheasant told Waguli that the soldiers wanted to give the new clothes to the Cherokees and at the same time to get the names of all the Cherokees written down in their book. The Cherokees refused the clothes and would not give their names. The rest of the day passed much as had the previous one.

On the morning of the third day at the camp, more wagons came. These brought more captive Cherokees, unloaded them, and left again, and then two more of the flat boats came. The boatmen tied the eight boats into four pairs, and the soldiers began to shout. The Cherokees were all loaded onto the boats again, along with the clothes they had refused, and the journey down the river was resumed.

Waguli soon noticed that the river was getting wider and deeper and the current more swift. The children began to be frightened again. Some cried, and some screamed in fear. The current grew faster, and soon the boats raced wildly down the river. Women and children screamed, and men shouted. The people clutched one another for safety. Waguli began to feel ill. The soldiers and boatmen called out in futile attempts to maintain order on the recklessly careening boats. Waguli wondered if maybe this would be the end. Maybe, he thought, we will be rushed headlong riding on these flat white-man boats to the far western edge of the world and then tossed screaming into the Darkening Land.

But no. The rapids slowed, the waters calmed, and the boats stopped once more and unloaded. Another camp was made. More rations were passed out, and the people, as soon as they had calmed down enough from their frenzied ride through the rapids, cooked and ate. What now? The question repeated itself over and over again in Waguli's head as he drifted off into a troubled sleep. What now?

Waguli was awakened the following morning by a loud, raucous clamor. There were shouts and screams and crying, and there were shrill whistles and puffings and chuggings, and strident, reverberating splashes. He jumped up from the ground, expecting at any moment to be hurled precipitously into the Darkening Land, and then he saw the big boat. He had seen one once before from the safety of a high hilltop. Someone had told him that the white men burned wood on them, and used the burning wood to boil water and produce steam. Somehow the steam made the big boats go. He had never seen one at such close range, and it was a dreadful sight to behold. Great clouds of ugly black smoke billowed from its two tall horns. The big boat had three levels and a giant wheel at its rear. In spite of his numbness, Waguli felt twinges of fright deep in his bowels. A hand touched his shoulder, and he jumped. It was Pheasant.

"Have you ever seen one before?" asked Pheasant.

"Once," said Waguli.

"Have you ever ridden on one?"

"No."

"I did. Once. It's not so bad. Don't be afraid."

"I'm not afraid," said Waguli. "It doesn't matter anymore."

The supplies were loaded on the big boat, and four of the flat boats were lashed to it on each side.

"Ha. Waguli," said Pheasant.

"What?"

"White men name their boats. Do you know what this one's name is?"

"No."

"It's called the *George Guess*."

"How do you know that?" said Waguli.

"My woman reads the white man's writing. The name is there on its side. *George Guess*. Do you know who that is?"

"No."

"That's Sequoyah's white man name. George Guess. They're making Sequoyah take us to the west."

"Sequoyah?" said Waguli. "He's the Cherokee who gave us the writing, isn't he?"

"Yes," said Pheasant, "and now the white men are making Sequoyah take his own people to the west. The *George Guess*. Ha."

The loading of supplies and securing of the flat boats were accomplished, and the soldiers began to herd the Cherokees onto the boats like so many cattle. Waguli found himself on the third deck of the big boat, far above the water. He had lied to Pheasant. He was afraid. And when the great boat began to move, so did Waguli's insides. Pheasant had been right. The ride was not so frightening as the ride in the small boats through the rapids, but the motion was of a different kind, and it was that motion which made Waguli ill. He felt the need to vomit, yet he did not.

The chuffing and banging, the hissing and clanking, the

occasional loud, explosive blasts soon actually became a comfort to Waguli. For the first time since his incarceration in the stockade, he could not hear the crying of the children. He curled himself up on the boards of the upper deck and pressed himself against the railing at the edge. He closed his eyes. All the misery was shut out of his senses, and even though he had slept the night before and even though his stomach still churned from the motions of the big boat, he soon slept, and in his dreams he found himself back home at Old Town. It was the time of the busk, the green corn festival, the celebration of the beginning of a new year.

They had played the four sacred ball games, the men against the women, and the women had won them all, of course. Waguli had scored a point, though. He had reached out with his two ballsticks and caught the ball in flight. Then, still using the sticks, he had tossed the ball high into the air, and it had struck the carved wooden fish perched high atop the pole and it had made the fish spin. And they had danced the four dances, the stomp dances that lasted all night long. All this had taken place over a period of several weeks. Then came the four days together with the cleansing of the arbors and the stomp ground, the feasting and the fasting, the dancing of the special dances and the preparation of the sacred black drink, and the scratching. Waguli had been scratched, and he had bled, but he knew that the scratching and the bleeding would help to purify his body. Then came the time to drink the special drink. The men all drank, and then one at a time when they felt the urge, they went into the woods to vomit. When the ceremony was done, all the impurities gathered over the past year, all the pollution in the bodies of the people, would be gone. Everything and everybody would be clean and pure, and the balance and harmony of the world would be restored. Waguli drank, and he felt the uprising deep within. He went to the woods and fell to his knees, and he gagged, and there were spasms and convulsions in his guts that twisted his body grotesquely, and the tears ran down his face, but he could not vomit.

Suddenly he was awake. The boat had stopped, as had its noises. Waguli decided that he had been awakened by the silence. He could hear the crying again. The Cherokees were urged ashore to camp again beside the river. They built their small cooking fires, and the soldiers began to distribute food. The boatmen were gathering wood for their ravenous vessel. Waguli's stomach felt queasy. When his rations were handed to him, he put them on the ground. Pheasant came over to him and picked them up. He started to go back to his wife's cooking fire, but changed his mind. He squatted down beside Waguli.

"While you slept," he said, "a child died on the boat."

Waguli looked at Pheasant, but he didn't respond. His stomach churned. He wanted to vomit.

"And another was born," said Pheasant. "I'll take this to cook."

While the Cherokees were eating, the soldier chief began to talk to them again. Waguli paid no attention. He couldn't understand anyway. When the soldier stopped talking, Pheasant interpreted for Waguli.

"They are offering us the clothes again," he said. "Look. Some are going to take them."

Waguli shrugged.

"It doesn't matter, I guess," he said.

Soon Pheasant, with Sally and Yudi, was in line. Everyone was in line except Waguli. Pheasant looked back at him from his place in line.

"Waguli," he said. "Come on."

Waguli stood up then and took his place in line. After he had been handed the new clothes, he went to the river and stripped. He bathed himself, then put on the white man's clothing. Looking down, he couldn't recognize his own body. He put his hands to his head and rubbed them over what had been his slick-shaven head. He found it rough with stubble. He felt a convulsion in his guts, and he walked back to his spot near Pheasant's fire.

They rode the big boats again the next day, and then they camped again, and in the camp an old woman died. They buried her there, and some Cherokees sang a few strange songs over the grave. They sang in Cherokee, but Waguli didn't know the songs. Pheasant told him that they were Christian songs. White man songs, thought Waguli. By this time he had simply learned to live with the constant uneasiness in his stomach. They slept there by the river, by the fresh grave of the old woman.

The Sun was just peeking out from under the far eastern edge of the Sky Vault when Waguli was startled out of his sleep by the noise of the big boat. He sat up and saw that the boat was leaving. The other Cherokees were looking at the boat and at each other in confusion. The soldiers were standing around, some watching the Cherokees, some watching the boat. Then the soldier chief turned away from the boat to face the Cherokees, and he yelled some orders.

"We're going," said Pheasant.

Waguli stood up, and it was only then that he noticed the crowd of white people up on the hill watching them. They must want to watch us die, he thought. On up the hillside was a white man's town. They had spent the night just beside a white man's town, and he had not even known it. When the direction of their march became apparent, Waguli saw that they were going right into the town. They walked past the crowd of whites on the hillside, and Waguli could hear them talking. He didn't know what they were saying. He had no idea what their attitudes were. He wouldn't look at them. But as they walked into the town, he did look. He looked long enough to see that the streets were lined with the curious whites. He didn't look long enough to discover the expressions on their faces. The crowds of whites became a blur in his mind, another vague image of horror to add to those which already swirled inside his head. They walked through the town, and then they stopped. Up ahead, over the crying, Waguli could hear the surprised murmurs of the Cherokees at the head of the line. A child began to scream.

"They're loading us onto *ajila-dihyeg*," said Pheasant.

Waguli had heard about these fire-carriers that hauled white people long distances over iron roads, but he had never seen one. He had never before been sure he really believed in their existence. And now he was about to ride in one. He still couldn't see it for the hordes of people ahead of him. The crowd of Cherokees, urged on by the soldiers, began to inch forward. Soon Waguli found himself up close to *ujana,* the thing one gets into. Pheasant was climbing up, going inside, and Waguli was next. He hesitated. Pheasant looked back at him, just as a soldier standing nearby shouted.

"Come on, Waguli," said Pheasant. "It's all right. It's better than walking."

Waguli crawled into the great iron thing, and he found that it was like a house. It was a house on wheels, and it was tied to other houses, and somewhere up ahead there was a monstrous, smoke-belching engine that pulled all of them along the iron road. When all of the people were crowded onto the fire-carrier, Waguli heard a long and shrill whistle that nearly pierced his soul. Then there was a loud, inhuman coughing, followed by a great lurch forward. Mothers clutched their crying, terrified children. Even Pheasant's Sally was hugging little Yudi to her breast, little Yudi, who was always so brave, who did his best to imitate the manly behavior of his father. Yudi was coughing, but he did not cry. Waguli's stomach turned over, but nothing came up. He thought he heard a hideous scream from somewhere, but the noise of the fire-carrier and the crying of the children was too much. He couldn't be sure. Soon the house-pulling monster picked up speed, and it was racing across the face of the earth like a giant iron snake. Waguli closed his eyes. He tried to sleep. Something was crawling inside his stomach.

The fire-carrier filled with Cherokees raced on, but for Waguli time seemed to stand still. Now and then Pheasant tried to engage him in conversation, but Waguli's answers were always brief, terse, dissuading, and when Yudi's coughing grew worse, Pheasant turned all his attention to his wife and child. Waguli spent the day drifting in and out of sleep.

He had been sleeping again when he was jarred back to the waking world by the sound of a woman's scream close by, so close that it seemed the woman had screamed right into his ear. He came awake, but everything was black. He could see nothing in the darkness around him, but he could feel the forward, mad rush of the fire-carrier. Again he had the powerful sensation that he was being hurled into the Darkening Land. Perhaps they were already there. Slowly his eyes adjusted to the darkness, and he saw Pheasant and Sally beside him, wrapped in each other's arms, wailing in despair and grief, and he saw that they were holding between them the lifeless body of their young son. Yudi was dead. Waguli felt a great heaving surge from deep down inside him. He leaned forward and gagged and gasped for air, but he did not vomit.

They buried Yudi by the light of the following morning there in a strange land, not far from the iron road of the fire-carrier. They had kept racing forward all through the night, and shortly after the appearance of daylight the fire-carrier had slowed, then stopped. The soldiers had ordered the Cherokees off, and they had discovered that Yudi and another child had died during the night. And Waguli had overheard bits of a conversation that explained the hideous scream he had heard back at the beginning of the journey on the iron road. Somehow, it seemed, a man had fallen under the wheels of the fire-carrier. Waguli never heard anything more about the man, never heard his name, never heard where he had been buried or when or even if he had been buried. How much more, he wondered, must they endure?

15

They were taken a short distance away from the iron road to a place beside a river, and there they were told to make another camp. Rations were again distributed. Cooking fires were built. Waguli heard rumors that twenty-five Indians had escaped. For a moment he thought of trying to escape too, but no, he thought, he had already tried—twice—and then he had said that he would not try again. Had he not said so, he would surely still be bound. He wondered what those twenty-five would do. Where would they go? Did they know where they were? Waguli had no idea. Even if he could manage to escape, he would be hopelessly lost. And if he could somehow find his way back home, what would he find there? Still he wished success for the twenty-five, and still something in him wished that he was with them—wherever they were.

During the first night in this new camp, two more small children died. It seemed as if all the children were sick. And the old were all sick as well. And the sickness was spreading. Many Waguli's age were catching it. Soon, Waguli figured, all would be ill, and soon all would die, and then the soldiers would all go home. Their job would be done. His stomach churned with revulsion.

They stayed in the camp for six days, and then some of the flat white-man boats came. Again they were loaded on the clumsy boats and floated down the river. The trip only lasted a day, and they were unloaded to make yet another camp, and there three more children died. Another was born there, too. And someone said that 118 Cherokees escaped into the night. After two days, another of the big, noisy boats came. This one, according to Pheasant, was named *Smelter*. The name meant nothing to Waguli. They were loaded onto *Smelter* and their journey resumed.

The next day *Smelter* stopped so that the boatmen could gather more wood, and a Cherokee child died there. Its mother sent forth a piercing wail that was immediately followed by a streak of lightning that slashed across the horizon. Then there was a deafening clap of thunder. The soldiers hurried the Cherokees back onto *Smelter,* and the boatmen rushed to get their wood loaded. The mother's wailing continued, and the thunder and lightning increased. Strong winds brought sideways rain, and *Smelter* rocked violently on the thrashing river waters. Boatmen shouted desperate orders at each other. Some people found shelter, but most were crowded onto *Smelter*'s open decks, exposed to the fury of the pounding wind and the slashing rain. The storm raged the rest of that day and throughout the night, but the morning light brought calm, and *Smelter* started to move again. They rode *Smelter* for a few days. Waguli did not keep track of the number. He did know that three more children died.

Then they stopped at a white man's town. It was large and noisy and dirty. Pheasant told Waguli that the town was called Little Rock and that they were in the Arkansas country. He said that meant they were near the end of their journey. Waguli wondered if it meant they would all soon be dead. They stayed in Little Rock only a short time before being loaded onto another big boat. This one, Pheasant said, was named *Tecumseh*. Waguli had heard of Tecumseh. Another white man's boat with an Indian's name.

"What does it mean," Waguli said, "when the white men give a big boat a name?"

"I don't know," said Pheasant. "I guess it's some kind of

honor. They give their boat the name of some great man."

"If they think so highly of Indians," said Waguli, "that they name their boats after them, then why do they treat us so badly?"

Pheasant just shook his head, slowly and sadly.

"I don't know, Waguli," he said. "There is much about white men that I don't understand."

They rode *Tecumseh* for only one day. Then they unloaded and camped, and wagons were brought. There were twenty-three wagons, and the soldiers loaded them up with the sick. There was not enough room. Some sick were left. The soldiers said that more wagons would come the next day for the rest of the sick. Waguli, Pheasant, and Sally, along with the rest of the well, walked behind the wagons. Most of the soldiers went with them.

"There is no one left behind but the sick," said Pheasant. "It won't take many soldiers to watch them."

To watch them die, thought Waguli. It was hot and humid. The very air in this place, this Arkansas, was sick, Waguli thought. Flies, gnats, and mosquitoes tormented animals and humans, sick and well. Waguli noticed with a sense of horror that the children were no longer crying. They were too sick to cry. Waguli trudged along listlessly, he thought beside Pheasant and Sally. He wasn't sure. The dust from the wagons ahead was too thick. It was too hot even for the soldiers. About noon they called a halt. They would wait, they said, until early morning, before sunup. Three had died that day. Waguli assumed that they had been buried.

The next day the wagons with the rest of the sick, those they had left behind, caught up with them, and the rest of the walk became one blur in Waguli's mind. He didn't know how many days they walked. He knew only that each day three or four or five died along the way. One day, somewhere in the middle of the trip, one of the ones to die was Sally. Waguli stopped beside the road with Pheasant to put her in the ground. A soldier sat on his horse, rifle in hand, and watched them until they had finished. Then he rode along behind them while they followed the rest, who had gone on without them. They caught up with the others where they had stopped at noon to wait out the hottest part of the day. Pheasant did not talk for the rest of the trip. Finally they stopped, and someone said they had reached the end of the trail. It was over. Waguli listened to the talk. He heard that their trip from the stockades had taken six weeks. Along the way 70 had died, and 203 had escaped. The soldiers had left with 875 Cherokee captives, of whom 602 remained. Of those, about 200 were sick. Waguli looked around at the strange country and the rabble of wretched immigrants of whom he was a part. The contents of his stomach roiled and rumbled, and he felt a sudden and violent cramp which caused him to double over in pain and clutch at his middle. On his knees in the western dirt he twisted in agony. He choked. He gasped for breath. And all of his heaves were dry.

Early in June several parties, aggregating about five thousand persons, were brought down by the troops to the old agency, on Hiwassee, at the present Calhoun, Tennessee, and to Ross's landing (now Chattanooga), and Gunter's landing (now Guntersville, Alabama), lower down on the Tennessee, where they were put upon steamers and transported down the Tennessee and Ohio to the farther side of the Mississippi, when the journey was continued by land to Indian Territory. This removal, in the hottest part of the year, was attended with so great sickness and mortality that, by resolution of the Cherokee national council, Ross and the other chiefs submitted to General Scott a proposition that the Cherokee be allowed to remove themselves in the fall, after the sickly season had ended. This was granted on condition that all should have started by the 20th of October, excepting the sick and aged who might not be able to move so rapidly. Accordingly, officers were appointed by the Cherokee council to take charge of the emigration; the Indians being organized into detachments averaging one thousand each, with two leaders in charge of each detachment, and a sufficient number of wagons and horses for the purpose. In this way the remainder, enrolled at about 13,000 (including negro slaves), started on the long march overland late in the fall.

Those who thus emigrated under the management of their own officers assembled at Rattlesnake springs, about two miles south of Hiwassee river, near the present Charleston, Tennessee, where a final council was held, in which it was decided to continue their old constitution and laws in their new home. Then, in October, 1838, the long procession of exiles was set in motion.

A very few went by the river route; the rest, nearly all of the 13,000, went overland. Crossing to the north side of the Hiwassee at a ferry above Gunstocker creek, they proceeded down along the river, the sick, the old people, and the smaller children, with the blankets, cooking pots, and other belongings in wagons, the rest on foot or on horses. The number of wagons was 645.

It was like the march of an army, regiment after regiment, the wagons in the center, the officers along the line and the horsemen on the flanks and at the rear. Tennessee river was crossed at Tuckers ferry, a short distance above Jollys island, at the mouth of Hiwassee. Thence the route lay south of Pikeville, through McMinnville and on to Nashville, where the Cumberland was crossed. Then they went on to Hopkinsville, Kentucky, where the noted chief White-path, in charge of a detachment, sickened and died. His people buried him by the roadside, with a box over the grave and poles with streamers around it, that the others coming on behind might note the spot and remember him. Somewhere also along that march of death—for the exiles died by tens and twenties every day of the journey—the devoted wife of John Ross sank down, leaving him to go on with the bitter pain of bereavement added to heartbreak at the ruin of his nation. The Ohio was crossed at a ferry near the mouth of the Cumberland, and the army passed on through southern Illinois until the great Mississippi was reached opposite Cape Giradeau, Missouri. It was now the middle of winter, with the river running full of ice, so that several detachments were obliged to wait some time on the eastern bank for the channel to become clear. In talking with old men and women at Tahlequah the author found that the lapse of over half a century had not sufficed to wipe out the memory of the miseries of that halt beside the frozen river, with hundreds of sick and dying penned up in wagons or stretched upon the ground, with only a blanket overhead to keep out the January blast. The crossing was made at last in two divisions, at Cape Girardeau and at Green's ferry, a short distance below, whence the march was on through Missouri to Indian Territory, the later detachments making a northerly circuit by Springfield, because those who had gone before had killed off all the game along the direct route. At last their destination was reached. They had started in October, 1838, and it was now March, 1839, the journey having occupied nearly six months of the hardest part of the year.

It is difficult to arrive at any accurate statement of the number of Cherokee who died as the result of the Removal. According to the official figures those who removed under the direction of Ross lost over 1,600 on the journey. The proportionate mortality among those previously removed under military supervision was probably greater, as it was their suffering that led to the proposition of the Cherokee national officers to take charge of the emigration. Hundreds died in the stockades and the waiting camps, chiefly by reason of the rations furnished, which were of flour and other provisions to which they were unaccustomed and which they did not know how to prepare properly. Hundreds of others died soon after their arrival in Indian territory, from sickness and exposure on the journey. Altogether it is asserted, probably with reason, that over 4,000 Cherokee died as the direct result of the removal.

From James Mooney,
Historical Sketch of the Cherokee, 1900.

The removal of the Cherokees having at last been accomplished, the next important object of the Government was to insure their internal tranquility, with a view to the increase and encouragement of those habits of industry, thrift, and respect for lawfully constituted authority which had made so much progress among them in their eastern home. But this was an undertaking of much difficulty. The instrumentalities used by the Government in securing the conclusion and approval of not only the treaty of 1835 but also those of 1817 and 1819 had caused much division and bitterness in their ranks, which had on many occasions in the past cropped out in acts of injustice and even violence.

Upon the coming together of the body of the nation in their new country west of the Mississippi, they found themselves torn and distracted by party dissensions and bitterness almost beyond hope of reconciliation. The parties were respectively denominated:

1. The "Old Settler" party, composed of those Cherokees who had prior to the treaty of 1835 voluntarily removed west of the Mississippi, and who were living under a regularly established form of government of their own.

2. The "Treaty" or "Ridge" party, being that portion of the nation led by John Ridge, and who encouraged and approved the negotiation of the treaty of 1835.

3. The "Government" or "Ross" party, comprising numeri-

cally a large majority of the nation, who followed in the lead of John Ross, for many years the principal chief of the nation, and who had been consistently and bitterly hostile to the treaty of 1835 and to any surrender of their territorial rights east of the Mississippi.

Upon the arrival of the emigrants in their new homes, the Ross party insisted upon the adoption of a new system of government and a code of laws for the whole nation. To this the Old Settler party objected, and were supported by the Ridge party, claiming that the government and laws already adopted and in force among the Old Settlers should continue to be binding until the general election should take place in the following October, when the newly elected legislature could enact such changes as wisdom and good policy should dictate. A general council of the whole nation was, however, called to meet at the new council-house at Takuttokah, having in view a unification of interests and the pacification of all animosities. The council lasted from the 10th to the 22nd of June, but resulted in no agreement. Some six thousand Cherokees were present. A second council was called by John Ross for a similar purpose, to meet at the Illinois camp-ground on the 1st of July, 1839.

From Charles C. Royce,
The Cherokee Nation of Indians, 1887.

16

Well, I had heard about the Trail of Tears, of course. I knew that there were Cherokees in Oklahoma, and I knew that they had got there because the government made them move. There was even a little box down on the bottom of one page of my history book at school, and it had a color picture of Indians on horses and in wagons and some of them on foot with some soldiers riding along beside them, and there was a little story there. It was called "The Trail of Tears," and it said that the Trail of Tears was a dark page in the history of the United States because the govern- ment had made all the Cherokees move out west and some of them had died along the way. I recall that I asked Mr. Grimes, that was my history teacher, how come if they moved all of the Cherokees out west, how come there was still some of us here, and I told him that my Grandpa and Grandma lived out on the Cherokee Reservation not too far away from here with a lot of other Cherokees. He just said that he didn't know. Some of us must have come back later, he said. So anyhow I knew about the Trail of Tears, but I guess that it had never really soaked in on me just what it really meant. And listening to Grandpa tell it to me the way he done, with all the details about people having to go all that way in wagons and on

steamboats and flatboats and a little ways on a train and how some
of them walked the whole way and how so many of them got sick
and died, so many little kids and babies too, well, I guess that it was
like I had never heard about it before at all.

I just sat there real quiet when Grandpa had finished telling it. I
felt sick, kind of. Really, I guess, I was stunned. I didn't know
what to say, and I could feel tears building up, but I was fighting
real hard to hold them back. I didn't want to cry. Grandpa could tell
though. He could always tell. He got up and walked over to me,
and he put his big hand right on top of my head, and he kind of
ruffled my hair all up. Then he pulled me sideways into his body
and hugged me to him, and I could smell all those Grandpa smells
that were so warm and friendly and comfortable.

"It all happened a long time ago, chooj," he said.

Oconeechee knew that she was being followed, and she was
pretty sure she knew who it was. They had said the soldiers
weren't looking for any more Cherokees in the hills, so it
wasn't likely to be soldiers. It could be Georgians, she supposed, but she didn't really think so. She hadn't seen any
Georgians around so far up in the hills, and she couldn't think
of any real reason for them to be up there. Certainly if any
had run across her, it would have been by accident. They
didn't know where the caves were in which the people were
hiding, and she hadn't gotten very far away from the caves
yet. No. She didn't think it was soldiers or Georgians. The
only other possibility, the only explanation that made any
sense to her, was that Mouse and Badger were on her trail
with plans to get even with her for what she had done to
them at their last encounter, with plans to finish what they
had intended to do then. She was intent on finding Waguli,
but she knew that she would have to be careful, would have
to watch her back trail, make sure that they did not catch up
with her or catch her off guard.

She had been walking all day, headed back for Old Town.
Perhaps Waguli would go back there. It was a place to start
at least. She had to start somewhere. Waguli had escaped
from the stockade, and he was not with the others who were
hiding out in the hills. He had to be someplace. She would
start at Old Town. The people in the cave had given her some
supplies for the trail, some *guhwisda,* parched cornmeal, some

dried bear meat, and some *kanutche,* pounded hickory nuts rolled into balls. Grasshopper had given her a knife, and an old man had given her a blowgun and six darts. She felt well prepared for a long journey.

The sun was low on the western underside of the Sky Vault, and soon she would crawl under the edge and vanish for the night. Old Town, or what was left of it, was not far, Oconeechee knew, and she also knew that she had a problem to resolve. If Badger and Mouse were on her trail, as she was almost certain they were, any pause she might make would give them the chance to catch up with her. She could not just keep running from them. That would defeat her purpose. She was searching for Waguli, and she had no intention of allowing her pursuers to interfere with her sacred intent. Sacred. Yes. There was no other word to describe her love of Waguli, the Whippoorwill. She knew that if she never found him, there would be no other man in her life, no matter how long she should live. But it was unthinkable to her that she should not find him. She must find him. She would find him. And Badger and Mouse would not stop her, would not interfere. She was determined that they would not.

In spite of the fact that the mountain trail could be treacherous after dark, Oconeechee decided to continue traveling for a few hours. Badger and Mouse would surely make camp for the night. They would think they could easily catch a girl, so they would not worry about the loss of time resulting from a good night's sleep. She would get a couple of hours more between her and them. That would give her some needed time to think and plan and prepare, time to decide just how to deal with Badger and Mouse. She walked on into the night. Her pace was slowed, but she didn't mind. She was sure that those who followed her had already stopped to sleep. So she walked on. She had been over the trail only once before, but she remembered that it would narrow and that on one side, her left in the direction she was traveling, would be a dangerous precipice. The night was clear and the moon was full, yet the trail was almost black because of the heavy canopy of overhead leaves. She felt her way slowly and cautiously along the narrow, winding path.

One time she slipped, and she heard the rocks dislodged by her misstep bounding their way down the side of the abyss. She pressed herself into the rock wall on her right and looked over her shoulder, but she could not distinguish between the path on which she stood and the space beyond. Suddenly she was afraid. Her over-confidence, her arrogance, had gotten her into this trouble. She couldn't move, couldn't go forward or backward. She wondered if she could cling to the rock all night or if she would be overcome by sleep and fall into the black nothing behind her. She thought about sitting down, or kneeling, or getting down onto her hands and knees to crawl along the way, but she couldn't make herself move. Then from out of the blackness ahead came the clean, clear call of the whippoorwill. It called four times, it seemed to Oconeechee directly to her, and then it ceased. Her determination returned, and with it, her courage. She moved ahead, and she did not falter.

Oconeechee was up before the sunlight. She had made her way in the darkness of the night before past the dangerously narrow part of the trail, and when she found herself on safer ground, she had stopped to sleep. After a few hours she felt rested and refreshed, but she was hungry. She took part of the dried bear meat out of her pouch. She would much have preferred it pounded, like cornmeal, and then boiled in water, but she was still in a hurry. She tore a piece off between her teeth and chewed it as she slung the pouch and the blowgun over her shoulder. Then she started walking again. It was only a short way to Old Town from where she had stopped, and by the time the sun was peeking out from the east, she could hear the rushing waters of the stream that ran by the townsite. Soon after, the ruins of Old Town came into her sight.

At the opposite end of the town from which Oconeechee approached, two white men entered the ruins. Each carried an ancient Kentucky long rifle and had two Kentucky flintlock pistols tucked in the waistband of his trousers and a long knife in his belt. They held their rifles at the ready, and their eyes shifted nervously from side to side. The tallest and lankiest of the two men walked to a pile of ashes and burnt wood that had been a house and kicked at the rubble.

"Damn it, John," he said. "Everywhere we go, someone's beat us to it."

By then the one called John was shoving at another pile
with the butt of his long rifle.

"Looky here, Luke," he said. "They didn't even take the
good stuff. They just burned it all. There was good stuff in
here. Look."

Luke walked over to see what good stuff John was looking
at. He knelt and picked up a pistol from the ash pile.

"We might be able to fix this," he said. "It's burnt pretty
bad, but we might fix it."

He dropped it in a pocket of his loose-fitting vest.

"That's just meanspirited," said John. "To burn up good
stuff like that, that's just mean."

Luke kept sifting through the rubble until he found the
steel blade of a knife. Its wooden handgrips had been burned
away.

"Hey," he said. "This is good. Get busy looking through
all this stuff. There's good salvage here. Get to looking."

Their initial disappointment soon turned to exultation, for
in a short while out of the ash heaps of Old Town, Luke and
John had created a pile of small treasure: silver gorgets and
bracelets, the metal parts of pistols, rifles, knives, swords,
and axes, iron pots and pans, even a few gold trinkets. Their
clothes, their hands, even their faces were black from scav-
enging through the ashes.

"Luke," said John, "we're rich. Ain't we? We rich, Luke?"

"Well," said Luke, "I don't know if we'll get rich off this
stuff, but it'll sure bring us a nice little pile of money. It'll at
least last us awhile."

"Hot damn. Whiskey and women," said John.

"Time enough for all that later, boy. We only about halfway through this mess. Keep a digging."

"Hell, I can talk, can't I? Can't I talk while I dig?" He
pulled a blackened but otherwise undamaged pair of spectacles from the black residue. "Hey, Luke. Looky here. You
ever see a damn injun wearing eyeglasses?"

"Toss them in the pile," said Luke.

John pitched the spectacles over with the rest of the salvage. Then a sudden thought caused him to drop to both
knees and lean forward eagerly toward his accomplice.

"Hey, John. If this here was a town where people lived,
they must be a burying ground nearby. Ain't that right? I

heard that injuns bury valuable stuff with their dead. That right?"

"I've already thought that out," said John. "When we finish here, we'll find the graves, and we'll dig them up and see what can we get us. Now keep a looking."

Up the mountain path not far from the other end of town, Oconeechee stood. She had been marching steadily toward the one-time home of her lost love when she saw the two white men, and she had stopped. Had the scavengers looked up from their dirty work, they would easily have seen her standing there. Realizing at last that she was clearly visible, that she was vulnerable there, she moved off the path and into the shelter of thick bramble. Behind her, she wasn't sure just how far, were Badger and Mouse, and now, before her, these white men. What should she do? She could alter her course and find her own new path through the woods, but what would that accomplish? Old Town was her immediate goal. And even if she cut through the woods, there was no guarantee that Badger and Mouse, or even the white men, for that matter, would not discover her new trail and pursue her there. She had to think of something. She would not run. That would mean that she would no longer be the searcher; she would be a fugitive, a fugitive from worthless whites and worthless Cherokees, less than worthless. No. She would not let these men turn her from her purpose.

She wondered how long it would be before Badger and Mouse caught up with her. Then, realizing that she must do more than wonder, she began to backtrack, slipping along the edge of the trail until she was well out of range of vision of the two white men in the village. Only then did she move back out onto the trail. For awhile she hurried along her way, but soon caution made her slow down to watch and listen for any evidence of the approach of Badger and Mouse. At last she achieved a high spot on the trail, a place she had not taken note of the night before. She must have passed it in the darkness. From a safe vantage point, she could see well back down the mountain path, almost, it seemed, to that place where the path narrowed so dangerously. She settled down to wait and watch. She still had no specific plan.

She was in danger of falling asleep when she finally saw

them. Badger and Mouse appeared on the trail having just made their way through the narrow, winding hazard beyond. She was awake again and alert. She watched them for a few moments as they drew nearer, and she felt a new sense of strength, a new advantage, a new power. True, they were stalking her, but she saw them. She knew where they were. They had not yet seen her, nor did they know about the two scavengers ahead. She let them get a little closer, then she headed back toward Old Town. She got back to the spot where she had first seen the white men. They were closer to that end of the village by then. They were closer, but it would still be a long shot. She wondered if she could make it. She would try. Even if she should miss, she reasoned, it wouldn't matter too much. The main thing was to get their attention. She unhooked the strap from the top end of the blowgun which was slung across her back and took the blow-gun in hand. She removed one of the sharp darts from the thong that held it to the cane pole. She fitted the dart into one end of the gun and raised the gun to her lips. She was on higher ground than were the white men, so an aim more or less straight forward would give her shot a high trajectory. She took a deep breath. It was not enough. She let it out slowly and drew in another. This time she filled her lungs. She drew in breath until she could draw no more. She pressed her lips tightly to the blowgun and pulled in even more air through her nostrils, filling her mouth as well as her lungs. Her cheeks puffed out, stretching the skin almost painfully. Then she blew, a powerful puff of wind that emptied cheeks and lungs in an instant into the small hollow of the long tube. The dart flew forward for a distance, then began to arc in descent.

"Ow!"

John, who was bending over an ash heap, slapped at a sharp pain between his shoulder blades. Luke looked up from his work to see what was the matter, and saw the dart sticking into John's back. He looked from John to the trail that led out of Old Town, and his eyes followed the trail up to Oconeechee, standing defiantly in plain view.

"By God," he said. "Just look up there."

John by then had managed to twist his arm around awkwardly until he could pull the offending missile from the middle of his back. He held it in his hand and looked at it, angry and puzzled. Then he looked at Luke. He followed Luke's gaze up the trail, and his eyes widened.

"A squaw," he said. "She shot me. Did she shoot me with this thing?"

"I reckon she did," said Luke.

John stood up and raised his long rifle to his shoulder. He cocked it, but just as he pulled the trigger, Luke knocked the butt of his own rifle against it, causing the shot to go wild.

"Hey," shouted John.

"You damn fool," said Luke. "Is that the best thing you can think of to do with a good-looking squaw? Come on. Let's get her."

Luke started up the trail toward Oconeechee.

"Oh," said John. "Oh, yeah. I get your meaning. Okay."

He began to follow Luke, dropping his rifle as he moved. Oconeechee stood arrogantly in the trail for a moment and watched the two white men move in her direction. Then she turned and ran.

"Come on," said Luke, and he started to run after her. John broke into a run a short distance behind his companion.

Oconeechee knew that her judgment of time and distance was crucial. She ran on around a curve, then dashed into the brambles off the side of the trail. Crouching beside the trunk of a tall oak tree, she felt her heart pounding in her breast. She took out another dart and reloaded the blowgun, just in case she should need it. She could hear the pounding feet of the two white men as they raced up the trail after her. She had seen the one man aim his rifle and the other deliberately spoil his aim, and she knew what they wanted. They were the same as Badger and Mouse, so different in so many ways, yet the same. The pounding came nearer, and soon she could hear as well their puffing breaths and the whining, complaining voice of one man. Then they rushed past her. the first part of her plan had worked. She waited, but she didn't have to wait long.

The two Cherokees who soon came trotting around the bend were as startled as were the two running white men when the four came suddenly and unexpectedly face to face. John tried to stop running so abruptly that his feet skidded out from under him, and he fell hard on his backside with a loud curse. Luke came to a more graceful halt and immediately raised his long rifle to his shoulder. Badger shouted and made a dive for the cover of the brush at the side of the trail, so the lead ball which was aimed at him sped harmlessly by. Mouse raised his steel ax over his head, shouted, and ran straight at Luke, who dropped his useless empty rifle and reached for one of the two pistols at his belt. Mouse's ax split Luke's breastbone just as Luke pulled the trigger, sending a ball into Mouse's stomach. Luke went over backwards with the force of the blow and lay lifeless on his back, the ax still embedded in his chest, the rich red blood oozing forth. Mouse, a stupid expression on his face, sank slowly to his knees, his hands clutching at the hole in his belly.

John had scrambled to his knees, and he stared for a horrified instant at his dead partner before his wits returned to him. He pulled a pistol from his waistband and fired it almost point-blank into the side of the head of the wounded Mouse. Mouse's head jerked. His whole body relaxed and crumpled down in a heap at the feet of the body of his own victim. Then Badger came running out of his hiding place, an old-fashioned stone-headed war club in his hand. John tossed aside his empty pistol and grabbed for the second one, but it was hung up on the waistband of his trousers. Badger was almost on top of him. He screamed and dodged the blow that Badger had aimed at his head, then quickly got up onto his feet. He wanted his pistol, but it took all of his concentration to keep away from the club that Badger was swinging at him. Badger took another swipe and missed, and John pulled the pistol free. He cocked it and was starting to bring it up to position for firing, when Badger surprised him with a backhand swing of the club, smashing the stone head into the softness of John's right temple. John was dead on his feet, but the impact of the blow caused a reflex action throughout his body. His hand tightened on the pistol, and his finger jerked the trigger. The ball shattered Badger's left kneecap.

Oconeechee peered cautiously out from her place of security in the brambles. She saw the two dead white men and the dead Mouse lying there in the trail and, sitting in the midst of the bodies, his knee crushed and bloody, his leg turned out at a grotesque and unnatural angle, Badger. She stepped out into the path, and Badger saw her. He looked up at her with pleading eyes.

"I need help," he said.

"You won't get it from me."

Satisfied that she was safe from pursuit by any of them, Oconeechee turned to walk away.

"Wait," said Badger. "Help me. If you leave me here like this, I'll die."

Oconeechee turned fiercely on the pathetic Badger.

"Why were you following me?" she said. "What were your plans for me? You think I don't know?"

"Help me, Oconeechee."

She stood there for a moment, exasperated yet undecided. She should ignore him. Then she pulled the strap of the pouch over her head and tossed it down at Badger's side.

"There's food," she said.

She put the blowgun and remaining darts where he could reach it with only a slight effort. Then she looked around. There were several weapons at his disposal—his own club, Mouse's ax, the white men's guns and knives. Her eyes lit on the long rifle lying near the tall white man's body. She picked it up, putting the muzzle to the ground and the butt under her arm.

"Look," she said. It was like a crutch. "This is the best I will do for you, and it's more than you deserve."

She placed the rifle by his side, turned, and walked away.

"Oconeechee," Badger shouted at her back. "Don't leave me. I'm a Cherokee. You're a Cherokee. Come back."

But she did not go back. She did not even look back. She walked down the trail that would take her into the ashen ruins of Old Town.

17

That day that Grandpa had to go to town on some kind of business, I don't remember just what it was, probably because I didn't even really understand it at the time, but anyway they said that I'd be bored if I went with him, so that day I stayed home with Grandma. Well, she had all kinds of stuff in the house laid out on the table. She had a big sack of beans, and she had a whole bunch of shelled corn in a pan, and she had got both of them right out of her own garden just out behind the house. She had some long blades of grass laid out there on the table and some leaves, and she had the shucks or blades off of the ears of corn there, too. And she had several pots and pans and different kinds of baskets all out and lined up ready to use, and it was a warm day, but she had a little fire going in the fireplace.

"What are you going to do, Grandma?" I said.

"Make some bean bread, Sonny," she said. "You can help me."

"Okay."

"First let me put the beans on the fire," she said, and she put the beans in a big black pot with some water and set the pot in the fireplace. "There. Now let's go out to the creek. Here, you take this."

She handed me a big bucket, and I followed her outside and ran ahead of her to the creek. Pretty soon she came on down.

"Over here," she said.

I ran over to her, and she had a fireplace made out of big rocks right out there by the creek. She had brought along another black pot with a lid and a basket. She set them down and built her a fire there in those rocks. When it got to going pretty good, she had me go to the creek with my bucket and fill it up with water and bring it back to her, and I did, too, without spilling too much, even though it was heavy. She put her black pot right on the fire, and then she took my bucket and poured the water into the pot.

"There," she said. "We have to get some more stuff from the house now."

We went back to the house, and Grandma checked the beans and said they were just fine, and then she picked up the pan of corn and handed it to me.

"You carry this for me," she said.

"Okay."

Then she went over to the fireplace and picked up a box that was full of ashes from the fire, and she got one of the baskets, and we went back outside and back down to the creek. We put down all that stuff, and I got a good look at her basket. She was just about to pour some ashes into it.

"Grandma," I said, "your basket's got holes in it."

She kind of chuckled and just went ahead and poured the ashes right in there.

"This is my sieve basket, Sonny," she said. "I'm going to sift these ashes into the water to make good, strong lye water."

She bent over the pot and kind of shook the basket back and forth, and ashes fell through the holes and went down into the bucket of water. Then pretty soon she got the corn I had carried down for her, and she poured that in there, too. Then she got a stick and stirred it. She'd stir it for awhile, and then she'd stop and just watch and wait, and then she'd stir again. Up in a tree pretty close by, a gray squirrel chattered. He was looking right at us, and he sounded like he was fussing at us for being there.

"Oh, hush, saloli," said Grandma. "We live here, too."

She stirred the pot some more, and I got bored and started looking around and wandering, not too far away, just down to the edge of the water and back and along the creek bank a ways. Like that. Across the creek a whole flock of cardinals came down and settled in a big bush.

"Look, Grandma," I said.

"Dojuwha," she said.

"What?"

"Dojuwha. *That's what we call him in Cherokee. The redbird.* Dojuwha."

"*Some of them are brown,*" I said. "*Well, they're kind of red—a little.*"

"*Those are the mamas,*" said Grandma.

"Dojuwha," I said. "Redbird."

Grandma was stirring the pot again, and she bent over and fished out one kernel of corn on her stirring stick. Then she got it between a finger and her thumb.

"What are you doing now?" I said.

"I have to test it," she said, "to see if it's ready. Yes. The skin is ready to slip."

"Let me see," I said, and she showed me the slippery skin on that corn kernel.

"Now," she said, "we got to wash it off."

She took the handle of the black pot in her hand, using her thick apron as a potholder, and poured the corn into the sieve basket. Then she took the basket to the creek and put it down into the water to wash the corn off and to get rid of the skins. She put a pot full of clean, fresh creek water on the fire, and then we gathered up all of the rest of the stuff and went back to the house, except Grandma didn't go inside. She took the corn around to the side of the house where her wooden beater was. Kanona, I had heard her call it before. It was really a tree stump was what it was, and it was about up to Grandma's knees. On top it had been kind of hollowed out, or rather scooped out, so it was like a bowl. Grandma put all the corn in there, and she picked up a long pole that was leaning against the side of the house there by the beater. It had one real big end, and she held it in both hands so that the big end was up on top. Then she started to pound the corn with the little end. Well, she pounded and pounded, and finally she bent over and felt of that corn with her fingers, but I guess that by then it wasn't just corn any more. It was cornmeal. That's what Grandma said. That's what she had done was to make cornmeal.

"Grandma," I said, "Mom buys cornmeal in a bag at the grocery store. How come you go to all this trouble to make it?"

"It tastes better, Sonny," she said. "You just ask your momma. Now run inside and get that big white pan for me."

I found the pan, a big kind of flat one with white enamel with a couple of chips out of the enamel here and there, and I took it to her. She scooped all the meal out into the pan, and we went in the house.

Grandma put the pan on the table. She went over to the fireplace and got the big pot of beans, and she took it to the table and poured the whole thing in on top of the cornmeal and mixed it all up with a big wooden spoon. Finally she just reached right down in there and pulled out a handful of that dough she had made, and she patted it around awhile until she had a ball.

"You want to make some?" she asked me.

"Sure," I said, and I grabbed a handful just the way she had done and made me a ball.

"Now we kind of flatten it out," said Grandma, "like this. We call them broadswords when we make them flat like this."

Well, I copied everything she did, and when we had our broadswords all flat, she picked up a corn shuck, a blade, she called it, and she gave it to me and got another one for herself. We wrapped up our broadswords in those blades, and then we tied them together with long pieces of grass, the ones that she had laid out there on the table, and I had wondered what in the world they were for. After we had wrapped up several broadswords in blades, we made some more and wrapped them in oak leaves. Finally we had used up all the dough, and we had a big basket full of wrapped-up broadswords. Grandma picked it up, and I followed her back outside and on down to the creek, where the pot of water she had left on the fire was just boiling away. Grandma put all the wrapped-up broadswords into the boiling water and put the lid on the pot.

"Now we wait awhile," she said.

Well, after awhile we just sat right down there on the ground by that fire beside the creek, and we ate some of those broadswords, hot and fresh, and I tell you, that was the best bean bread I ever ate.

"Will Grandpa be home before they get cold?" I asked her.

"He ought to be coming along pretty soon now," she said. "We should get some coffee ready. He likes coffee with his bread."

Pretty soon we had practically moved to the creek. Grandma made coffee over that same fire, and we had moved the two metal chairs, the green one and the red one from behind the house, down there. And we even had cups down there, too, so everything was ready when Grandpa came driving back in his old brown station wagon with wood on its sides. He didn't even drive on up to the house where he usually parked it. He stopped right there by the creek when he saw us, and he got out and came over where we were and sat down in his red chair. Grandma poured him a cup of coffee, and I handed him a broadsword.

"Oh," he said, "you been busy while I was gone."

Now I don't know who ate the most, but we ate up all that bread right there that evening, and I even drank hot coffee, too. Momma never gave me coffee to drink at home, but sometimes with Grandpa I drank it. The sun was going down, and Grandma and Grandpa were sitting in the chairs. I was stretched out on the ground just feeling full and happy. Then I heard a funny kind of sound from out in the woods. I knew what an owl sounds like. At least I thought I did, and it didn't sound like an owl to me. Not really. I sat up and listened, and I heard it again.

"What was that?" I said.

"Waguli," said Grandpa.

"Whippoorwill?"

"That's right, chooj."

"Grandpa," I said, "what happened to Whippoorwill after the Trail of Tears was over?"

"Oh, well," he said, "first of all, it wasn't over just after he got out there. The army took three different bunches, I think. I think it was three. Waguli was just in one of those bunches, but there was two more. They had to go, too."

"Were those other two as bad as the one Waguli was on?"

"They were all bad, chooj. Lots of people died. It was a hot summer, and lots of people were sick. And then it was a tough trip. Not like it would be today in a car on paved roads. They were all bad."

"They called it ahuhsidasdi," said Grandma, "or digejiluhstanuh."

"What's that mean?" I asked.

"Ahuhsidasdi," she said, "to move things around. Digejiluhstanuh. That means kind of like, the way they were forced, or herded, down there, away from where they wanted to be. It means something like that. It's hard to put it in English."

"But there was more yet," said Grandpa. "The first three trips were so bad, so many people died, that old John Ross, you know, the Chief, Cooweescoowee, he went to the army, and he said let us move ourselves. We can do a better job of it, he said. At least we can't do no worse than you guys are doing. And he finally talked them into it, but it was way into October before he was able to get it started. When the rest of the Cherokees, those that were captured, started to move themselves, it was cold winter, and the Cherokees took about twelve different groups, waves, they called them."

"Thirteen," said Grandma.

"Thirteen waves," said Grandpa. "And lots of people died then, *too. The first bunch that the army took went in June, I guess, of eighteen-and-thirty-eight, and the last bunch led by Cherokees got out west in March of 'thirty-nine. Almost nine months."*

"The Trail of Tears lasted for nine months?" I said.

"Yeah, chooj. *All told. About that. And then the real trouble started. Out west at least."*

"What trouble?" I said.

"You recall those Cherokees I told you about who signed the treaty? Major Ridge and John Ridge and Elias Boudinot were their names, and Stand Watie, and there were some others, but those were their leaders. Remember?"

"Yeah."

"Those were the main ones. They signed that treaty, and then they just took themselves on out west. Well, after the Trail of Tears, after the whole nine months, those people who suffered and who watched so many of their friends and their relatives die along the way, they just had to try to get even somehow. And I guess they knew that they couldn't go attack Washington, D.C., or Georgia or Alabama. They couldn't start a war with the United States or against the whites, not one that they could win, so they went after the treaty signers. They called them traitors, and they blamed them for all the suffering. So then on top of everything else that had happened, there was Cherokees killing Cherokees out there in the west."

Murder of Boudinot and the Ridges.—Immediately following the adjournment of the Takuttokah council three of the leaders of the Treaty party, John Ridge, Major Ridge his father, and Elias Boudinot were murdered in the most brutal and atrocious manner. The excitement throughout the nation became intense. Boudinot was murdered within 300 yards of his house, and only 2 miles distant from the residence of John Ross. The friends of the murdered men were persuaded that the crimes had been committed at the instigation of Ross, as it was well known that the murderers were among his followers. Ross's friends, however, at once rallied to his protection and a volunteer guard of six hundred patrolled the country in the vicinity of his residence.

From Charles C. Royce,
The Cherokee Nation of Indians, 1887.

On their arrival in Indian Territory the emigrants at once set about building houses and planting crops, the government having agreed under the treaty to furnish them with rations for one year after arrival. They were welcomed by their kindred, the "Arkansas Cherokee"—hereafter to be known for distinction as the "Old Settlers"—who held the country under previous treaties in 1828 and 1833. These, however, being already regularly organized under a government and chiefs of their own, were by no means disposed to be swallowed by the governmental authority of the newcomers. Jealousies developed in which the minority or treaty party of the emigrants, headed by Ridge, took sides with the Old Settlers against the Ross or national party, which outnumbered both the others nearly three to one.

While these differences were at their height the Nation was thrown into a fever of excitement by the news that Major Ridge, his son John Ridge, and Elias Boudinot—all leaders of the treaty party—had been killed by adherents of the national party, immediately after the close of a general council, which had adjourned after nearly two weeks of debate without having been able to bring about harmonious action. Major Ridge was waylaid and shot close to the Arkansas line, his son was taken from bed and cut to pieces with hatchets, while Boudinot was treacherously killed at his home at Park Hill, Indian territory, all three being killed upon the same day, June 22, 1839.

From James Mooney,
Historical Sketch of the Cherokee, 1900.

18

aguli had been in the West for almost six months when the last of the waves of Cherokees had been ushered into their new homes over what was already being called the Trail of Tears. They were saying that 4,000 Cherokees had died. Whenever Waguli heard that, he wondered how many more, like him, were walking dead and therefore had not been counted among the fatalities. He had done next to nothing since the dreadful journey's end. He and Pheasant together had managed to construct a small lean-to near the river at the edge of the woods not far from the army post, Fort Gibson. It was not substantial enough to call a cabin. It was built not of logs, but of long branches, sticks, and it was plastered, hastily and sloppily, with river mud. It was small, but they did not need much room. They had few possessions: a change of clothes and a blanket each. Their rations were issued from Fort Gibson, the United States government having agreed to support the Cherokees with rations for one year after the Removal, and Waguli and Pheasant gave theirs to neighbors who in turn invited the two bachelors to eat with them. Sometimes when they could find someone with money they sold their rations or a portion of them. Around Fort Gibson there was whiskey to be had. It was illegal, but anyone with money who wanted it could get it.

Pheasant had lost his wife and child. Waguli had lost, he thought, everything: Oconeechee, his pride, his manhood, his country, his entire conception of the way the universe was constructed and the manner in which it operated. As time crept slowly by, more and more of their rations were sold for money and more and more of the money was spent on the white man's whiskey—*wisgi*, they called it. More and more, they were drunk. When they could afford it, they stayed drunk. When sober, they longed for the soothing liquor, the forgetfulness, the numbness of body and brain. More and more, Waguli and Pheasant kept company only with others who, like them, craved the solace of the white man's strongly flavored water. At first Waguli had not been able to drink much of it. It had burned his tongue and his throat and his stomach. It had made him cough and splutter. Soon, though, he was drinking along with the others.

Almost from the first time, Waguli felt the burning liquor roll around uneasily in his stomach, felt it move as if it was alive and did not want to stay where he had put it. He had welcomed the unsettling sensation in his guts, thinking, hoping that it would lead to an eruption down there, but it did not. So he drank the brown liquor for the numbing effect on his brain and the queasy effect on his insides, and he continued to hope. He hoped that he would forget, forget the pain and the suffering, the anguish and the misery, the sickness and the deaths and the humiliation. He longed to forget the loss of home and the loss of the security of knowing how the world was put together and just what it all meant. He yearned for the temporary oblivion achieved by the ingestion of the unsettling flavored water to become permanent forgetfulness, complete nothingness, absolute fuzziness of brain, and total absorption into the black mist. And he hoped that he would vomit.

Sometimes Waguli and Pheasant, even with their new drinking acquaintances, could not get any *wisgi*, and they would slowly and painfully grow sober, regain their feelings and memories and thought processes. Waguli's head would ache and throb, and he would taste the nauseating, noxious, gaseous vapors of the contents of his stomach which he was still unable to cast up. But worst of all, he would think. He thought about all the things he had been taught as a child, those things he had always believed without question: how there were three worlds, one up on top of the great Sky Vault, another down below the waters, and the one in the middle, the one upon which Waguli walked. Up on top was a world much like the one with which Waguli was familiar, but up there were all the original life-forms, as well as all those ancestors who had gone before. And at the Seventh Height dwelt the great Apportioner, the god of all gods, the one who was a mystery to all men. Down below, the world was the opposite of Waguli's world. The unexpected was ordinary. It was a world of chaos, ruled by strange and dangerous creatures, and the Cherokees performed their rituals and ceremonies in order to maintain a precarious balance between these two other worlds and a harmony in their lives.

What had happened? What had upset the balance? Had the old prophet been right? Had the Cherokees brought this doom on themselves by introducing into their delicately balanced world things obtained from white men? Or was none of it true to begin with? A steel knife was useful, and Waguli could see no real harm in a cup of coffee. He did not know. All was confusion and chaos. It was as if the world below had come up to replace the one he had known before. He did not even know where he was, only that he was someplace west, far west from home. He did not talk about these things with anyone, not even Pheasant. He kept them to himself, kept them inside where they festered and fomented and poisoned his brain and made him long all the more for the sweet, soothing, fuzzy drunkenness which came from the *wisgi*.

Waguli sat alone in the lean-to. He sat on the ground, his elbows on his knees, his head in his hands. His head hurt and his stomach churned. He was sober. He was thinking. He was remembering. Then he could hear loud voices, raucous laughter, and footsteps, getting louder, coming nearer. He did not bother to get up and look to see who might be approaching. He did not even lift his head, not until the voices were inside the lean-to with him, and he recognized the one that addressed him, called him by name.

"Waguli."

It was Pheasant. Waguli slowly raised his heavy head. Pheasant was there with four others. They were men Waguli had never seen before. They were all Indians. Waguli grunted a nonverbal response.

"Look," said Pheasant, "my new friends have *wisgi.*"

The jug was handed to Waguli, and he took a long, soothing draught. It burned its way down his throat and roiled in his guts. He coughed and took another. His head began to clear. The throbbing went away, and with it the painful recollections and the tormenting questions. He handed the jug to Pheasant.

"This is Waguli," Pheasant said to the strangers. "He's my *unaligohi,* my partner. We came out here together—under the soldiers' guns. *Unaligohi.* He was with me when my wife died. When my child died."

Pheasant began to blubber. Waguli could see that Pheasant was already well ahead of him with the *wisgi.* He glanced at the others.

"Pheasant," he said, "who are these?"

He didn't really care who they were, but he wanted to get Pheasant's mind off his grief.

"Oh," said Pheasant, "I forgot. Thigh, Swim, Bud Soldier, Dirt Thrower."

"Sit down," said Waguli.

The other five men sat in the lean-to, and they passed the jug around.

"You two came in the summer," said Thigh, "in the sick time, marched along by the white soldiers."

"Yes," said Waguli.

"It was bad," said Thigh. "I know. I heard about it. We came in winter, brought out by other Cherokees. I came with Chief Ross. His own wife was one of the ones we buried along the way. It was bad enough, but at least we didn't have the soldiers."

Waguli grunted and shrugged.

"They had to keep Waguli tied," said Pheasant, "because he fought them."

Pheasant grabbed Waguli's wrists and held them out for the others to see.

"See the scars?" he said. "And on his back are whip marks

yet. This one didn't give up. He fought them. And he escaped once. Yes. He's my partner. *Unaligohi.*"

Waguli was ashamed. Pheasant was bragging about him, trying to make him into a hero. And it was not true what Pheasant was saying. He had given up, and he had given up in the worst possible way, in his heart. He reached out eagerly for the jug which was coming his way again, and he sucked into his system some more of the warm forgetfulness.

"Many died," said Thigh.

"They say four thousand," said Bud Soldier. "Four thousand. Old people. Women. Babies."

Dirt Thrower took the jug and had a long drink, then he passed it on to Swim.

"It was those traitors," he said, "the ones who signed the treaty. They sold our lands to the white man. If they hadn't signed that paper, we would still be in our homes."

"That's right," said Thigh. "They're the ones to blame."

"Our law calls for death for anyone who sells Cherokee land," said Dirt Thrower. "Well? Isn't that right?"

"Yes, it is," said Pheasant.

The jug had found its way back to Waguli, who briefly turned it up to his lips, then tossed it to the ground in the middle of the lean-to.

"It's empty," he said.

"Someone should kill those men," said Thigh.

Dirt Thrower stood up, almost steady.

"Come on," he said. "I know where we can get some more."

"*Inena,*" said Pheasant.

When Waguli stood up to follow along with the others, his head spun, his stomach churned, and his legs were wobbly beneath him, but he kept his feet, and he walked after them. He did not know where they walked. He followed. He did not know where they obtained more *wisgi* or how they managed to pay for it, but he sat down with them beneath a large walnut tree and helped to empty another jug. Waguli's world was spinning by the time the second jug was done, but Thigh had a third, and someone suggested that they go back to the lean-to of Waguli and Pheasant to drink that one. Waguli managed to make it back to his new home somehow. He staggered and weaved the whole way. Sometimes he thought that the world had tilted up on one side, and he was trying to walk on it as if he were trying to walk along the side of a sheer cliff. He fell down a few times, but he managed to keep up with the others. Back at the lean-to he passed out on the ground before the third jug was empty. He remembered hearing the voices around him, but he had not understood the words since somewhere in the middle of the second jug. He drifted into oblivion with the earth whirling around his head. The night was chilling, and Pheasant and Thigh built up the fire. Then one by one the others passed out along with Waguli, and the fire blazed unattended in the lean-to.

Waguli's consciousness tried to assert itself as he felt himself being dragged along the ground. He felt the temperature drop drastically, and he heard around him frantic voices, shouting, and screams, but as soon as his body was released and ceased to be dragged his consciousness gave up the fight, and he was gone again into the realm of senselessness.

He woke up finally, slowly and painfully. Gradually he took in the scene around him. The lean-to was burned to the ground. Pheasant saw him trying to get up, and moved over to his side to talk to him.

"We burned our house down," he said.

Waguli grunted.

"We burned up Bud Soldier. He's dead."

Waguli looked up into Pheasant's face for just an instant, then he looked back down at the ground. His head was hurting. He did not know Bud Soldier. He was not hurt by the news that the man had died in his lean-to. He had seen so much death, so much senseless death, that one more did not hurt. He was numb to pain and suffering and misery. However, he thought that he should express some interest, if not concern.

"The others?" he asked.

"All here," said Pheasant, "except Thigh. He messed his pants in the night, and he's gone to the woods."

Waguli laughed, but it was a hollow, almost a painful laugh. He forced himself to stand up, and his legs felt like they had no bones in them.

"How did I get out here?" he said.

"I brought you."

Waguli put his hands to his throbbing head.

"What about the *wisgi?*" he said.

"It's okay," said Pheasant. "We drank it up before we all went to sleep."

"I feel sick," said Waguli. "I wish I could vomit. Can we get more *wisgi?*"

19

They drank some *wisgi* to give them some fire inside, but they were not staggering drunk. Dirt Thrower tossed a blanket on the ground and unfolded its corners to reveal what he had brought. There were knives and hatchets. He did not say where he had gotten those things. He then reached out, and picked up a rusty hatchet with nicks in its blade. It was slightly larger and heavier than a real war ax or war club. Pheasant reached for a knife. Swim picked out a knife. Thigh grabbed for the remaining hatchet, and then there were two steel knives left. Waguli sat staring. Dirt Thrower picked up both knives and thrust one, handle first, toward Waguli. Waguli clutched the handle in his right hand. Dirt Thrower stuck the other knife in his belt. It was late evening, and the sun was low in the west. Dirt Thrower stood up, his hatchet in his hand.

"Let's go," he said.

They had gathered at a place near Tahlequah, some miles away from Fort Gibson, the place that had been newly selected for the Cherokee national capital. Just a few miles through the woods from the capital was the community of

Park Hill. There Chief John Ross and other prominent Cherokees had built new, fine homes. The five crudely armed Cherokees walked silently through the woods toward Park Hill. Dirt Thrower had discovered that Elias Boudinot, who lived in Park Hill, would be near his home helping a neighbor to build a house. The homesite was two miles from the fancy house in which the Chief lived, the place that was called Rose Cottage. Elias Boudinot, full-blood Cherokee, formerly known as Buck Watie, was the brother of Stand Watie. As a young man he had been sent to a white man's college, and he had met and married a white woman from the north. He had also changed his name at that time. He had taken the name of a white man who had helped him while he was in school in the north. Before the Cherokees were moved, Boudinot had been clerk of the Cherokee National Council and editor of the *Cherokee Phoenix,* the bilingual newspaper published by the Cherokee Nation after Sequoyah had presented his people with a system for writing their language. He had helped the missionary, Reverend Samuel Worcester, translate the New Testament of the white man's Bible into the Cherokee language, and he had even written a novel. With his cousin John Ridge, Boudinot had traveled extensively among the whites making speeches against removal, trying to win sympathy for the Cherokee cause among the white Americans. He had gone to Washington to talk with members of the white man's government there. But one day, suddenly, Boudinot and his brother Stand Watie and their cousin John Ridge and Ridge's father, known as Major Ridge, had changed their minds. They had begun to talk to Cherokees, trying to convince them to give up the fight and move west. They had said that there was no hope in trying to remain in their homelands. Removal, they said, was inevitable. It would be easier on all the people if they cooperated with the United States and moved west voluntarily. Then they had signed the treaty that Andrew Jackson, the white man's president, had wanted them to sign. They had sold the land and promised that all the Cherokees would move west.

The small gathering of Cherokees who moved through the woods, Waguli among them, had decided that for this crime, Boudinot must die. There were others who were going that same night to John Ridge's house. And still others who had

the names of the other treaty signers. The law said that anyone who sold Cherokee land must die. These men had decided that they were the ones who would carry out the law.
Their faces were grim, and even though the *wisgi* still burned
slightly inside, their long walk and the nature of their task
had sobered them. Waguli's head was throbbing. His stomach churned. He had dreamed of being a warrior and achiev-
ing honor and respect by killing the enemies of the Cherokees, but the warrior days of the Cherokees were gone before
his birth. Now he was going with these others—men, excepting Pheasant, he did not even know—to kill another Cherokee. He tried to recall the misery he had gone through, the
suffering he had witnessed, and to blame it all on this man,
to focus all his hatred and resentment on this man, but he
could not call up much hatred. Inside he was still numb. He
had no real feelings. They had been beaten out of him, or
he had pushed them out in order to endure. Still he followed,
the knife stuck in his belt.

Dirt Thrower held up his hand to stop the procession, then
gathered the four men around him in a tight circle.

"There they are," he said.

Up ahead was a group of men in a clearing at the end of
the path. The frame of a house was up. It looked like they
were just about to stop work for the day. Soon the sun would
crawl under the western edge of the Sky Vault, and it would
be dark. Waguli's heart began to pound in his chest.

"Swim and Pheasant will go get him. You know which
one is Boudinot?"

"I know him," said Swim.

"Good. Tell him that your friend is sick with *onisquagani-
junahisna*. He has pain in his side, and it hurts him to breathe.
He has chills and fever. He is coughing and spitting up phlegm.
Budinot is known to have medicine for this sickness. He'll
come with you. One of you walk on each side of him, and
bring him down this path. Look at this tree here. Remember
this spot. When you get him back here, right here where we
are, grab his arms so he can't run. Hold him tight. We'll do
the rest."

"*Hawa,*" said Swim, and he and Pheasant began walking
toward the unfinished house and the small group of men
standing around it. Waguli was sweating. Dirt Thrower put

his hands on Waguli and Thigh and pushed them back off the path behind the trees.

"Wait for me," he said. "I'll strike the first blow. Then you can strike him, too, but wait for me. Don't move until I have struck."

Waguli felt sick. He leaned against the big tree behind which he was secreted. His head throbbed with the poundings of his heart, and the contents of his stomach roiled and churned. He longed for a drink of *wisgi*. Down at the end of the path he could see three men begin walking toward the spot where he and the others lay in wait. The plan was working, it seemed. He couldn't make out their features, but it must be Pheasant and Swim with Boudinot between them. They came closer, and he could hear their voices.

"We'll have to go to my house first so I can get the medicine," he heard Boudinot say.

"*Hawa.* That's okay," said Swim. "My friend's house is not far from here."

Suddenly, too soon for Waguli, they were beside him. Another few steps and they were beyond him. Then Swim grabbed one of Boudinot's arms, and Pheasant grabbed the other. They stopped walking, and they held him tight. Boudinot struggled.

"What is this?" he said.

Dirt Thrower sprang from hiding, raised the old hatchet high above his head, and with a mighty swing, buried it between Boudinot's shoulder blades. Boudinot screamed once, not long. Waguli thought the single blow must have killed him. Nevertheless, Thigh stepped out of the darkness and swung his ax, smashing Boudinot's skull. The victim's body hung lifeless between its two supporters for an instant, then they let it drop. Dirt Thrower, with great difficulty, wrenched his hatchet from the body's back, and he swung it again and again. Thigh did the same, and Pheasant and Swim plunted their knives into the body over and over. Waguli had stepped out into the road. He stood watching in horrified fascination, but glancing back down the path toward the construction site, he saw men running toward them. They had heard the scream.

"They're coming," he said.

"Let's go," said Dirt Thrower, and he began to run down

the path, back in the direction they had come from. The others followed him. They ran down the path for a distance, then turned into the woods. The darkness had fully descended, and soon Waguli was crashing through the thick woods, blindly, alone. He had lost sight of the others. He had dropped his knife, unused. He ran. He ran until he no longer knew where he was. He ran until he thought that he was far enough away from the site of the brutal slaying of which he had almost been a part. Or had he been a part of it? He ran until he could run no longer, and until he no longer had any idea which way to run. Then he collapsed upon the ground. The ground was cold, and the night air was cold. The bloody scene he had witnessed kept running through his mind. He heard the scream and the vicious chops and stabs over and over again, and he saw the blood. Boudinot was a traitor, he told himself. But still he felt sick, and he wanted to vomit.

The night passed, and the sun came out to the east, and Waguli had a vague notion which direction to travel to make his way back toward Fort Gibson. He couldn't say just why he was going back there. His home had burned, and it hadn't ever really been a home anyway. He had no family, no real friends. He didn't want to see Dirt Thrower and Swim and Thigh again, not ever, and he didn't particularly want to see Pheasant either, not for awhile at least. Yet he walked toward Fort Gibson. Why? It was familiar at least. Perhaps that was the reason. No. The reason came to him, and it was simple. It was easy. It was too obvious. He wanted the *wisgi*. At Fort Gibson he knew where to get it, and he wanted it. He wanted it badly.

He found Pheasant and the others lying on the ground just off to one side of the ashes that had been the wretched lean-to. They were all asleep, or passed out, all except Dirt Thrower, who began to stir when Waguli approached. He walked into the midst of them as Dirt Thrower sat up slowly and rubbed his face.

"You made it back," said Dirt Thrower.

"*Wisgi agwaduli,*" said Waguli.

Dirt Thrower got slowly to his feet and looked around. He walked over to where Swim lay on his stomach, his face in his folded arms, one arm wrapped around a jug. He picked up the jug and shook it, then turned it up to his own lips and took a drink. He turned to face Waguli and tossed the jug through the air. Waguli caught it and drank greedily.

"Did you hear the news?" asked Dirt Thrower.

"I heard nothing."

"The others got old Ridge and John Ridge, but Watie escaped."

Waguli took another long drink. He didn't care about the Ridges. He didn't want to hear it. He wanted to be drunk and to pass out like the others around him. He certainly didn't want to listen to Dirt Thrower talk. All of a sudden he hated Dirt Thrower. He wished that it had been Dirt Thrower they had chopped up instead of—that other man. Waguli had forgotten the man's name.

"Give me some more of that," said Dirt Thrower.

Waguli handed the jug to him and watched him drink. I should kill this man, he thought. Instead, when Dirt Thrower gave him back the jug, he drank.

"That one won't sign any more white man's papers," said Dirt Thrower, and he laughed, an ugly guffaw, Waguli thought. "We saw to that. We fixed him up real good. Give me the *wisgi*."

Waguli had just lowered the jug from his mouth after having sucked out the last burning drops.

"It's gone," he said.

Dirt Thrower suddenly resorted to English.

"Shit," he said. He turned his back on Waguli to search the ground for another jug which might contain a little liquor, and just as he did, Waguli took a swing with the empty jug, bouncing it off the back of Dirt Thrower's head. Dirt Thrower's knees buckled and he stood for an instant on his toes, knees bent, arms hanging slightly out to his sides, then he pitched forward, landing on the rocky ground face first. Waguli tossed the jug aside. He wondered if he had killed the hateful Dirt Thrower. He bent over the seemingly lifeless form and rolled it over, and he could see that Dirt Thrower was still alive. He was a little disappointed, but not enough to finish the job. He had not really planned to murder the man. He had simply struck out on an impulse. He checked Dirt Thrower's pockets and found a few coins. Then he went through the pockets of the others, who were still out cold from the drink. He found a little more money. Maybe with all the money from all of them he would have enough to buy some more *wisgi*. He shoved the coins down deep in the pocket of his white man's trousers and walked away. He could find the *wisgi* man by himself, he thought. He did not need any of the others.

As the weeks dragged slowly and painfully by, Oconeechee continued her lonely search. She found her own old home-town, Soco Gap, in much the same condition as Old Town had been: abandoned, burned, picked over. In fact, all of the Cherokee towns she visited were much the same. She found some fine Cherokee homes still standing but occupied by white people, and she found white people building new homes on Cherokee land. She was cautious, careful not to let herself be spotted by these whites. She traveled the old Cherokee country patiently and diligently, searching for Wa-guli. When she had exhausted her supply of food and worn out her clothing, she would return to the people hidden in the mountains to rest and get new supplies. Then she would go again. Her search was not only frustrating but also depressing. The land she had known all her life was changed. It was hostile, because it was no longer populated by her own people, but by white people. And there were already beginning to be more white people on the land than there had ever been Cherokees. In some places the whites were building new white-man towns. Land that had been farmed for years by Cherokee farmers was now being plowed and planted by white farmers. Yet she continued her search. She continued, for she had no life without Waguli.

20

Waguli was not surprised when within a short time after the killing of the Ridges and Boudinot, friends, relatives, and supporters of those men began to retaliate. The Cherokee Nation became embroiled in a civil war. The one side became known as the Treaty Party or, sometimes, the Ridge Party. The other was usually called the Ross Party. Soon the killers from the Ross Party were known to their enemies, at least some of them. Waguli was not surprised at that either. He had heard Dirt Thrower brag about his own role in the assassination of Boudinot when he was drunk and not careful of who was within earshot. Waguli tried to stay away from Dirt Thrower and his friends, but not because he was afraid of being attacked and killed by members of the Treaty Party. He had not felt like he was alive since his recapture at the stockade. He was not afraid of death. He thought he would even welcome it. Sometimes he wondered why he did not just go ahead and kill himself and bring it all to an end. Why did he continue walking through this shadow existence, enduring it with the help of *wisgi?* He couldn't answer that question.

He was hanging around the fort, looking for an opportunity to earn some money, or beg it. He had approached a white soldier who had brushed him aside roughly and said something in English that sounded menacing. He decided to keep away from the soldiers. There were plenty of other people around the fort: white civilians and Indians. He thought about going somewhere else, but he could not think of any-place he wanted to go. He found a spot by the stockade fence and sat down, leaning back against the fence and drawing up his knees. It reminded him of the other stockade, and he felt an urge to turn around and dig under the fence. It was a stu-pid urge, he knew. He lowered his head between his knees and tried to shut out the world around him, but he kept wanting to dig.

"Waguli."

Waguli lifted his head. It was Pheasant. He was standing there in front of Waguli, a big grin on his face.

"Let's go," he said.

Waguli didn't move.

"Come on," said Pheasant.

"Where?"

Pheasant held out his hand toward Waguli, still grinning, and he slowly opened his fist to reveal a handful of coins.

"Where did you get all that money?" said Waguli.

"Never mind where," said Pheasant. "Let's go."

Waguli stood up and walked along beside Pheasant. He knew where they were heading. He knew as soon as he saw that Pheasant had money. The direction they began walking only confirmed the knowledge. They would get *wisgi,* and they would get drunk.

The jug was already half empty, and Pheasant and Waguli were walking toward the partially finished lean-to beside the ashes. No one had suggested that they go there. They were walking, and there was no place else to go. It did, after all, serve as home. Waguli took the jug from Pheasant and drank as he walked. By the time they reached the lean-to, he was staggering. And there lounging around the hovel were Dirt Thrower and his friends.

" *'Siyo,*" said Dirt Thrower. "We've been waiting for you here."

"Hello, friends," said Pheasant. "We have a little *wisgi* here. Have a drink."

He took the jug from Waguli and handed it to Dirt Thrower. Dirt Thrower took a long drink, then handed the jug to Thigh. While Thigh was drinking, Waguli felt the need to urinate. He welcomed the excuse to take himself away from the company of his uninvited guests, and he walked around behind the lean-to and a few feet into the thick woods. Then he heard the sounds of approaching horses, and he heard the voices of the riders.

"Who is coming?" Dirt Thrower said.

"I don't know," said Pheasant.

Waguli waited in the woods. He heard the horses draw closer, and he got himself into a position where he could see at least some of what was happening but not, he thought, be seen himself. The riders looked like mixed-bloods or white people. The paper signers, he thought. As they rode even closer, each rider drew a pistol from his belt.

"Run," said Dirt Thrower, but the reaction had been too slow. One rider fired his pistol right into the back of Dirt Thrower's head. Waguli saw Dirt Thrower pitch forward life-less onto the ground. Thigh had been sitting, and as he scrambled to his feet, one of the riders shot him in the chest. Swim was running down the path toward the fort. A rider turned his horse and raced after him. Coming up beside the fleeing Swim, the rider reached down with his pistol, get-ting it within a foot of the side of Swim's head, then pulled the trigger. Swim's head jerked sideways. He ran three or four more stumbling steps and flopped off the side of the road. Pheasant jumped toward the rider who had shot Dirt Thrower, grabbing him by his jacket. The man fought to stay in the saddle. He struck at Pheasant's head with his empty pistol while his horse spun nervously. Another man who still had a loaded pistol dismounted and ran up behind Pheasant. He pointed the pistol at Pheasant's back just be-tween the shoulder blades. Waguli sprang from his cover.

"No," he shouted.

The man fired, and Pheasant screamed and fell backward. The riders all turned toward Waguli, who had given himself away with his shout. One of them aimed a pistol at him, and Waguli stood mesmerized by the sight of its barrel staring him in the face. The man pulled the trigger and the hammer fell with a harmless click. Waguli turned and ran back into the woods. He heard someone on foot crash into the woods behind him in pursuit, then heard another one cry out.

"Come on. Let him go. Let's get out of here."

Waguli kept running anyway. He went on into the woods until he was sure that no one was chasing him. He stopped and watched and waited. Finally he started walking back to the scene of the carnage. He made his way back to the spot where he had been hidden when the men first rode up, and he stood there for a long moment. Birds were singing in the trees, and a gentle breeze was rustling the dry leaves. Waguli became aware for the first time that his white man's trousers were wet. He stepped out into the open, and the sight of the bodies around made him feel ill. Slowly he walked over to the body of Pheasant. It was on its back, and except for the fact that its eyes were wide open and staring blankly up at the sky and there was a bloody hole at its sternum, it would have looked to Waguli like Pheasant was just drunk again and passed out. He dropped to his knees and looked at Pheasant's face, and he thought of Sally and of Yudi, and he wondered if Pheasant would find them waiting for him in the Darkening Land on the other side of the Sky Vault. He felt a tremendous cramp develop in his stomach, and he clutched at it. It turned into a violent spasm, as if giant, unseen hands had gripped him fast by the middle and were wrenching his body, wringing it like a wet rag. He opened his mouth wide in anticipation of a coming upsurge, but it did not come. The spasms subsided, leaving in their wake the familiar uneasiness in the pit of his stomach.

Waguli buried Pheasant and covered the grave with a small wooden structure like the roof of a house. At first he thought that he wouldn't bother with the others, Dirt Thrower and his friends, but he found that he couldn't bring himself to just let them lie and rot out in the open. He buried them too, not far from the grave of Pheasant, but he didn't bother to mark their graves. Then he gathered his few belongings, including one knife and one ax left over from the store of assassination weapons, and left the place that had served as his home, never to go back. He found himself a new homesite, still not far from Fort Gibson, and he built himself a rude log cabin.

Then he gradually settled into a routine existence. He drew his rations, and he planted a small crop: corn, beans, squash, pumpkins, potatoes, sweet potatoes, and tomatoes. At the right times of year, he gathered the wild food plants that he knew and could find in his new environment: walnuts, chestnuts, hickory nuts, possum grapes, mushrooms, ramps, creases. He began to fish and to catch crawdads from the river and the abundant streams and creeks nearby. He found river cane and honey locust trees and bull thistle and boi d'arc, and he made himself a blowgun and darts, a bow and some arrows for hunting.

Soon he discovered that he could harvest much more from the land than he needed for his own subsistence, and he could sell the surplus to the white people at the fort or to Cherokees who had money. He was apparently not known as one of the assassins of Boudinot and not identified as an adherent of any faction. However, in the back of his mind there was always the realization that he had been seen, however briefly, by the killers of Pheasant and the others. They could spot him at some time and recognize him. Yet he moved freely around the fort, and he found that he could obtain odd jobs from the whites: cutting and hauling wood, cleaning, anything that the white men or their women wanted done but did not want to do for themselves. And with the money he made from selling his surplus harvest and from these odd jobs, he bought *wisgi,* and in the evenings, he drank himself into a deep sleep.

21

know you think the white man, the federal government, has stolen your lands from you," Wil Usdi was saying, "but that's not exactly what happened. He bought it. It was a sale that he forced on you, yes, but it was a sale nonetheless. And even though you escaped the removal, you are still Cherokees. The land was yours no less than it was theirs who have been forced west, and you, by rights, should share in the proceeds from that sale. Do you understand me? Some of that money is yours."

Oconeechee was only half listening to Will Thomas, Little Will, the white trading-post man who had been raised by Cherokees. She had just returned from an extended trek throughout the old Cherokee country in search of Waguli. She was tired and despondent. She had returned to the fugitives in the mountain caves for a brief respite to regain her strength, to replenish her trail supplies, to gather her thoughts for further search, to ask herself some questions and try to answer them. Where had she not looked? Where else should she travel? Where could he be? And when she had arrived, the little white man was there.

"I have been in Washington City," Wil Usdi continued.

"I'm trying to get the government there to give you your money. If I can get your money for you, I can use it to buy back some of this land. It will have to be bought by me and deeded to me. They won't let you buy it. But if you will authorize me to use your money, I will buy the land, and I will provide you with a secure place to live."

A big Cherokee named Ut'sala, or Lichen, stepped forward. This man, Oconeechee had learned, had assumed the leadership of this band of refugees in their own land.

"If we let you have our money," said Lichen to Wil Usdi, "how do we know you will use it to our advantage? Even if you do as you say and buy some of this land, which is ours anyway, given to us by God, how do we know that you won't kick us out just like we were kicked out before?"

"I know that it's difficult for you to accept the word of a white man after all that has happened," said Wil Usdi, "but most of you have known me for many years. I was raised among you. The only father I have ever known was Yonaguska, the Drowning Bear. Believe me, I have only your interest at heart."

It was hard for Oconeechee to concentrate on the words of Wil Usdi. Her mind was occupied with her own thoughts and concerns. Her heart was not with her there in the mountains. It was somewhere else. It was with Waguli—somewhere. Yet she heard, and she tended to believe the little white man. She had known him, though not well, all of her life. Her father had often taken her with him when he went to trade with Wil Usdi, and they had always considered him to be fair and honest. Still, it was hard to believe that anyone, even a trustworthy white man, could do anything to alleviate the misery the white man's government had brought on the Cherokees. Wil Usdi had paused in his speech. When he could see that no response was forthcoming from Lichen, he broke the silence.

"What good will your money do you if you are hiding in these mountains?" he said. "Can you go to the government and get it? Even if you could do that, could you buy the land? Where could you go to spend the money? Let me try this for you. If you say okay to this, I will go back to Washington City, and I will not leave that place until I accomplish the task or die in the attempt."

Ut'sala turned his back on Wil Usdi and ambled, seemingly aimlessly, into the crowd of assembled Cherokees. Now
and then he would pause and speak low into someone's ear,
then listen while that person responded to him in the same
manner. He spoke in that way to men and to women. When
he drew near Oconeechee, he put a hand on her shoulder and
his head close to hers.

"What do you think of this man's proposal to us?" he said.

"I haven't really been living with you," she said. "I've only
been taking advantage of your kindness. I shouldn't speak."

"You're one of us. What do you think?"

"I don't know what to think of the plan. I don't know anything about the government or money or buying land. My
father always spoke well of the little white man. He trusted
him, and he liked him."

"Your father was a great man," said Ut'sala, then he strolled
on and spoke to some others. The last one he stopped by was
an old woman, and he talked with her for some time. Then
he moved back through the crowd to stand beside Wil Usdi.

"We all know you," he said. "We all trust you. Go back to
Washington City. Get our money for us if you can. Buy our
land—in your name. We will all wait here to hear from you."

"I'll leave in the morning," said Little Will.

The rest of the day was spent in eating and visiting. Different
ones found their opportunities to talk to Wil Usdi, to remi-
nisce about old times or to ask what he thought about his
chances with the government. He told them that his task was
not going to be an easy one. It would take some time, he said,
but he thought he had a good chance. Some of the Congress-
men were softening on the issue—slowly. Large numbers of
white people were feeling guilty for what their government
had done to the Cherokees. Some were even angry. It would
probably take some time yet, but Wil Usdi was guardedly
confident that he eventually would be able to get the job
done. He had brought some coffee up the mountain with
him, and the people were enjoying its taste. Little Will eventually got a break from the nearly constant interviews, and
he sat down with a cup of the steaming black drink. Oconeechee saw her chance and went to his side and sat down.

"I'm Oconeechee," she said.

"I remember you," said Wil Usdi, "and I remember your father. I'm glad to see you here safe."

"Thank you."

Wil Usdi sipped some hot coffee from his tin cup.

"Your father has been gone from us now for some time," he said. "Are you alone, or do you have a husband now?"

"I have a husband," said Oconeechee. She ducked her head. "Well, I was going to be married—before the troubles started. In my heart I'm married."

"Your—husband was taken west?"

"No. He was captured, but he escaped. There are some here who saw him escape."

"Perhaps," said Wil Usdi, "perhaps he was killed."

"No. I don't believe that. I came to talk to you because you've been places that I haven't been, places that I can't go. Maybe you've seen him or heard something about him."

Wil Usdi put his tin cup down on the ground beside him and folded his arms across his knees. He glanced at Oconeechee's face, then looked down at his crossed arms.

"What is his name?" he asked.

"Waguli. From Old Town. He is old-fashioned in his dress and with his shaved head. But he is a young man."

"Hmm. No," said Wil Usdi. "I don't know him. I never knew many people from Old Town. They didn't get down to my trading post often. I haven't heard anything about your Whippoorwill. I'm sorry. It would probably be best for you to try to forget. Start your life over. There are other young men."

"There is no one else for me," said Oconeechee.

"You may feel that way now. You're young. Time heals wounds. Many people lost the ones they loved. It's sad, but you have to go on. You have your own life to live."

"Not without Waguli. Without Waguli I have no life. He's out there somewhere, and I'm going to find him. Some day, somehow, I'll find him."

She stood up and started to walk away from him.

"Oconeechee," said Wil Usdi, "wait."

She stopped and turned back to face him. The little white man stood up and walked to her. She stood taller than he did, waiting there to see what it was he wanted.

"You are very determined," he said.

"He is my life."

"If he is alive," said Wil Usdi, "and if anyone knows anything about him, Gun Rod will know."

"Gun Rod?"

"He's an old man. He's a white man who was once married to a Cherokee woman. They had children, but they lost them all years ago to a sickness. More recently Gun Rod lost his wife, too, so he is all alone in the world. I've seen him not long ago, and he seems to know all about what has happened to the People, to many of them. His knowledge amazed me."

"Where can I find Gun Rod?" Oconeechee asked.

He was with your father at the fight at Horseshoe Bend," said Little Will. "Do you know that place?"

"Yes," she said. "My father took me there once to show me where it happened."

"Gun Rod lives near there. It's a long trip for you to make."

"I'll make it."

"He's an old man with long white hair and a long white beard. He lives alone in a small cabin near the battlefield. The Cherokees knew him as Gun Rod, but his white man name is Titus Hooker. Can you remember that? Titus Hooker."

"Titus Hooker," repeated Oconeechee, pronouncing the English sounds with some difficulty. "Titus Hooker. Gun Rod."

"If you are really determined to go there to continue this search of yours," said Wil Usdi, "I'll draw you a map to show you the way to Gun Rod's house from the battleground."

The following morning Wil Usdi left. His ultimate destination was Washington City. At almost the same time, Oconeechee left. She left well supplied for a long journey, but she left with a much lighter heart than she had had on her previous excursions. This time she had a destination. She would not be wandering aimlessly. She had a man's name, and she had a map. In her mind she could see this Gun Rod, this white man with the hairy white head, and he seemed to her to be the very image of the white man's God, and the longer she walked, the more her trek took on in her mind the characteristics of a sacred pilgrimage. This god-like white man, this Gun Rod who had so much knowledge

in his hoary head, he would give her the answers to her
questions.

The first day of her trip she did not even stop to eat, so
anxious was she to get to Gun Rod there by Horseshoe Bend
in the land that the whites called Alabama. But the second
day, in spite of her eagerness, she deliberately slowed her
pace. She was weary from her haste the previous day, and she
knew that she must eat to maintain her strength. She also
realized that the farther she traveled away from the mountain
fastness of Ut'sala and the others, the more dangerous her
situation became. She could not allow herself to be captured
or harmed, perhaps killed, when she was finally getting close
to her goal. And she knew that she was getting close. Wil
Usdi had sent her to Gun Rod, and Gun Rod would have the
answers. She began to travel more cautiously. When it was
possible, she moved at night and found daylight hideaways
in which to sleep. She kept away from main-traveled roads,
and when she saw people, she quickly hid herself and kept
still and quiet until they were gone. She had heard it said that
the whites were no longer trying to catch Cherokees to send
them west, but Ut'sala and his people still hid in the mountains, and she would be at least as skeptical as they. She would
not take any unnecessary chances. She would not trust rumor. She would not be caught being careless or neglectful or
overconfident.

Oconeechee was confident, though. Not only had Wil
Usdi given her hope by telling her of Gun Rod, but she had
also gone to see the old man known as the Breath who lived
there among the fugitives and was said to be a conjuror. She
had told him about her search for Waguli. The old man had
taken from a little bag two beads, one black and one red.
Oconeechee did not have to be told the significance of the
colors. She knew that the red one stood for success, and the
black was ominous and indicated disaster. She had stopped
breathing without realizing it, and she could feel her heart
pounding in her breast as the old man took up the beads. He
held them, the black one in his left hand, the red one in his
right, between his thumbs and index fingers. He stared hard
at the beads, and mumbled something to them, low, too low
for Oconeechee to understand what he was saying. Time
seemed to stop. Then suddenly, frightfully, the black bead

seemed to take on life. It began to crawl along the leathery old finger of the Breath, and Oconeechee's heart skipped a beat. Then the red bead moved, and the black one moved back to its original position. The red bead seemed to quiver for an instant, then it shot along all the way to the first joint of old Breath's finger. The stored-up wind came out of Oconeechee's lungs. She would have success, the old man had told her. She would find Waguli.

She was sleeping in an open field late one evening. She had found the country through which she was moving to be heavily populated with whites, and she was afraid to travel by day. The field was covered with tall grass, and she had moved a distance away from the road to lie down in the cover of the grass. When the sun was down, she would crawl out and resume her travel. The sky had been clear all day, and she expected a bright, starry night. It would be all right for traveling. She was awakened from her sleep by the noise of a barking dog. She sat up to listen. The dog seemed to be coming closer, and she could hear the voices of white men, could hear them trampling through the grass. She raised herself up as much as she dared and strained to see through the dimming light of evening. There were three white men with guns following a dog, and they were coming straight towards her. They had not seen her, could not know of her presence there. The direction of their movement was just bad luck. Panic-stricken, she wondered what to do. If she sat still, they would surely come upon her. Even if the men walked by without noticing her there, the dog surely would not. If she jumped up and ran, they would be bound to chase her. She might outrun the men, but she could not outrun the dog.

Then off to her left, back in the direction from which she had come, sounded the loud, clear call of a mountain whippoorwill, followed by a rustling of dry grass and a flapping of wings. The dog barked and ran after the sound, and the men yelled and ran after the dog. Oconeechee watched until they had run almost out of her sight, then got up and began to move quickly in the opposite direction.

"Waguli," she said out loud.

She recognized the battlefield when she found it. She could remember it from the time years before when Junaluska had brought her there. Not much had changed. She saw the spot her father had pointed out to her with pride, pride which would later turn to regret, the spot where he had saved the life of Old Hickory, Tseg'sgin. Thoughts of her father brought tears to her eyes, but she brushed them away and brought out the map Wil Usdi had drawn for her. The house of Gun Rod would be just over the hill off to her right. She was almost there, and a good thing, too, for she had run out of food and had been traveling for a day without anything to eat. She was weak and weary from hunger and from physical exertion.

"Gun Rod is just there," she said.

She was pleased with the accuracy of Wil Usdi's map and with how easily she could read it. She started to walk directly across the open battlefield toward the hill which was hiding her goal from her eyes. Her legs seemed to move of their own will. She seemed to be plunging forward. She saw nothing but the hill. She moved across the field in long, jerking strides. Reaching the hillside shortened her steps, but still she moved forward, still straight ahead. As the climb grew steeper, she leaned more and more forward until at last her hands touched the ground that seemed to be rising before her. Then she was crawling. And then she was on top of the hill.

She stood up straight and drew in lungs full of air, her breast heaving in labored motion. Her head felt light, and her vision was beginning to blur, but down below she could see a cabin with blue-gray smoke rising lazily from its stone chimney. It was Gun Rod's cabin. It could be no other. Oconeechee started walking again. She walked faster. She was almost running when she reached the steep downhill grade, and she fell forward tumbling. She scrambled to her feet once, only to pitch forward, rolling again. At the bottom of the hill, she stood up on unsteady legs and walked to the front of the cabin. The old man must have heard her approach, for he opened the front door and stepped out onto the small porch. He was short, though not so short as Wil Usdi, and he was powerfully built. His blue-gray eyes, red nose, and bit of loose flesh below each eye were all that showed of a face through the mass of white hair and beard. He looked down off the raised porch at Oconee-chee, dirty and battered there before him, and she thought she could read in those clear old eyes both curiosity and compassion.

"Gun Rod," she said, and then the world began to spin around her, and the last bit of strength left her tired legs. Her knees buckled beneath her, and she sank to the ground unconscious.

22

She went into Alabama
to a place they call Big Bend,
where her father had saved Old Hickory,
and that's where she found a friend.
Bitterly she wailed in sorrow,
"Why am I crying still,
and who has taken from me
my noble Whippoorwill?"

Old Titus Hooker practically jumped off the porch when he saw the girl faint. He ran the few steps from the porch to where she lay, and he knelt heavily beside her with a loud groan. Carefully he rolled her over onto her back and straightened her arms and legs. He listened to her breathing for a moment, and then, satisfied that it was regular enough, he shoved his thick arms underneath her body and lifted her to carry her into the house. Inside, he lowered her gently onto his bed. Then he located a clean rag which he soaked in water that stood in a basin on a small table. He wrung the excess water out of the rag and went back to her side to bathe her face and lower legs. He touched a hand to her cheek and to her forehead.

"No fever," he said. "I expect she's just wore out."

He was speaking English, talking to himself out loud, as he spread a blanket over the unconscious girl. Then he stepped back to look at her. He wondered who this strange young woman could be and what had brought her to his lonely cabin. He was sure that he had not seen her before, but, he thought, she called me by my Indian name. Looks like she's come a long, hard ways to find me. Wonder why? Oh, well, I reckon she'll come around in a while. I'll find out then.

Realizing that he could do nothing more for her for the time being, he went back to what he had been doing before her arrival. He had been busy putting together a stew—building a stew, he called it. When the girl comes around, he thought, she'll need something to eat anyhow. I just as well get back to this. He tossed the last of the ingredients into the black pot and hung the pot on the iron rod which swung into and out of the fireplace. Then he swung it into the fireplace so that the pot was over the fire.

"That's good," he said. He had gotten used to hearing his own voice, and he found it a comfort. For quite a few years now there had been no one else around the house to talk to, no one regular. Of course, there were occasional visitors, but usually he was alone, so he talked to himself. Well, the stew was cooking, and the girl was still unconscious. He took up a short clay pipe and a tobacco pouch from off his table and filled the pipe bowl. Then he went to the fire and stuck one end of a long stick into the flames. When the stick was burning he used it to light the pipe, then he moved back to the table, pulled out a chair, and sat down to smoke. He stared across the small room at the girl lying unconscious in his bed. He knew she was a Cherokee, because she had said the name the Cherokees had called him, and she had spoken it in the Cherokee language. She was young. Gun Rod judged her to be no more than twenty, probably not that old. It was hard to tell in her present condition, but still, he thought, no more than twenty. And she was beautiful. He could tell that. Almost as beautiful as—. His thoughts drifted back to his own youth and another young and beautiful Cherokee girl. He had thought there would never be another like her, and he had loved her, he was sure, more than any man had ever loved a woman, or than anyone would ever love again. He had thought he could not live without her, but he had been doing just that now for several years. Often he wondered what the next life would bring. Would there be a next life? And if there would be, would he find her there waiting for him? Would she be young and beautiful again as she had been? And would he be the young man she had fallen in love with? Would they be together throughout eternity in everlasting bliss? Would they make love the way they had done on earth? Did spirits do that? And the children—were they out there somewhere with their mother and would the whole family be once again united in that spirit land, the Darkening Land of the Cherokees on the other side of the Sky Vault or the heaven of the white man? Which would it be? Or would it be neither? Was what came after death a mere nothingness, oblivion, an end to all consciousness and all caring and feeling and knowing, a melting into the universe? Ah, God, how he missed them all—the children, yes, but her especially. Especially her.

Oconeechee slowly opened her eyes. Their lids felt uncommonly heavy. The first thing she saw was the wooden roof over her head. She stared at it for a moment, then rolled her eyes cautiously to one side and looked at the wall. Then carefully, as if she were afraid she might hurt something, she turned her head in the other direction. The old man saw her head move as soon as she saw him sitting there at the table.

"Ah," he said, "so you're back in this world."

She tried to sit up, but she was weak, and her head was still light.

"Just lie easy," he said. "Be patient. I'll get you some food."

"Gun Rod," she said.

"That's the name the Cherokees call me," he said. "If you're looking for old Gun Rod, you've found him, and I'm just as curious about what brought you here as you are anxious to tell me. But we can both wait. First you'll eat."

He had ladled out a bowl of stew, and with it he moved to the side of the bed. He set down the bowl and helped her sit up enough so she could eat comfortably. Then he picked up the bowl again and dipped a wooden spoon into it. He held the spoon to her lips.

"Here," he said. "Sip this. It'll bring back your strength."

She sipped from the spoon, and the stew was hot and good. She felt it course through her body, felt, she imagined, the strength already beginning to return. When she had finished the stew Gun Rod gave her tea in a cup, and she drank that. Then she sat up.

"*Wado*," she said. "I feel much better."

"I'm glad," said Gun Rod, "but don't get too anxious. Take it easy."

"I'm called Oconeechee," she said. "My father was Juna-luska."

The old man raised his eyebrows and looked hard into her face. He looked long enough and straight enough at her that she began to get nervous. Then, remembering the Cherokee's aversion to such direct stares, he looked away.

"Yes," he said. "I can see that you're my old friend's daughter. He was a fine man and a good friend, and I miss him. I liked him and respected him while he lived, and now that he's no longer with us, I honor his memory. I'm glad that you're here. I'm glad for the chance to get to know you, but I don't believe you came just to give me that opportunity."

Oconeechee ducked her head.

"No," she said. "I came for your help. Wil Usdi said you could help me. He said that you know more things about what has happened to people during these bad times than anyone else."

"Well, I have tried to keep up with events," said Gun Rod. "Tell me what it is you want to know, and I'll see if I can help."

"I was to be married," said Oconeechee. "My father approved just before he went away. Waguli is the man who was to be my husband. Waguli of Old Town. Before we could be married, the soldiers went to Old Town and captured everyone. They took Waguli to one of their stockades, but he escaped. He escaped, but I have never seen him again. I've been looking all this time."

"It's been over three years now, girl," said Gun Rod, his voice incredulous.

"I've been looking for him."

Gun Rod looked at her again, and again he saw in her that other young Cherokee woman of long ago. He thought of his longing, of his own lost love, and he believed the girl. She had been looking for her lover all this time. She would keep looking. He knew that about her.

"How do you know that he escaped?" he said.

"Some of the people up in the mountains were captured and escaped. Some who are up there now saw him. They told me. He dug a hole under the wall with his hands and ran away after dark."

Gun Rod stood up and began to pace the floor.

"Waguli," he said. "Waguli of Old Town. I don't know him. I never knew many of the Old Town people. Tell me about Waguli."

"I—I don't know much about him," she said. "I didn't know him very long before they captured him. He was young and very handsome. He dressed like some of the very old men, in the old way, and he shaved his head the old way. People in Soco Gap stared at him and thought that he looked funny. His clan is the Wolf Clan, and I love him. I cannot go on long in this life without him. That's all I can tell you. That's all I know."

"Maybe that's enough," said Gun Rod. "At least for now. There are some people I can talk to about this. I'll see what I can find out."

Oconeechee stood up quickly and eagerly.

"When can we go?" she said.

"You can't go with me, girl. I have to go alone. You need to rest and get your strength back. Besides that, some of these people I'm going to see are white men—soldiers. You'll be safer here. Stay here and use my house as if it were your own. I'll be back in a few days. Maybe then I'll know something."

For the next four days, Oconeechee, alone at the cabin of Gun Rod, felt like an animal in a cage, but she tried to make the best of her time. She bathed in the nearby stream, and nursed her cuts and bruises. She prepared her meals from the old man's stores, and she mended the tears in her clothing. She busied herself cleaning Gun Rod's cabin and looking for things in need of repair, but Gun Rod was a good house-keeper. There wasn't much to be done. She did find a garden behind the house, and she managed to pass some time taking care of it. Mostly, though, she thought about where Gun Rod could be and wondered what he would find out for her. And she thought about Waguli and longed to see him again, longed to touch him, and at night she listened for the call of a whippoorwill. On the afternoon of the fourth day, Gun Rod returned.

"Yes," he said to her, "I believe he's alive. What you heard was true, but it was only part of the truth. Waguli, I believe, was captured as you said at Old Town. He fought the soldiers, so they tied his hands. They put him in the stockade at Hiwassee Island, and after awhile they unbound him. That's when he dug his way out to escape, but they caught him again. He was taken away to the West by the soldiers in one of the first groups to go. Many people died along the way, you know, but I believe that Waguli is alive. He's alive in the West."

"I must go find him," said Oconeechee.

"No," said Gun Rod. "It's too far and too dangerous. There are too many whites along the way. You would have to go through their towns and cities. I'll go get him and bring him back to you."

"Why will you do that?" she asked.

Titus Hooker stepped to a window and looked out at the mountains in the distance. He heard the chirping of cardinals somewhere outside, and he thought of the love this young woman had for her man. For over three years she had searched, and she would not give up. And he thought of his own love, a long ago love that still burned in his heart. He did not know if he could answer her question.

"It gets lonely here," he said. "I'd like to take a trip. Don't worry. I'll find him. If he's alive out there, as I believe he is, I'll find him, and I'll bring him back to you. Where will you be when he comes? Do you want to wait here?"

Oconeechee thought for a moment.

"No," she said. "I'll be waiting at the place where he first saw me."

> Then the old man held her tightly,
> and to the maid he said,
> "I'll go and find your lover,
> for I don't believe he's dead.
> I will go to the land of flowers,
> the home of the Seminole.
> I will wander to Kentucky.
> I will travel to and fro.
> I will cross the mighty river,
> and I will not stop until

I have find your one true lover
and bring back your Whippoorwill.

Gun Rod removed a loose stone from the fireplace and reached into the recess. He brought out a bag of something obviously heavy for its size and carried it to the table.

"I'll need some money for this trip," he said. "I always knew there was a reason for hoarding this stuff."

They spent the evening getting things ready for their separate journeys, Oconeechee's back to the mountain people, Gun Rod's to the new Cherokee country in the west. He told how long he thought the trip should take.

"Don't get too anxious until then," he said.

He offered her some of the money, but she declined it with thanks and with a question.

"Where would I spend it?"

They slept that night in Gun Rod's cabin, Oconeechee in the bed, the old man on a pallet on the floor near the fireplace, and in the morning they traveled together to Gun Rod's nearest neighbor, who had horses to sell. Gun Rod picked out two and bought them. He gave one to Oconeechee.

"This will make your return trip a little easier," he said.

Mounted and ready to go, they looked a last time at one another.

"Be careful going back," said Gun Rod, "and when you get there, be patient. If I don't die first, and if he's alive, I'll bring your Waguli back to you."

"I believe that you will bring him back," said Oconeechee.

They turned their horses in opposite directions and started to ride. Wil Usdi was right about this old man, Oconeechee was thinking. He will do what he says. He will bring Waguli back to me. And Breath was right. The red bead told the truth. Behind her riding in the other direction, old Gun Rod, Titus Hooker, was lost in his own thoughts. He thought about the past, the lost past, and he thought about the nature of love. At last, because his mind needed the comfort of words, he forced himself to cut through the jumble of abstractions for one thought he could verbalize, and he spoke aloud to himself, or to his horse, or to the winds.

"My last days," he said, "will have a grand purpose."

Whippoorwill, Whippoorwill,
Don't you know how she's searched all these hills?
She's searched every glen and glade
not knowing why you went away.
Can't you feel she loves you still,
Whippoorwill?

23

Old Titus couldn't stop himself from feeling a little guilty. Oconeechee's journey would be much more difficult, he thought, than would his own. She had a long way to go, and she was a woman traveling alone. Not only that, she was a Cherokee Indian woman traveling alone through country recently divested of its Indian population by a hostile white horde. It was not quite possible, he thought, to accurately assess current white attitudes in that part of the country towards the Cherokees. Surely some of the fervor for removal and death had subsided over the years, but how much, he couldn't guess. Oconeechee was determined, though—resourceful and tough. She would make it. She'd be all right. He hoped that he was being reasonable and not just trying to make himself feel better.

His own trip, while certainly a greater distance, could be largely accomplished by boat travel on the waterways. He would ride horseback the first hundred miles or so going just about due north to reach the southernmost point of the Tennessee River, where it sliced through the northern part of Alabama. There he would sell his horse and book passage on a steamboat which would take him even farther north, all the way through Tennessee and into Kentucky. Then he would travel the Ohio River over to the Mississippi, which would finally take him south and down into Arkansas. There the Arkansas River ran west to Fort Smith and at last into the new Cherokee Nation West. Gun Rod wasn't sure how much of the end of the trip would have to be accomplished by land, but surely, he thought, not as much as at the start—not a hundred miles. It would be a long journey by water, but it would be much faster that way than going the shorter, more direct overland route. He estimated that he would actually spend more time in the saddle in Alabama and later in the Cherokee Nation than he would on the steamboats.

Gun Rod found that he liked the feel of the horse beneath him again, the easy rhythm of the beast's gait. Had he not felt a sense of urgency for his mission, he would have enjoyed this trip at a more leisurely pace. It carried him back through the years to be wandering. He thought it made him, in a way, young again. But no, he decided, it's probably the nature of my mission that's taking the years off this old frame of mine. His first night on the trail he slept under the stars beside a woods. As he crawled groaning into his bedroll for the night, he heard the soft cooing of a whippoorwill from somewhere in the trees. He propped himself up on one elbow and looked into the darkness in the direction from which the sound had come.

"Ah," he said out loud, "I hear you in there. Would you be trying to tell me something now? Would you?"

The second day on the trail was uneventful and long. Gun Rod found himself thinking over and over again the same thoughts he had drifted with all the day before. His initial enthusiasm for the trip had worn away during the first day of riding and on the second day tedium had set in. Gun Rod had anticipated the tedium, however, and so he endured it well and with the patience of the gracefully aged. The rest of the journey would have to be accomplished on determination, and the old man was determined. Toward the end of the day, he found a roadside inn where he stopped to eat a meal prepared for him by someone else and served to him at a table. He paid for a room and slept the night under a roof and in a bed. In the morning he bought a breakfast, and after he had eaten well, he resumed his journey refreshed and almost energetic.

In the late afternoon of the fourth day a weary old Gun Rod arrived at Gunter's Landing on the Tennessee River. It had been several years since he had visited the place, and he found that it had changed from not much more than a spot where steamboats, flatboats, and keelboats stopped to pick up wood and occasional passengers to a thriving little economic center of somewhat questionable character. Gunter's Landing was a cluster of small log buildings, most of them commercial. Obviously the freight and passenger business had grown considerably, as had other business which depended on river traffic. There were wood sellers, and there were taverns where the traveler could eat, put up for the night, buy a drink, gamble, or purchase the temporary charms of a prostitute. There was no school, no church. Gun Rod thought, a man could get a knife stuck between his ribs here right quick if he's not careful. He found an inn where he bought himself a meal and managed to wrest from a tight-lipped proprietor information about steamboat schedules and local horse-trading. He then paid for a room for the night, having been told that the next steamboat west would not arrive until the following morning, and went out to sell his horse. He was pleased when he managed to make a small profit on the beast, but the hard stares of two scruffy-looking river rats lounging nearby made him more than a little uneasy. They were a rough pair, he could tell, and they had seen him sell the horse and pocket the money.

Gun Rod pulled open the front of his Cherokee hunting jacket to make obvious to any interested observers the two pistols tucked into the sash which he wore tied round his ample waist. Then he removed the traveling pack from the horse, hefted it up onto his broad shoulders, and started back for the inn. He resisted the constant urge to look back and see what the river rats were doing behind him. At the inn he went immediately to his room, dropped the pack to the floor, and closed the door. He was going to have a long wait. He wasn't afraid of any man, but neither did he believe in taking foolish chances, and he felt like he had an important mission to accomplish. Going out with his pack on his shoulders, he would feel conspicuous and vulnerable. If he went out and left the pack unattended in the room, he would probably never see it again, and he couldn't bring himself to trust the weasel-faced proprietor of the inn to watch it for him. That left him with only one choice: sit in the room with the pack until morning.

He thought about the youth and beauty and bravery of Oconeechee, and he was more than content to be spending his money, time, energy, perhaps even his final days, in helping to end her search, her—sacred search. Yes, he thought, it is a sacred mission: it has as sacred a purpose as any there ever was. And his thoughts drifted back again to his own love. In his mind it was only yesterday. He was young and vigorous, and she was perfect beauty and symmetry. His business had been trade with the Cherokees, and he had ended up marrying and staying among them. When Junaluska and other Cherokees had joined Old Hickory's army and gone to fight the Creeks, Gun Rod, as he had come to be known, went with them. He had fought with them at the decisive and famous Battle of Horseshoe Bend. He had cast his lot with the Cherokee, and he would be among them yet had not—. But he forced his mind in another direction. He did not care to dwell on the painful loss. He could think about the past long past when they were young and happy in their love, or he could think of the future with its hope of a reunion—somewhere.

Finally he began to feel drowsy. The door of his room had no latch, so he shoved his heavy pack against it. He was a light sleeper. If anyone tried to open the door, he would hear the noise of the pack being shoved across the rough floorboards, and he would awaken. He pulled off his tall boots, removed his jacket and sash, and lay down heavily on the narrow bed with a long and loud sigh. Soon he was asleep.

It was somewhere around midnight when he heard the footsteps in the hall. He was instantly awake, and he opened his eyes wide. He listened intently while waiting for his eyes to grow used to looking in the dark. The footsteps stopped, and he heard a harsh whisper. They were just outside. Slowly, carefully, quietly, he got out of bed. He stuffed the lumpy pillow under the worn blanket and stepped across the room in his bare feet to stand beside the door. He stood where he would be behind it when it was opened. He waited.

His breathing was heavy and sounded loud to his own ears. He thought maybe the ones on the other side of the door could hear it and would know where he was, what he was up to. He waited, and then someone from the other side gave the door a tentative push. When the door encountered the weight of the pack it stopped, and he heard another rough whisper. There was a brief answer, and the door was pushed again, this time slowly and steadily. The pack was being shoved along the floor. Then the movement stopped. Gun Rod became acutely aware of each throb of his heart. There was a pause and then another whisper. The door was pushed again, this time until it stood almost wide open and the pack was nearly against Gun Rod's feet. There was another pause, not so long as the previous one, and then two men rushed into the room. The two men hesitated and looked across the bed at one another, and from his spot in the corner of the room Gun Rod recognized the two river rats he had seen earlier in the day. One of them reached down and ripped the blanket away from the bed, and Gun Rod sprang into action.

Two long strides took him to the foot of the bed. His two hands reached out, each grabbing a handful of hair. He spread his arms wide to his sides, pulling the heads back, then with a roar, bashed them together. The man in his right hand collapsed, unconscious, perhaps dead, and fell across the bed, then slid off and on down to the floor. The other cried out and grabbed for his head with his left hand. His right still clutched his deadly skinning knife. Gun Rod jerked the man backwards by the hair, and he noticed the knife just as the man raised it up over his head. Gun Rod swung his right hand, still clutching the man by the hair, shoving the river rat's face into the mattress. With his left hand he reached across the man's back and gripped the right wrist. He twisted the arm up behind the back. The man screamed.

"Drop the knife," said Gun Rod through his teeth.

The man struggled, and Gun Rod gave a vicious wrench to the arm, which was already grotesquely twisted well beyond where it should have been. There was a loud crack followed by another scream. Gun Rod pulled the man up to his feet and shoved him across the room to the door. Then he threw him out into the hall. The man staggered a few steps, his broken arm flopping foolishly at his side, then fell sprawling on his face. Then Gun Rod went back for the other one, who had not moved since he had dropped him to the floor. His face was covered with blood. Gun Rod grabbed the collar of the man's jacket and dragged him out into the hall beside his partner, who was still on his face on the floor, writhing in pain and whimpering. Then he went back into the room and shut the door. He stood for a moment looking around the room, shoved the pack on into the corner, then dragged the bed across the room and pushed it firmly against the door. It would take a powerful man to open the door against the weight of the bed with Gun Rod lying on it. I should have done this in the first place, he thought. He stretched himself out on the bed and noticed at once how heavily he was breathing. I'm an old man, he told himself. Old. But by God I took care of those two scurvy knaves. I did.

He slept well, and in the morning he got himself ready to leave. He pushed the bed back where it came from and picked up the pack. Out in the hall the man with the bloody face was lying where Gun Rod had tossed him. The other was nowhere to be seen. Gun Rod wondered as he passed by the bloody-faced one whether or not the man still breathed, but he wasn't interested enough to stop and check. He bought himself a breakfast and ate it, and noticed with interest that the proprietor of the inn seemed to take care not to look in his direction. When he had finished his meal, he went deliberately up to the innkeeper and looked him in the face.

"Is there a sheriff in this settlement?" he said.

"Huh?"

"Is there any kind of law here?"

The proprietor looked at Gun Rod stupidly.

"I didn't really think that there would be," said Gun Rod, and he turned and walked out of the inn. He went straight to the river's edge, to the landing spot where the boat would nose up to the bank. There was no dock. There were two large tree stumps for the boat to be tied to. Gun Rod dropped his pack to the ground beside one of the stumps and sat down on it to await the boat's arrival.

It was midmorning before the steamer appeared, and when it had nosed up to the landing its crew busied themselves gathering wood. There was also some freight to be loaded, and there were a few new passengers in addition to Gun Rod.

It was noon before the boat got underway. Gun Rod was hungry. He had missed his lunch, but he was relieved to be on the boat at last. The rest of the trip, the bulk of it at least, would be easy, and it would be speedy. He was also relieved to be away from the riffraff at Gunter's Landing. Gunter's Landing. Not long ago it had been a part of the Cherokee country. It had not taken much time, Gun Rod mused, for white trash to make a ruin and a shame of it. He tried to put the place and the bad times out of his mind and passed his time studying the boat. His pack was stashed in a private cabin just behind the hurricane deck on the second level and above the firebox. He could walk forward out of his cabin and stand on the hurricane deck overlooking the deck passengers below. The boat was a stern-wheeler with a draft of only fourteen inches, a wide, low hull, and an open-sided main deck which was stacked with cordwood and with crates, barrels, bales, and bags representing a variety of westbound cargo and crowded with low-paying passengers who lounged or strolled aimlessly about. On top of the cabins was a third deck on which, forty feet above the water, was mounted the wheelhouse, and just forward of that, two iron chimneys, or smokestacks, rose another twenty or twenty-five feet into the air. The boat was named the *Lucy Walker* and was owned by Rich Joe Vann, a Cherokee who had lost a mansion and plantation in Georgia, but not before he had preceded the Trail of Tears west and established himself a new home there to rival his old one.

This last discovery sent Gun Rod to the boiler deck behind the cabins, where he could stare out over the big wheel and its churning wake to watch the riverscape recede behind him. He felt suddenly overwhelmed by the perplexing ironies of life. He found a deck chair and sat down to fill and light his pipe, and he left a wake of smoke behind him which trailed in the air above the larger and more insistent wake below. He was conscious that he was also traveling in the wake of the Cherokees' bitter trail of sorrow.

Rich Joe Vann. So he was riding on Rich Joe's boat. He had seen Rich Joe once back in Georgia, a full-blood Cherokee dressed like a southern dandy, preceded and trailed and constantly pampered by black servants, his slaves. It was said that he owned three hundred. And Rich Joe was not the only one of his kind. Many Cherokees were more sophisticated and more successful in the white man's world than were the vast majority of the whites who thonged greedily around them. Perhaps that had been their problem. Perhaps the whites couldn't stand to watch these Indians, these people they wanted desperately to believe were ignorant savages, beneath them, besting them in their own ways. And then there was old Titus Hooker, the white man who would have been content to live out his days as a Cherokee, who preferred to be known as Gun Rod.

Of course, not all Cherokees were like Rich Joe. Gun Rod knew that well. And sitting on the boiler deck of the *Lucy Walker,* he thought about the hundreds who had been herded onto boats like her, herded and shipped like cattle. Many were unfamiliar with the ways of the whites, could not speak or understand the English language, probably had never seen a steamboat before being loaded onto one to be taken they knew not where. Ah, God, he thought, it must have been a burning hell.

There was no way to make sense of any of it: whites moving Indians west because they didn't want savages in their midst, then turning the Indians' land into a haven for thieves, cutthroats and harlots; white men who wanted to live like Indians, and Indians who did live like whites—only better; a president whose life had been saved, whose political career had been at the least greatly aided by the Cherokees, coldly masterminding the malevolent removal of those very Cherokee people; white intellectuals in the North verbally attacking their own government for its cruelty and cupidity; white preachers among the Indians, and whites throwing the preachers into prison for being there; at least two bold southern politicians, Crockett and Houston, both former Indian fighters, standing up for the rights of the Indians to their own political detriment, both of them now gone to Texas, Crockett to his death there; and somewhere in the heart of all this madness, this chaos of insanity, cruelty, insufferable inhumanity, there was love. The fire in Gun Rod's pipe went out. He stared back at the churning wake of the *Lucy Walker,* and secretly, silently, he wept.

24

They stopped briefly at Decatur to pick up three more passengers and take on several barrels of something. Gun Rod's curiosity regarding the cargo was not strong enough to cause him to put forth any effort or inquiry. And they took on a little more wood while they were there. He was pleased that the stop was brief. Decatur appeared to him to be very much like Gunter's Landing, but larger and more firmly established. He stayed on the hurricane deck during the stop, casually observing the procedures. There were similar stops at Tuscumbia and Waterloo, and then they were out of Alabama and traveling north into Tennessee. When darkness fell the boat, tied to trees along the riverbank, settled for the night.

The second day was spent traversing western Tennessee from north to south in order to reach the Ohio River. At one place they stopped while the crew went ashore to chop and load wood. At another they stopped to purchase wood from two seedy flatboatmen who, it seemed, simply tied up on the bank with their barge of cordwood and waited for their noisy customers to come along the river. At the end of the day,

with the confluence of the Tennessee and Ohio rivers just
ahead, they tied up again for the night.

Gun Rod's cabin on board the *Lucy Walker* was nicely furnished, and it included, at the foot of the bed, a nightstand
with a pitcher of water and a basin, so the old man was able
to keep himself reasonably fresh. For two days he had kept
pretty much to himself, but on the morning of the third day,
as the boat churned its way into the Ohio River and headed
west, he made himself as presentable as possible under the
circumstances and ventured into the main cabin, a spacious
room between the men's cabins toward the bow and the la-
dies' cabins toward the stern, also called the dining room,
saloon, and social hall. Indeed, it served all of those purposes.
Ornately furnished, it was lighted by bright crystal chande-
liers and stained glass skylights. The floor was carpeted and
the windows draped. The tables were all covered with ele-
gant cloths. Gun Rod had been in the social hall before, of
course, but only long enough to take his meals. This time,
he decided, he would see how much of the day he could pass
away in its opulence. There was a card game in progress at
one table, and near the bar another table was occupied by a
group of men who were listening to a backwoodsman (by his
looks) telling tales. Gun Rod took a seat at an unoccupied
table near that one and ordered himself a pot of tea and some
cakes. He said to himself, this is certainly a genteel life I am
leading, for however short a time it may be.

Gun Rod had barely settled himself at the table when he
realized that the voice of the backwoodsman irritated him.
He had never liked the bragging of the southern woodsmen
and rivermen. This one was telling a long-winded fabrica-
tion concerning a bear hunt. His rapt audience consisted of a
slimy-looking fellow that Gun Rod took to be a professional
riverboat gambler, a member of the boat's crew, a man taste-
fully dressed with the appearance and manner of a northern
businessman, and a young southern gentleman. Gun Rod's
opinion of the entire gathering was not very high. The story
of the bear hunt was finished to loud guffaws, and when they
began to subside, the young southerner spoke.

"Do you really expect us to believe that tall tale, sir?" he
said, but he asked the question with a good-natured smile on
his face.

"Why, hell, no," roared the yarn spinner. "I scarcely believe it myself, it's so ferocious, and I was there to live through it."

There was more laughter, and a round of drinks was poured.

"But now, my young friend," said the bear hunter, "if you can stand to hear it, I'll tell you a tale that no one here will believe one word of, even though it's all as true as the very gospel."

"Let's hear it then," said the southerner, and there was lighthearted chuckling all around the table.

"Well, it was back in 'fourteen at the Horseshoe, and I was riding right alongside Old Hickory himself, the most fiercest white man that ever drew breath. Why, the man's eyes looked like two red-hot, glowing coals was set right into his face, and his skin was hard, dried leather. But the hardest thing about him was inside the seat of his pants. The man could set a saddle longer than any man alive, except for maybe the devil, and there's been considerable argument over that. There was some that thought old Andy was the very devil and leading us into the jaws of hell. We knew the hostile Creeks was all holed up on that horseshoe-shaped peninsula there in the Tallapoosa, and they was the most ferocious savages ever yet encountered in the wilds. When we got there, we found that they had built a eight-foot-high wall of logs across the neck of that there peninsula, closing up the horseshoe, and they was in it, and we was out. Old Hickory drew his sword, and I was right there, and Sam Houston and Davy Crockett, too. We was all there.

"'Charge,' he said, and we did charge, but the cowardly Cherokees that was with us ran away and hid, so—"

"Damn you and your filthy lies," roared Gun Rod, coming to his feet and pounding his huge fist down onto the table. The whole social hall became instantly quiet. Even the card game at the table at the far end of the room stopped, and the gamblers stared, alternately at Gun Rod and at the hunter. The hunter stood still, staring straight ahead, apparently trying to fathom the almost unbelievable challenge he had just received. Gun Rod, too, stood and glared, wondering why he had allowed his temper to get the best of him. Men had been killed for less than what he had just said. And what if

he were to die on the *Lucy Walker* for such a thing? For calling
a liar a liar when everyone knew the man told lies? Lying was
expected of the man. It was in the very nature of the entertainment. And for this he had endangered the hopes of Oconeechee. What an old fool I am, he thought, but he was in no
way prepared to back off. The hunter slowly turned to face
old Gun Rod.

"I'm half horse and half alligator," he said. "I once et a man
twice your size for breakfast, and I picked my teeth with a
wagon tongue. I've wrestled grizzler bears and wildcats with
my bare hands and lived to tell about it, and once a rattlesnake bit me on the bare ass and died of blood poison. Every
man that ever dared to call me a liar to my face is dead but
not in his grave, because you couldn't find all their pieces to
bury them after I had got done, and I'm a fixing to scatter
pieces of you all up and down this here Ohio River to feed
the fishes."

He whipped a long-bladed knife out from under his fringed
jacket and assumed a menacing stance. Those men who had
been his audience retreated toward the card players. Gun Rod
pulled out one of his pistols, thumbed back the hammer, and
aimed it at the man's chest.

"One little lead ball won't even slow me down," said the
hunter. "Why, I'm carrying nigh onto twenty pounds of lead
around with me in my guts wherever I go."

Gun Rod pulled out the second pistol in his left hand.

"I can accommodate you with two more," he said. "Now
if you want to fight me, put down your pig-sticker, and I'll
put down my pistols, and we can fight like men."

The hunter raised his knife high over his head and swung
it down hard to stick in the tabletop.

"Now that's the kind of talk I like to hear," he said. "Put
away your peashooters, friend, and let's see who the best
man is."

Gun Rod walked over to the man, looking him in the eyes.
He released the hammer of the cocked pistol, then laid both
pistols on the table, one on each side of the standing knife.
Then two more ominous clicks were heard, and the two an-
tagonists turned their heads simultaneously toward the bar,
where the bartender had just laid a Manton flintlock shotgun
across the bar, aimed generally at both of them.

"Sorry," he said, "but I can't have you breaking the place up."

Gun Rod eyed the expensive side-by-side English import. "It's just like Rich Joe to have a man killed in style," he said.

"Take your fight out onto the main deck."

"That's just fine with me," said the hunter. "It don't make me no nevermind where I pound out his brains." Then he looked at Gun Rod. "You coming?"

"After you," said Gun Rod.

The card players at the far table and the hunter's scattered audience all ran together out the door. When Gun Rod and the hunter got down the stairs to the main deck, the others had already cleared a large space for them and were standing around it in a circle.

"Fight," they were shouting, "fight," and other passengers and crewmen, hungry for entertainment, were joining the circle. The combatants got themselves into the circle and squared off. The crowd shouted encouragement. With a sudden roar, the hunter ducked his head and ran for Gun Rod, who quickly stepped aside and hammered a heavy fist down between the man's shoulder blades as he hurled past, sending him sprawling on the deck. Gun Rod stepped back and waited. The other man got up to his knees, shook his head, then stood. He braced himself, then ran at Gun Rod again. This time he hit his target, and with a full embrace bore him backward, breaking through the circle of onlookers, knocking down two gamblers, and finally falling on top of him on the deck. Gun Rod gave a mighty heave and flung the man aside, and both of them got quickly to their feet. The hunter swung a fist, but Gun Rod saw it coming and dodged soon enough to catch only a stinging, glancing blow to the jaw. He countered with his own hamlike right fist, catching the hunter a solid blow on the side of the head. It was a powerful blow. The hunter stood on wobbly legs, stunned. Gun Rod moved in, stepped to the side, caught up his opponent by the collar and the seat of his pants, and with a powerful pitch, tossed him headlong off the starboard side of the boat and into the river. A general roar went up from the crowd, and some rushed to give Gun Rod congratulatory slaps on the back. A crewman ran aft with a roustabout's pole and fished the hunter out of the drink just in time. The hunter, revived by his dunking, shook himself like a wet dog, then walked back to the forward deck.

"I've been soundly thrashed," he announced to the crowd, and a cheer was offered up for his good sporting manner. Then the dripping hunter approached Gun Rod, who stood by red-faced and panting. "I would like to know just what it was that set you off," he said.

"I was at Horseshoe Bend," said Gun Rod, "with the Cherokees. And I'll lay the lie on any man who calls them cowards. They won the day."

"I own the truth of what you say," said the hunter. "I was making a tall tale, and I got caught in my own snare. Can I have your name?"

"I was given the name of Titus Hooker at my birth, but I lived among the Cherokee for nearly twenty year, and they call me Gun Rod."

"Gun Rod," shouted the hunter. "By God. Sure, I know you. Can I shake your hand?"

Gun Rod shook the other's hand, though without exhibiting much enthusiasm.

"I'm Abner Breeze," the hunter said. "Even though I was fixing to tell a hell of a lie awhile ago when you so cheerfully interrupted me, I was at the Horseshoe, and I remember you." Then he turned and shouted to the crowd. "This is Gun Rod, one of the bravest men in the country, and every word he speaks is true."

Almost before he could realize what was happening, Gun Rod had been escorted back into the large social hall, where he found himself surrounded by an admiring crowd. Whiskey was bought all around, and a glass of the brown liquor was set before him.

"I'll sit with you, and I'll talk with you," he said, "but I'll not get drunk, for I'm on a sacred mission."

Abner Breeze looked astonished for an instant, even seemed as if he might issue another challenge, then recovered himself and held up a hand.

"Then, by God," he said, "bring him his pot of tea."

Before long the *Lucy Walker* hove to larboard and soon entered the waters of the mighty Mississippi River to head south at last. For the rest of the trip, Gun Rod had an almost constant companion in Abner Breeze and was treated generally as a celebrity by passengers and crew alike. He was slightly embarrassed by all the attention, but it did help make the time pass more quickly, and, Gun Rod admitted reluctantly to himself, he sort of enjoyed it. One day Gun Rod and Breeze were seated together at a table in the social hall, Breeze with his whiskey, Gun Rod with tea, and Breeze leaned confidentially across the table, speaking in a low voice.

"Tell me," he said, "just what is this here 'sacred mission' of yours?"

"I'll keep it to myself," said Gun Rod. "You'd either think me a fool, which I may well be, or you'd make it into one of your tall tales."

"I swear to you that I'll never breathe a word of it as long as I live, and my word's as good as a Washington City bond. I can't swear that I won't think you a fool, though."

Gun Rod surprised himself by starting to answer Breeze's question.

"I'm going after a man," he said. He took out his pipe and started to fill it.

"To kill?" asked Breeze.

Gun Rod was lighting his pipe from a candle which burned on the table, and he answered Breeze between puffs.

"No," he said. "Not to kill. There's a lovely Cherokee girl back in the old country—the old Cherokee country in North Carolina. She was going to be married to her sweetheart, and then the soldiers came. She escaped and hid in the mountains, but he was captured and carried west. She didn't know that, and for these four years, she's searched for him. She's remained faithful to him. Hers is a rare love and sacred. I believe it is."

Gun Rod stared into a puff of smoke and thought about that other rare and sacred love he knew.

"Well, I be damned," said Breeze. "And you're a-going after the man to take him back to her. Is that it?"

"Yes," said Gun Rod. "That is it."

Breeze fell back in his chair, uncharacteristically speechless for a moment. Then he leaned forward again, resting his arms on the table.

"My friend," he said, "that is the most noblest thing I have ever heard of a man set out to do."

After a long voyage down the Mississippi River, the *Lucy Walker* found the Arkansas River and headed west again, and

Gun Rod felt his anxiety increase. Just across Arkansas was
the new Cherokee Nation West. He would be there soon, and
then his search for Waguli would begin. How easy would it
be to find the man, a man he had never seen? He did not
know. He did not even know if he would find Waguli alive,
but his faith told him that he would. Oconeechee was waiting, trusting in him, and he would not let her down. He
stood alone on the hurricane deck looking west. He's out
there somewhere, he said to himself. Somewhere just ahead
of me. And I will find him.

Fort Smith, Arkansas, was bustling. It was a trade center for
Cherokees, Choctaws, Chickasaws, Creeks, and Seminoles,
and Gun Rod saw some representatives of each of these tribes
moving about in their colorful garments to accomplish their
business. The Indians brought their produce: corn, cotton,
beans, squash, pumpkins, and traded for flour, coffee, sugar—
and whiskey. Gun Rod saw a good many drunken whites and
Indians. He was pleased to discover in Fort Smith that he
could stay with the steamer all the way in to Fort Gibson.
The river was full. He had no desire to stop longer than was
necessary in Fort Smith, so he paid for the rest of his passage,
bade farewell to Breeze, who had reached his destination, and
continued west on the *Lucy Walker,* which arrived at Fort
Gibson later that same day. Gun Rod debarked from the
steamboat with his pack thrown over his left shoulder. The
journey's over, he thought. The search has just begun.

   Looking around, he saw the same degradation he had seen
at Fort Smith. Outside the post itself a small community of
grog shops and brothels had developed. Indians and whites
alike were involved in the lucrative trade, both as vendors
and as customers. He grit his teeth and shifted the weight of
the pack on his shoulders, then started walking toward the
military post. There he would make his initial inquiries. Was
there a place he could stay as a boarder for an indefinite period of time? Where could he buy a horse or two? Had anyone heard of a man from Old Town, a recent emigrant, by
the name of Waguli?

 25

Oconeechee made her way back safely to the mountain haven of the Cherokees. She was welcomed back once more and fed, and some curious ones asked her where she had gotten her horse. Perhaps they were afraid she had stolen it from a white man, who would follow her to get it back, and then they would all suffer.

"It was a gift from someone," she said. That was all they needed to know. Then Wildcat came to her to ask if she would finally give up her hopeless search and think about taking another man. He made it clear to her that he was interested and available. Oconeechee liked Wildcat. He had helped her once, and she was grateful. She wanted to be careful not to say anything that would hurt him unnecessarily.

"Thank you for your interest, my good friend," she said. "Waguli is coming back—soon."

And she would say no more. Behind her back the people talked. Who could have given her a horse? There was no one out there but white people. That made no sense. And it was a fine horse, too. Had her long devotion to a man probably dead made her crazy? If not dead, this Waguli was surely lost somewhere in the west. Or maybe he was okay but married to another woman. A man wouldn't wait four years. Neither would a woman—unless she was crazy. And now she's bragging that he's coming back to her. Ha. How could she know that? She doesn't even know where he is. She should take one of the young men here. But no. She's crazy. Our young men don't deserve that. And she's not getting any younger either, you know. Who does she think she is, anyway? You know who her mother was. She's not even really a Cherokee. No clan.

Oconeechee knew what they were saying. She also knew that some were not involved in the gossip. Wildcat, in spite of her rejection of his advances toward her, remained her friend, and so did Grasshopper and Lichen and Breath. Breath, the old conjurer, he knew she wasn't crazy. He was the one who had told her that she would be successful in her quest. Whenever she passed by the old man she would smile, and he would smile back, a sly smile that said, yes, you and I have a secret between us. No matter what they are saying, you and I know the truth. Strange, Oconeechee thought one day, that all my friends are men. She knew that she had a long wait, but she knew what she was waiting for. Waguli would come. She wanted to be ready for that day. She gathered wild honeysuckle, prepared the vines, and made baskets. She made pots from clay. Using river cane, she made woven mats, floor mats, and sleeping mats. She made more than she would need for her home, and she gathered more material than she could use. The extra baskets, pots, and raw material she traded to hunters for skins. She needed to make clothes for herself and for Waguli. Hiding out in the mountains, the people could obtain no cloth, no manufactured material with which to weave cloth, so they once again relied on skins.

And Oconeechee worked with the others in the garden and received her share of the produce. She ate what she needed, prepared what she could that would store and keep, and traded what surplus she had. If she could be, if anyone could be under the circumstances, she would be ready to set up housekeeping when Waguli came back to her.

One day Will Thomas did come back. He rode up the narrow trail to the secret hideaway of the Cherokee fugitives. He rode one horse and he led another. The second horse was a packhorse, and it carried a heavy load which Wil Usdi unpacked as soon as he arrived. He distributed cloth, beads, tobacco, coffee, sugar, flour, and other things the people had been doing without since they had gone into hiding. The mountain Cherokees prepared a big feast for Little Will with what they had. All of them were anxious to hear his news, but they followed form and fed him first. Wil Usdi also knew proper Cherokee behavior, and he kept his information to himself until the time was right to tell it. Finally he stood before them, Lichen by his side.

"My good friends," he said, "it is done."

He reached into an inside coat pocket and withdrew a paper which he held up high for all to see.

"This is the deed," he said. "It's in my name, and it's for 38,000 acres of land, some of which we are standing and sitting on right now. According to the laws of the United States government and the government of the state of North Carolina, the land belongs to me. That means that no one will bother you here. In my heart and in my mind, the land is yours, and I will continue working to get it in your name."

Little Will told the people as well as he could where their new boundaries were, and he answered questions. Yes, they could move anywhere they wanted on this land and establish new towns for themselves and clear new fields. They could roam the entire tract at will and hunt. And, yes, they could leave the land and go to town to trade and then come back. It was hard for the Cherokees to believe that they were safe again and relatively free, yet they accepted the words of Wil Usdi, and they had a great feast all the rest of that day. Once again, Oconeechee waited for a chance to catch the little white man alone.

"I found Gun Rod at his home," she said. "He's gone out west to find Waguli and bring him back to me."

"I'm glad to hear that," said Wil Usdi. "If it can be done, I believe that Gun Rod will do it."

"I know he will," said Oconeechee. "And now I want to know something else. Beside Soco Gap, where I used to live, is a mountain stream. Not far from the town is a place where the water falls and a pool is made. The pool is still and clear and deep. Yet it is almost a secret place, even though the trail to Soco Gap is just above."

"I think I know where you mean," said Wil Usdi.

"I want to live there."

"Go there before anyone else and build your house, and you can stay," he said. "That place is well within our boundaries."

"*Wado,* Wil Usdi," she said. "That's the place Waguli will come to find me."

26

Then he came to Oklahoma,
to the town of Tahlequah,
where he found the chieftain,
told him what he had come for.
"The whites won't let me go," he answered
but he listened to the tale,
then he said, "I will go with you
if I have to crash the gates of hell."

t was so damned easy. The first soldier Gun Rod had spoken to had known Waguli. He had done some small chores around the post that very day, the soldier had said. He had even known where Waguli lived. Not far from the post. A tiny cabin. He had given Gun Rod the directions. So easy. Gun Rod didn't even bother looking for horses. He would find Waguli, bring him back with him to the fort, and buy them both passage on the next steamboat east. He was amazed at his luck, though he had begun to regret not having gotten himself a horse to ride. By the time he spotted the cabin ahead, if one could really quite call it that, the pack was becoming a considerable burden, and his old back was tired. His feet were sore. He walked up to the cabin and dropped his pack to the ground.

"Waguli?" he called out.

Slowly a head appeared, peering around the corner of the open doorway from inside the cabin. It was an Indian, a young man, Gun Rod thought, though it was hard to tell. The face was rugged, lined. The eyes were red and bloodshot. The long hair was tangled and uneven. The face was dirty, as was the hand which was also visible in the doorway, clutching a jug.

"What do you want?" asked the Indian, speaking in Cherokee.

"I'm looking for Waguli," said Gun Rod.

"I am Waguli, or—I once was."

My God, thought Gun Rod, is this what I have come all this way for?

"What do you want with me?" said Waguli.

Gun Rod thought it best to work his way slowly to the real purpose of his visit.

"Can we talk?" he said.

"Come in."

"Can we sit outside?"

Waguli hesitated, then staggered out into the fresh air. A small fire burned on the ground in front of the cabin. Gun Rod sat down on the ground facing the cabin across the fire and waited. Waguli dropped heavily down to the ground across the fire from Gun Rod, took a pull from his jug, thought about it, then offered it to his guest.

"No," said the old man. "I have to stay sober."

"I can't stay sober," said Waguli. "You talk good Cherokee. Are you a mixed-blood?"

"I'm a white man, but I lived for twenty years among your people. My wife was a Cherokee. I loved her very much. She is gone now."

Gun Rod looked hard at Waguli for any sign that the mention of love might have an effect on him, but he saw no sign, just the same blank expression. Oh, God help me, he thought. How can I approach this man?

"Among the Cherokees," he said, "I was known as Gun Rod."

Waguli wrinkled his forehead and scratched his head. He looked up at Gun Rod briefly, then looked back down.

"You were a warrior," he said. "I heard them talk about you. If you need a place to stay, you're welcome to stay here."

Gun Rod took out his pipe and tobacco to smoke.

"I don't want to stay," he said. "I have to go back—to the old country."

Again he searched Waguli's face. Again he saw nothing there.

"Why did you come here?" said Waguli.

Gun Rod decided that he could no longer put off his purpose. He puffed his pipe, then looked directly at Waguli. It was a challenge.

"I came here for you," he said. "I came for Oconeechee, to bring you back to her."

Waguli was silent. He stared into the fire.

"Will you go with me?" said Gun Rod.

"They brought me here," said Waguli. "They won't let me go."

He took another drink from his jug, and he was seized by a coughing spell. The old nausea came over him strongly, and he wanted to go to the woods to vomit, but he knew he couldn't. He drank again, and he felt the *wisgi* rumbling in his stomach.

> Whippoorwill, Whippoorwill,
> don't you know how she's searched all these hills?
> She's searched every glen and glade,
> not knowing why you went away.
> Can't you feel she loves you still,
> Whippoorwill?
> And don't you know she always will,
> Whippoorwill?

"Waguli," said Gun Rod, "it's been four long years. Oconeechee didn't know what had become of you. She's been looking all over the old country all this time. Looking for you. She traveled as far as where I live in Alabama near Horseshoe Bend. She came alone and on foot. She wants you. She's waiting for you. She—she loves you."

"You've really seen her?" Waguli asked after a long pause.

A vision from the past swept into Waguli's mind and asserted itself through the muddle that was there. He was a young man on a mission traveling to Soco Gap, and he was getting close to his destination. He was walking along a ridge, and down below the waterfalls made a clear, blue pool. She was there in the pool. He kept his eyes straight ahead, did not allow her to know that he had seen her, but, of course, he had seen her. She was beautiful, and he loved her. And here was this old white man, telling him that she was there again, at that very spot, and she was waiting. She was waiting for

him. Four years. Waguli had tried not to think of Oconeechee, tried to suppress his feelings for her, to forget his love.
When he finally spoke, the suddenness of his decision came
as a surprise to him, as well as to old Gun Rod.

"I'll go back with you," he said. He stood up with his jug
in his hand and walked unsteadily to a spot where a large flat
rock exposed part of itself above the surface of the earth. He
raised the jug up as far as his face, then smashed it down on
the rock. He walked back over to the fire. "But I can't go like
this. I have to clean myself up. I have to—get sober. I have
tried to stay drunk on *wisgi* for these four years. I didn't want
to think of certain things. There's a creek back there behind
my house not far. I'm going there to wash."

While Waguli was at the creek undressing and bathing,
Gun Rod was digging into his pack. He found some coffee,
a pot for boiling water, two tin cups, a pair of deerskin leggings and breechclout, a pair of beaded moccasins, a clean
white shirt, a long red sash, and another long piece of colorful striped material, suitable for use as a turban. He also found
a small mirror and a pair of scissors. All these things he laid
out carefully on top of the pack. He took the pot out back to
the creek and filled it with water. Then he went back to the
fire and set the coffee on to boil. When Waguli returned to
the fire, still dripping, wearing only his dirty, ragged trousers, Gun Rod picked up the clean clothes he had unpacked
and handed them to Waguli.

"These are for you," he said.

Then he poured coffee into one of the tin cups and offered
that. Waguli took the cup in both his hands and sipped the
hot black drink. It was uneasy in his stomach. He finished the
cup of coffee, then used the mirror and scissors to trim his
hair. Gun Rod helped him to get the back trimmed straight.
Then Waguli dressed. The clothes were a little large for him,
but not ludicrously so. With the leggings, size didn't matter
nearly as much as it would have with white man's trousers,
and the loose-fitting shirt was okay, especially after the sash
had been tied on around it. The moccasins actually proved to
be a close fit. The colorful turban provided the final touch,
and Waguli felt like a well-dressed Cherokee dandy. Gun Rod
decided that he was beginning to see the man Oconeechee
had fallen in love with.

It was early evening. Gun Rod thought he should get some food into Waguli's stomach as soon as possible. And he was getting hungry himself. There were places around the fort where a meal could be bought. He had seen some of them when he had gotten off the boat.

"Let's go eat," he said.

Cleaned up, in new clothes, walking toward the fort with this old white man who was also an old-time Cherokee warrior, Waguli felt—sober. And he felt good. He walked straight. He held his head high. He was not a captive. He was free, and he was going home with this man. He was going to his Oconeechee. The long nightmare at long last was over.

27

The steamboat east would not arrive at Fort Gibson until the next morning, so when they had eaten a good meal, the best meal Waguli had eaten in some time, the two men walked back to Waguli's cabin where they would sleep that night. They smoked, and they talked. As time wore on, Waguli's new-found confidence began to wane. He paced. He was nervous. His body wanted *wisgi*. He had made a quick decision earlier. It had been easy to make the decision. But now only a few hours later, he could see that it would not be so easy to stick to that decision. He took deep breaths. He drank more *kawhi*. He smoked. And he paced. Gun Rod decided that they should sleep inside the cabin with Gun Rod right in the doorway. Waguli reluctantly agreed. When Gun Rod settled his bulk in the small escape hatch, Waguli felt trapped in the tiny cabin. The old man was soon asleep, but Waguli was wide awake. Still he paced. He thought about trying to get past the old man without waking him up, but he didn't have any money. He had spent the last of his meager earnings on the jug earlier. Why had he been so hasty? he asked himself. He had smashed the jug and wasted all that *wisgi.* If only he had it now. Then he remembered that the old man had money. He had seen it when Gun Rod had paid for their meal, and he had seen him put the money bag back into the pack. The pack was inside the cabin with Waguli. He could easily get the old man's money, then step carefully over him and out the door. He needed *wisgi.* But he thought of Oconeechee. He remembered the pride he had felt when walking along with Gun Rod to get their evening meal. He had not felt pride for a long time before that, and it had been good. His body wanted the *wisgi.* His mind did not. He decided to try to sleep.

In the middle of the night Gun Rod was startled out of his sleep by a loud, terrified cry. It was Waguli. He was sitting up, staring, trembling.

"What?" said Gun Rod. "What is it?"

"I'm sick," said Waguli. "I'm hurting."

"Do you need to go outside?"

"Yes."

Gun Rod followed Waguli outside. Waguli dropped to his knees and tried again to vomit. He twisted and gagged and coughed, but as before, nothing came up from his stomach. He was sweating profusely, and his whole midsection was gripped by painful cramps.

"I want some *wisgi,*" he said. "I need it."

"No," said Gun Rod. "Let's go back inside."

"I'm sick."

"Yes. I know you're sick. You're sick from all the poison you've been drinking these last four years. The way to get well is to get the poison out of you, not to put more in. It won't be easy, but you can do it, and I'll help you. Think of her. Think of her devotion, her courage, her love for you."

"Her love for me is misplaced," said Waguli. "I am not worthy of it. I'm not even a man."

"You're sick, and you can get well. Let's go back in."

Waguli groaned and tossed and whimpered for the rest of that night, and Gun Rod got little more sleep. He realized that he would have to change his plans. He had not really been sure what the reaction of the army would be when he bought steamboat passage east for a Cherokee the army had removed to the West, but he had thought he would try it. If challenged, he would try to bluff his way through. But now, knowing Waguli's condition, he knew that he would not be able to take him on the boat safely and discreetly. They would have to travel by land for however long it would take to get the alcohol out of the man's system. Gun Rod had seen men like this before. He knew it would take time. He also knew that there would be plenty of whiskey available along the way. He would have to watch Waguli like a mother hen. Men desperate for whiskey were capable of desperate deeds. Gun Rod's own life could be in danger from this man.

Gun Rod was up with the first light, and he made Waguli dress up again in the good clothes.

"You look just fine," he said.

"I feel bad."

"We'll get some breakfast and coffee, and then we'll be on our way."

"I don't want food. I feel sick."

"You'll eat. You have to eat. Come on."

They got some breakfast and Waguli did eat, at the insistence of Gun Rod. And he drank lots of black coffee. Then Gun Rod located a horse trader and bought two horses. He divided his pack in two, loading half behind the saddle of each horse.

"Watch yourselves," the trader had said. "There's horse thieves all along the trail from here clean to Fort Smith."

Gun Rod checked his pistols and tucked them into his sash.

"Well, then, let's get going," he said to Waguli.

All that day Gun Rod had to baby Waguli along, to pamper him and encourage him. He did his best to avoid any settlements or to hurry through them, and when they met other travelers on the road, Gun Rod nodded his greetings and kept riding. He was surprised at the number of people they met along the way, mostly immigrants bound for Texas on what was already being called the Texas Trail. Gun Rod stopped along the way to prepare their meals rather than venture into towns, and that night he made sure that they camped a good long way from any signs of human habitation. Waguli spent another fitful night, but Gun Rod managed to get a fairly

good night's sleep. In the morning he found Waguli sitting
up and trembling. Waguli would not eat. Gun Rod thought,
the way he's shaking, he probably couldn't get any food into
his mouth anyway. Waguli's trembling began to look more
like convulsions, and Gun Rod began to worry. I might be
killing the poor wretch, he thought. He didn't bother with
breakfast or coffee. Instead he packed the horses as quickly
as possible, got Waguli into the saddle, and resumed the trip.
He tried to hurry, but he had to watch Waguli carefully to
make sure he stayed in the saddle. He wanted to get to a
settlement as soon as possible, but he was afraid that at this
stage of the journey he would find nothing more until they
reached Fort Smith. Then he saw an immigrant wagon approaching from the east, and he raced ahead to meet it.

"Do you have any whiskey about you?" he asked. "I'll pay
you for it."

The immigrant went on his way well pleased with the
profit he had made on a jug of whiskey, and Gun Rod rode
quickly back to Waguli.

"Here," he said. "Take a drink of this."

From then on, Gun Rod's tactic was to save the whiskey
for mealtimes and bribe Waguli with it to make him eat.
Waguli got a drink after each meal and no more except for
one other time when the convulsions threatened again. After
four days, Gun Rod took away the after-breakfast drink. After eight days he withheld the liquor until after the evening
meal. On the fifteenth day, they were camped for the night
and had just finished eating. Gun Rod picked up the jug and
shook it. There was only a little whiskey left. He handed the
jug to Waguli. Waguli held the jug for a moment, then he
handed it back to Gun Rod.

"No more," he said. "I'm done with it."

Gun Rod took the jug and looked at Waguli. He smiled.

"Then, by God," he said, "I think I've earned a drink."

He tilted the jug up to his lips and emptied it, then tossed
the empty jug away. Waguli laughed. Gun Rod had not even
seen him smile until this time. He looked perplexed for a
moment, then he threw back his head and began to laugh
with Waguli.

28

They crossed the Wataunga,
the Missouri, Cumberland and Tennessee,
Nolichucky, land of the Tuckaleechee,
where his guide said, "I'm old and dying now,
but you must promise me
not to stop until you've found
beautiful Oconeechee.

This is my house," said Gun Rod, sitting in the saddle in front of the cabin at Horseshoe Bend. "We'll rest here for the night and go on in the morning."

He climbed wearily down out of the saddle and stretched himself. It had been a long, hard journey, and he was feeling all of his years. There was still a ways to go to get Waguli delivered safely to Oconeechee, but it would be nothing compared to what they had already done. He had gotten to know Waguli and to like him, and since the man had sobered up, Gun Rod thought he could see why the young woman was so much in love. They would make a fine couple, and Gun Rod was proud of his part in bringing them back together. But at the same time, it made him feel very lonely. He stared for a moment, it seemed at the front of his house, but in his mind he was looking through the house to a spot beyond the garden where there were three graves he had dug himself. He shook himself and turned to unpack and unsaddle his horse. Waguli swung easily down out of his saddle and began to unburden his mount. Gun Rod took note of the fact that while the trip had aged him, it seemed to have restored Waguli's youth. Gun Rod prepared a meal in his house, and after they had eaten, he and Waguli sat on the porch and smoked.

"I've not defeated this thing, Gun Rod," said Waguli, "this white man's poison, this *wisgi*. I still think of it. I want some right now."

"And you will for the rest of your days, my boy," said Gun Rod. "But you'll learn to live with it. You're a strong man with a strong will."

"And I'll have the strength of Oconeechee to help me," said Waguli. "I could never have come this far without your help. You've done a great thing for me, my friend, and I'll never forget you."

Gun Rod thought, I did it for love.

"Ah," he said, "I just wanted to take a trip and see the West."

They slept that night in the house, and in the morning they had breakfast and coffee and then went outside to saddle and pack the horses. Gun Rod swung the saddle up onto the back of his horse, and he felt a sharp, stabbing pain in his chest.

"Ahh."

The saddle slid off the horse's back and fell to the ground as Gun Rod staggered backward a few steps. Waguli ran to him and grabbed him around the shoulders to support him.

"What is it?" he said.

"Take me inside."

Waguli got Gun Rod into the house and laid him on his bed. The old man groaned as he stretched out, and Waguli could read the intense pain on the old face.

"What can I do for you?" he said.

"Ah," Gun Rod groaned, "there's nothing, I think. Nothing to do. Get that chair and sit here beside me."

Waguli pulled the chair up beside the bed and sat down. Gun Rod reached out and put his old hand on Waguli's arm.

"Don't forget what we talked about last night," he said. "Be strong. Do it for her sake as well as your own, and do it for me."

"I will," said Waguli. "I promise you."

"I'm afraid that I won't be able to go on with you, Waguli. My time has come. Behind my house, there's a garden. Beyond that, you'll find three graves. My wife and children. Bury me there beside them. Put me on the north end."

Waguli felt tears well up in his eyes.

"I will," he said.

"And make me one more promise. Go on without me. Find Oconeechee. Don't let anything stop you."

"I'll find her. Nothing will stop me."

Waguli sat with Gun Rod until the old man died, but before he died, Gun Rod wrote on a paper that he had given Waguli the two horses, two saddles, all the supplies in the packs, his two pistols, and his money. Waguli kept his promise and buried Gun Rod beside his wife, and he quietly sang a Cherokee funeral song for the old man who had given so much for him and for Oconeechee. Then he packed his horses and left. He did not know what the white people of Alabama, Georgia, and North Carolina would do to him if they found him riding through what they were now calling their country, so he rode carefully, almost fearfully. He kept remembering the soldiers who had captured him, the beatings, the bonds, the stockade, the seemingly endless forced march, and all the dead along the way. He carried his pistols the way their former owner had carried them, tucked into the sash he wore around his waist, and he was constantly on guard. When he saw white people approaching from any direction, he rode off the road to hide. He began to want *wisgi* more often and more desperately, but he remembered old Gun Rod, and he thought of Oconeechee waiting for him at the pool below the falls. When he finally reached the mountain trail leading to Soco Gap, he felt some sense of relief, though he still did not know what to expect. He began to hurry the horses along. At last he was looking down on the pool from the very spot where he had first seen her, but he did not see her there. There was a house, a Cherokee house, he could tell, on the ridge overlooking the pool. He dismounted and trailed the reins of his horses, then ran to the house.

"Oconeechee?"

There was no answer. He went to the house and looked inside. It was a clean house and nicely furnished, but there was no one in there. He ran to the edge of the ridge and looked down into the pool. There was no one to be seen. He felt a sense of panic from deep inside, and he ran back to his horses. Leaving the packhorse with its reins trailing on the

ground, he climbed back into the saddle of the other and
rode it fast along the trail into what had been Soco Gap.
There he found only ruins. He dismounted again and walked
aimlessly down the street. He felt very much alone and very
much afraid.

> Left alone, no one to guide him,
> Whippoorwill began to wail
> for a mystic hand to guide him
> down that long forgotten trail.
> As he listened in the silence,
> he heard a voice so sweet and clear,
> that he ran to try and find it,
> though his heart was full of fear.

Waguli walked like a man lost, and from his mouth came
a low, moaning wail. His head filled with questions and
doubts. Had it then been all a lie? Was nothing changed? Did
the old white man fill him full of hope only to dash those
hopes and make his torture worse? Ah, *wisgi*. Where could
he get some *wisgi*? He stumbled over something and nearly
fell, but he staggered on, blindly, for his eyes were filled with
tears. And still he moaned. A painful knot formed in his
stomach. Through the water in his eyes he could see that he
had wandered away from the village ruins and into the trees
behind, and his footsteps told him that he was no longer
walking on a traveled path. Up above him in a tree a squirrel
scolded angrily, and he could hear the song of a mountain
bluebird, totally indifferent to his pain. From just ahead came
the sound of rushing water. He staggered on a few more
steps and stopped beside a creek. The pain gave a sudden
twist to his guts that made him cry out, and he grabbed at
his belly, doubling over, and dropped to his knees. Then a
force from deep inside threw him forward, and he caught the
ground with his hands. His face was just above the rushing
water. His mouth came open wide and torrents of vomit
spewed out from the depths of his being.

He sat beside the creek exhausted and empty. The rushing
waters had carried away the evidence of his purge, and he had
rinsed his mouth with clean, cool water from the creek. He
had unwrapped the turban from his head, dipped it in the
water, and used that to wash his face. He felt refreshed—

fresh. He could see the world around him clearly, and he found it clean and lovely. He stood up, and he was aware that the uneasy feeling in his stomach, the queasiness that had been his constant companion for years, was no longer there. He walked the short distance through the woods back to the ruins of Soco Gap, where he found his horse patiently awaiting his return. He mounted and headed back toward the pool beneath the falls.

Oconeechee had just returned from a visit to a nearby neighbor where she had gone to trade for some fresh venison. She tried to keep near home and never stay away long, for she knew that Waguli was coming soon. She had just returned, and had seen the strange pack horse standing there. She had run the last steps to her house only to find it empty still. So who had left the horse? She built a fire outside the house and began to prepare the fresh meat for cooking.

When Waguli rode up to the new house on the ridge above the pool for the second time that day, he saw a fire. He urged his horse forward a little faster, and he saw her step anxiously out of the house to see who was riding in. He jumped from the horse's back and ran to her.

"Oconeechee."

"Waguli," she said. "I've been waiting for you. Come inside. It's your home."

Epilogue

She stepped out of the mountain laurel,
Ran to stand by his side.
"Oh, my Whippoorwill," she whispered,
"I knew you had not died."
Now they say that they were married,
And they lived up there for years,
Though most folks have forgotten
Their long bitter trail of tears.
Cherokees say that when the wind blows
Softly through those misty hills,
That's the love song of Oconeechee
And her noble Whippoorwill.
　　Whippoorwill, Whippoorwill,
　　Don't you know how she's searched all these hills?
　　She's searched every glen and glade
　　Not knowing why you went away.
　　Can't you feel she loves you still,
　　Whippoorwill?
　　And don't you know she always will,
　　Whippoorwill?

Grandpa leaned back against the big tree. I could tell that the story was over, and even though it had a happy ending, I was kind of sad. Grandpa took out his pipe and pulled his *tobacco pouch out of his pocket. He started filling his pipe bowl. A few feet away a brown creeper was scurrying up the side of a cotton-wood tree, looking almost like a little mouse. Grandpa struck a kitchen match on the sole of his shoe and lit his pipe, surrounding his old face momentarily with a blue-gray cloud. The wind was beginning to stir just a little.*

"Grandpa," I said. "What happened to them?"

"Hmm?"

"What happened to Waguli and Oconeechee after that?"

"Oh, well," he said, "I don't know for sure. That's the end of the story. They just lived here after that, I guess, and they had children. Their children got all growed up and had their own children, so they become Grandma and Grandpa. By and by, they died. That was all a long time ago."

I sat and stared at Grandpa. What he had just said made me realize for the first time for real that one day Grandpa would die. Grandma, too. I didn't want to grow up then. The breeze picked up a little more, and the leaves up above began to rustle. Then the breeze became a wind, and I stood up and went to the big tree Grandpa was leaning back against. I stood by Grandpa's shoulder and put my hands up high on the tree trunk and looked up into its branches and listened, and the wind picked up some more, and then I heard that sound again.

"Grandpa," I said, suddenly excited. "Grandpa, I can hear them. They're singing."